Stuart Pawson was born in Leeds and now lives in Fairburn, Yorkshire. He has worked for British Coal and, more recently, the Probation Service, as a mediator between offenders and victims. His interests include walking, painting and foreign travel.

Stuart Pawson's earlier novels, THE PICASSO SCAM, THE MUSHROOM MAN, THE JUDAS SHEEP and LAST REMINDER, which also feature Detective Inspector Charlie Priest, are available from Headline.

Find out more about Stuart Pawson at the following website:
http://www.twbooks.co.uk/authors/spawson.html

Acclaim for Stuart Pawson's previous titles:

'Priest is a welcome addition to the canon of fictional detectives' *Yorkshire Evening Post*

'Humorous and nicely plotted' *Irish Times*

'Well written, well characterised, funny but hard edged; what more could you want?' *Crime Time*

Also by Stuart Pawson

The Picasso Scam
The Mushroom Man
The Judas Sheep
Last Reminder

Deadly Friends

Stuart Pawson

HEADLINE

First published in 1998
by HEADLINE BOOK PUBLISHING

First published in paperback in 1998
by HEADLINE BOOK PUBLISHING

10 9 8 7 6 5 4 3 2

ISBN 0 7472 5778 7

Printed and bound in Great Britain by
Clays Ltd, St Ives plc

HEADLINE BOOK PUBLISHING
A division of Hodder Headline PLC
338 Euston Road
London NW1 3BH

To Doreen

Thanks to the following for their unfailing assistance and encouragement: Kath Gibson, Dennis Marshall, John Crawford, John Mills.

Prologue

Clive David Jordan, FRCS, FRCOG, had it made, and he knew it. Aged thirty-five, he was at the height of his powers and his appetites. For four days each week he worked at Heckley General Hospital, his tall fair presence spreading brisk bonhomie through wards, corridors, offices and staff rooms as he dispensed medicine, expertise and cheeriness to employees and clients alike. A hand on an arm here to comfort a patient, his best boyish grin to a nurse there, to give her an adrenalin boost that would take her to the end of her shift, it was all the same to Dr Jordan. Charm dripped from him like rainwater from a leaky gutter.

One, sometimes two, days a week he worked at the White Rose Clinic, just outside town, on the affluent side. Set in extensive grounds, the clinic was concealed by the last stand of decent trees before the moors began and nibbling sheep and gnawing winds stunted their growth. Word in the town was that the White Rose Clinic set standards of opulence that were not equalled by any hotel this side of Harrogate. Nobody knew anyone who had actually had treatment there, but the postman delivered their mail and saw what he saw, and the staff were recruited locally. The clinic paid good money, and was able to poach some of the best nurses from the National Health hospitals. Nurses have mortgages and electricity bills, just like everybody else. So, on Wednesdays and the occasional Saturday Dr Jordan's BMW 523i was parked outside the clinic while he doubled his income inside, ministering to the healthy. Strictly speaking, due to the perverse snobbery of the medical profession, he was *Mr* Jordan, having achieved the lofty rank of consultant.

He was in a relationship. Natasha Wilde – 'That's Wilde with an e' – was an actress who'd achieved a kind of fame playing a bimbo of doubtful sexuality in a Yorkshire soap opera called *Dales Diary*, known throughout the county as *Mrs Dale's Dairy*. Confident that her role in the show was secure, she had recently demanded more money, inspiring the producers to promptly write-in a dying sister in Australia and send her character off to the antipodes for six months. Clive Jordan didn't mind. It meant they could spend more time together, either in her rented cottage at Appletreewick, in Wharfedale, or at his modern executive-style penthouse apartment close to the centre of Heckley.

Dr Jordan was stage-struck. Natasha's friends, who he met regularly at parties, were often seen in a variety of hospital dramas. Sometimes applying the resuscitation electrodes to a stricken victim's chest with a terse: 'Stand back!' as the current was applied, sometimes gazing thoughtfully at an old x-ray of someone's kneecap while saying: 'It looks like pre-haemorrhoidal subcutaneous laparotomy to me. We'd better go in.'

But he, Clive Jordan, was the real thing. That was how he earned his living. Often he found himself taken to one side at a party and asked how a certain situation might be handled. He helped where he could, and once received a credit for technical assistance, but he knew they could never play the part as effectively as he did himself. He should really have been the one up there, in front of the cameras.

He certainly had the looks, and his own life would

have provided enough material for a couple of mini-series. Wednesdays he didn't start at the White Rose until eleven a.m., which gave ample time for the wife of one of his colleagues at the General to pop round and cook breakfast for him. She dressed up – or down – as a French maid, which was totally unnecessary as far as he was concerned, but she seemed to derive an extra *frisson* of pleasure from it.

Thursday nights, during term time, he had sex with one of the clinic's receptionists in the back seat of the BMW. Her husband thought she was at a pottery class. Occasionally he found the time and energy for a game of squash.

He wasn't serious about his acting ambitions, but found a more realistic way of melding his two worlds together in a sort of symbiosis. He always carried a couple of the clinic's glossy pamphlets in his pocket, and more than one of Natasha's friends found herself studying it, propped up against the cornflakes packet, after discussing her 'problem' with him. It was useful having an actress as a girlfriend, as well as being fun. He enjoyed it. When Natasha was in London, seeing her agent, she said, he enjoyed her friends, too.

But it all came to an end. One rainy evening, as the shoppers dashed from one tinsel-draped store to another, looking for that last elusive present before the shutters came down for two blessed days, someone gave Clive Jordan, FRCS, FRCOG, an injection.

In the ear.

With an Enfield 0.38 calibre revolver.

Chapter One

Christmas Eve we had a rape. The woman didn't report it until the day after Boxing day, so hers was the only Christmas it wrecked. We were having a social evening in the canteen when she walked into the station. Highlight of the celebrations was a bullseye quiz; the idea stolen, I am told, from television. The CID A-team, captained by yours truly, Charlie Priest, tied with the Angels for first place, so we had a sudden-death play-off to decide the winners.

'Mr Priest, of the CID, has won the toss and put Agnes of the Angels in to bat first,' Gareth Adey, my uniformed opposite number, informed the crowd. 'Select a category, please,' he ordered Agnes.

'Pop music,' she announced, predictably, and lined herself up with the dartboard. Pop music was the twenty. If she hit it the question was worth double points, and so far she hadn't missed.

Plunk!

'Number one,' Adey pronounced. 'Television. And here is your question.' Short pause while he shuffled his papers. He likes to do things properly, but he can be a bit of a prat at times. 'For five points, who played the part of Steed in the Aven—'

'Patrick MacNee!' Agnes interrupted, thumping the air with a calloused hand.

'Cor-rect. Would Inspector Charlie Priest now approach the oggy?'

I pulled Agnes's dart from the board and ambled to the line. If I threw well and knew the answer, we'd win. If I missed but still knew the answer, we'd draw. 'General knowledge,' I said.

'Number twelve,' Adey informed us for the hundred and fiftieth time.

Plunk!

'Number nine. Sport.'

'Useless,' I heard my DC, Dave 'Sparky' Sparkington, mutter. 'Absolutely useless.'

I wasn't worried – I know a bit about sport.

'And your question, with a chance to dead heat for first place, is as follows . . .'

'Get on with it,' someone shouted.

'Quiet, please. For five points, who was the first person to run the mile in four minutes?'

'Yes!' and 'Hooray!' I heard, *sotto voce*, from Sparky and Nigel Newley, my other team members.

I wasn't so confident. I let about five seconds tick away, then asked: 'Is this a trick question?'

'I am unable to enter into a discussion,' Adey replied in precisely the tone he uses for cautioning juveniles. 'You have five more seconds.'

'Do you mean in exactly four minutes, or under four minutes?' I demanded.

'I will repeat the question as it is written here. Who was the first person to run the mile in four minutes?'

I waited until he opened his mouth to tell me I'd run out of time, then said: 'Derek Ibbotson.'

'Derek bloody Ibbotson!' I heard from Sparky, over the groans and cheers from around the room.

'Wrong,' Adey pronounced. 'The answer is Roger Bannister. I declare the Angels as winners of the competition.'

Sparky and Nigel looked hurt and disappointed, as if I'd run over their toes with a Lada. 'Derek friggin' Ibbotson,' Sparky whined as I sat down with them and reached for my pint glass. 'What made you say Derek Ibbotson? Who ever thought that Derek Ibbotson ran the first four-minute mile? Even Nigel knows it was Bannister, don't you, Nigel?'

DS Nigel Newley nodded into his beer. ''Fraid so, Boss.'

'Roger Bannister . . .' I tapped the table with my forefinger for emphasis, '. . . was the first person to run the mile in *under* four minutes. Derek Ibbotson was the first person to run it in *exactly* four minutes. Four minutes, nought point nought nought *nought* seconds, and that's what I was asked.'

'Was he 'ummers-like!'

'He was!'

'Everybody knew what he meant!'

'Well he should have said what he meant. We're supposed to be detectives. Next time I'm giving evidence I'll say: "You know what I meant," to the defence barrister, see if he agrees with you.'

Sparky said: 'Talk about a minefield of useless information. That must be the most useless ever, if you ask me.'

'There's no such thing as useless information,' I stated, draining my glass and plonking it down to give the words maximum authority. 'Information is knowledge, and knowledge catches crooks. What does knowledge do, Nigel?'

'Catches crooks, Charlie.'

'Exactly.'

They drank their beer unforgivingly. If ever it was my

round, it was now. 'Anyway,' I declared. 'Ibbo's a local lad, not some toffee-nosed southerner. Sorry, Nigel,' I added. He's from Berkshire, so we have to make allowances.

I fetched the drinks and sat down again. Silence engulfed the table like a cloud of nerve gas. Maggie Madison, one of my DCs, was passing, so I reached out and pulled her towards me.

'Can I come and sit at your table, Maggie?' I asked. 'These two aren't talking to me.'

'I'm not surprised,' she replied. 'Everybody knows three universal facts: where they were when Kennedy was killed; who ran the first four-minute mile; and . . . something else.'

'We came second,' I protested. 'That can't be bad.'

Sparky broke his silence. 'We were beaten by the cleaning ladies. I ask you, the flippin' cleaning ladies!'

'It could have been worse,' Maggie assured us. 'You could have been beaten by the woodentops.'

'Or even traffic,' Nigel added.

'Nah!' Sparky said, grinning. 'Not traffic. That's being silly.'

It looked as if my lapse was forgiven. Not forgotten, though. I knew I'd be reminded of it every day until some greater calamity replaced it in the mythology of the police station.

Maggie said: ''Scuse me, I'm wanted,' and walked away from us.

I looked across the room and the other two swivelled round in their seats. A female PC was in the doorway and had evidently caught Maggie's attention. They stood there for a while, deep in conversation.

'She's attractive,' I said. 'Is she new?'

'Been with us about a month,' Nigel informed me.

'I thought you'd know. Is she in with a chance?' I asked, looking across at her. She was fair-haired, wearing it piled up so it wouldn't show when she wore her hat. I wondered if I had a thing about women in uniforms.

'No,' Nigel replied. 'She's too young for me.'

I nodded in agreement and pulled my glum face. She must have been nearly ten years younger than Nigel, and he was twice that younger than me. The trouble with growing old is that the people on the outside are more aware of it than you are. I took a long drink of denatured lager, but it didn't help a bit.

'Right,' I remarked, brightly, banging my glass down. 'So what sort of a Christmas have you both had?'

'Awful,' said Sparky. 'The kids say thank you for the presents.'

'They're welcome. Tell them thanks for mine. My CD collection was short of a Gary Glitter.'

'Sophie said he was your era.'

'Yeah, first time round.' I turned to Nigel. 'And what about you, Sunshine?'

'Same. We were working, remember. Some of us didn't have three days off.'

'I know. I'm thinking of doing it again next year, too. Murder, wasn't it?'

Nigel nodded. 'Christmas seems to be a good time for murders; it brings out the worst in people.'

'Don't remind me,' I told him. 'I had my fill last year.'

'I thought that was a suicide.'

'The mother was suicide. The baby was murder.'

'Of course it was. I'd forgotten the baby.'

I'd never forget the baby. That memory would be with me for ever. I said: 'And how do you like working for

DCI Makinson?' Regional HQ handle all murders, and had appointed one of their own as SIO.

Sparky chipped in with: 'Very nice. He's a good bloke, isn't he, Nigel?' I felt a movement under the table as he kicked Nigel.

'Er, yes,' Nigel confirmed, wincing with pain. 'He's good. Very . . . er, professional.'

'And very thorough,' Sparky added.

'Yes, very thorough – does everything by the book.'

'That's right, and he doesn't go chasing off in different directions without telling us.'

'No, he keeps us fully informed, all the time.'

'Yes, he's very good like that. And he listens to what we have to say.'

'What I really like about him is that . . .'

'OK! OK!' I interrupted. 'I get the message. So has the brilliant Mr Makinson caught the killer yet?'

They shook their heads.

'So what's he got you doing?'

Sparky looked downcast. 'Door to doors,' he replied.

'And you?'

'Interviewing staff at the White Rose Clinic.'

'Is that where the late departed doctor did his doctoring?'

'Only one day per week. I'm not complaining – I think they choose them for their looks rather than their medical qualifications.'

'I'll give Makinson a week,' I told them. 'Then they'll be asking me to take over and solve it.'

Maggie was heading back our way, looking serious. She bent down beside me and spoke softly. 'There's a woman at the front desk, Charlie. Says she's been raped. She's being taken to the suite. Shall I ring Mr Wood?'

Mr Wood is our superintendent, and Number 1 Cop at Heckley. In his absence I am most senior, mainly because of length of service. Officially, I was on leave until tomorrow.

'Is she . . . you know . . . all right?' Now I was asking the stupid questions, but she knew what I meant.

'I think so. She found her own way here and isn't hysterical, or anything.'

'OK.' I looked at my watch. 'I want to make a phone call from the office. You've done the training, Maggie, do you think you and the WPC can handle it?'

'No problem.'

'Right. Come on, then. I'll hang about in the office in case you want me. If she knows who did it we'll have to get moving.' I pushed my nearly-full glass towards Sparky. 'See if they'll give you a refund on that, please.'

'We'll be here if you want us,' he replied.

Going up the stairs Maggie said: 'Is it Annabelle you're ringing?'

'Yes.'

'Did you both have a good Christmas?'

'Not really,' I admitted. 'We went to her married sister's, in Guildford. I've left her down there, drove back yesterday. Not my types, I'm afraid.' I didn't mention the separate bedrooms.

'They're called the in-laws,' Maggie replied, knowingly.

She diverted to the front desk and I continued upwards to the CID office on the first floor. I unlocked the door and turned a few lights on. It hadn't changed much in three days. The balloon, our concession to the festive season, had nearly deflated, but everything else was just the same.

I met Annabelle that day about five years ago when the sun moved backwards in the sky and one of our tennis players hit one back against Boris Becker. She's tall and elegant, and looks just as beautiful when she's meeting ambassadors and statesmen as she does when she's halfway up Goredale Scar and the rain is running down her neck. I'll lean on a rock to gasp for breath, and she'll think it's the exertion and give me an encouraging smile. But her nose wrinkles when she smiles and all that does is make the lead weight sitting on my diaphragm feel heavier and heavier, and I have even more trouble trying to breathe.

Nobody answered at her sister's. She's called Rachel and they have hardly spoken since they were schoolgirls. Their family was well-off until daddy ran away with his secretary and their mother hit the bottle. Annabelle went to work in the Third World, married young, was widowed and fell in with me. Rachel married Harley Street's Osteopath to the Stars and enjoys the fruits of his success. Christmas was some sort of attempt at reconciliation and I think it worked. We had lunch at the golf club – fifty quid a head – and, while the sisters gossiped, George, Rachel's husband, introduced me to his friends and explained all the fascinating golfing memorabilia that adorned the walls of the clubhouse. I'd have preferred having extensive bridgework without anaesthesia.

I pushed the phone away and wandered into the annexe where we make the tea. Some kind person had washed all the mugs. I dropped a teabag into one with 'The Boss' in gold letters on the side and plugged the kettle in. There was a new notice above the sink, printed in forty-point Hippo. It said: 'Please do not leave your used teabags in the wastepaper bins.' The advent of the word processor has greatly improved the quality of informal notices. When I'd brewed I left the bag sitting in the spoon on the draining board because I couldn't see a more preferable alternative.

Nobody answered again. Or should that be still. They

must have gone out somewhere. I put my feet on the radiator and fished the top document out of my in-tray. It was a request for next year's budget forecasts. I wrote: 'Deal with this, please, Nigel,' in pencil across the top and dropped it on his desk. After a sip of tea I reached for the next document but immediately slid it back on to the pile – this was becoming too much like work. When my phone rang I grabbed it before realising it couldn't possibly be Annabelle.

'Charlie?' enquired Maggie's voice.

'Yep.'

'This woman. She's in the rape suite. Apparently the offence took place on Christmas Eve, so there's no point in a medical or anything, but she knows the bloke. I've asked her if she has any objection to a male officer being present and she says she hasn't.'

'I'm on my way.'

My tea was too hot to finish, and no doubt they were having one themselves, so I carried my mug down with me. The rape suite is a haven of luxury and calm in the midst of the normal utility and hurly-burly of the nick. It's all pastel tints and deep armchairs, but there's a sophisticated tape recorder on the wall and a medical examination room through a door. I chose the pictures. I was an art student before I became a policeman, so I get all those jobs. My own choice would have been Pollock and Kandinsky, but I'd reluctantly decided that they weren't to everybody's taste and settled for Monets. I knocked and went in, sliding the bolt across to the occupied position behind me and engaging my empathy mode at the same time.

I was right: they all had disposable cups from the machine. 'Hello, Mr Priest,' Maggie greeted me. 'This is Janet Saunders.' Turning to the woman she said: 'Inspector Priest is the senior officer at Heckley at the moment.' Looking back at me she said: 'You know PC Kent, don't you?'

It was the nearest I'd get to an introduction. I nodded at her without smiling.

'Do you need me, now?' PC Kent wondered.

I turned to Janet Saunders. 'We have you outnumbered, I'm afraid, but do you mind if PC Kent stays?'

She shook her head and mumbled: 'No.'

'Thank you,' I said. It was all experience for the young PC, and it didn't create the impression that she had something better to do.

Janet Saunders was about thirty and had once been blonde. There were crow's-feet around her eyes and deep lines down her cheeks, but you could still tell that she'd be attractive under different circumstances. She was wearing a black leather jacket and jeans. I couldn't fault that – I was wearing the same.

Maggie said: 'I'll bring you up to date, Boss, and Janet can interrupt if I get it wrong. She's single – divorced – with a five-year-old daughter. She lives on Marsden Road, about half a mile from the Tap and Spile public house, where she works as a barmaid three nights per week. She was working there on Christmas Eve, and a man she only knows as Darryl bought her a drink and later he offered to walk her home. She declined and walked home in the company of two neighbours.' Maggie turned to the alleged victim. 'Did you say they lived next door to you, Janet?'

'No. Next door but two. Mr and Mrs Brown, they're called.'

'Right. Janet's ex was bringing their daughter round at nine a.m. It was her turn to have her over Christmas. She left the pub at midnight, sharp, because she had presents to wrap and other things to do.' Maggie turned to Janet.

'Would you like to go on from there, Janet. I don't want to put words into your mouth.'

Janet gazed at the table for a moment. She was wearing a wedding ring but no other jewellery. Her fingernails were short and unpainted and the sleeves of the leather jacket were too long so she had to keep hitching them up. She shuffled her position until she was more upright and said: 'I wanted to make a trifle. Clean up a bit. And I had presents to wrap for Dilly.'

'Dilly's your daughter?' I asked.

'Mmm. Working at the pub, you come 'ome stinking of cigarettes. First thing I always do is have a shower. I had a good long soak and dried myself. I was going to put my jogging suit on and get stuck in for a couple of hours. Make things nice for . . .'

Up to then she'd been in control, but as we approached the offence she lost it and pulled a scrap of tissue out of her pocket. PC Kent produced a box of man-size and placed them alongside her.

'Thank you,' she sniffled, taking one.

I said: 'You normally only work three nights at the Tap and Spile, Janet?'

She nodded. 'Wednesdays, Thursdays and Fridays. They're not busy enough on Mondays and Tuesdays.'

'And not at weekends?'

'Not usually. I have Dilly at weekends.'

'Do you have a full-time job?'

She shook her head.

'Tell us what happened next, Janet, if you can.'

She bit her lip for a second before answering. 'I heard a noise. Thought it was someone outside, you know, revellers. I was drying my hair on the towel when, all of a sudden, I went cold. There was a draught and the light changed somehow. I lowered the towel and . . . he was standing there, with the door wide open. I screamed. Tried to cover myself. He just stood there, laughing.'

'This was the man you know as Darryl?' Maggie asked.

'Yes.'

I said: 'Janet, we're not recording this, but Maggie will do a statement later and we'll ask you to check it and sign it. If you're finding this too difficult would you prefer to write it down yourself?'

She shook her head. 'No, I'm all right.'

'Well, we can break off anytime you want.'

'You're doing fine,' Maggie assured her.

Janet had a drink of coffee and went on: 'I shouted: "What the 'ell do you want?" or something. He said: "What do you think I want?" and he waved a knife at me. He grabbed me by the 'air and dragged me into the bedroom and . . . he did it to me. On the bed.'

She took another tissue and blew her nose.

'You must have been terrified,' I said.

She looked at me and gave a little sniff of disdain at my description of her fear. Her eyes were blue.

'Did he say anything else?' Maggie asked.

'He pointed the knife at me, said he could kill me. But he said that was messy. He said if I reported 'im he'd just say I'd consented. Nobody would believe me. It would be my word against his. He said . . . he said . . .' She couldn't go on.

After a moment I asked: 'What did he say, Janet?'

'He said . . . that everybody knew I was a slag. It isn't true. I'm not. Then he went.'

We sat in silence for a minute. Maggie made several notes. PC Kent bit her lip and fidgeted with the cuffs of her blouse. I said: 'And then you had to pick up the pieces and get ready for little Dilly coming as if nothing had happened. And play the best mum in the world for the next three days while all this was churning away inside you.'

'Mmm.'

'And everybody around you was enjoying themselves,' Maggie added.

'Yes.'

I pointed at a disposable cup and held four fingers up to PC Kent. I was convinced that Maggie had deliberately not told me her first name. She asked how I liked my coffee. When she'd gone Janet said: 'I wasn't going to report it. I'm trying to win custody of Dilly again and I thought that this might go against me. Then I thought: No! It's my body. He's not getting away with it.'

'I admire your guts, Janet,' I told her, 'and we'll do everything we can to nail him, but I can't guarantee that we'll succeed. You'd better give us a description.'

He was about twenty-eight, liked to dress smartly in a three-piece suit, with close-cropped hair, no earrings or tattoos and stockily built. He answered to Darryl and drank occasionally in the Tap and Spile, leaning on the bar, chatting to the staff. If he lived locally we'd find him.

'You obviously haven't been back to the pub,' I suggested as WPC Kent came in with four cups in a purpose-designed tray.

'No. I've had Dilly with me until tonight.'

'Will you?'

'I don't think so, but I need the money.'

'Right. Can you describe the knife?'

'It was one of my kitchen knives. On Christmas Day Dilly came in from the garden carrying it. "Look what Dilly found, Mummy," she said. I nearly fainted.'

'Jesus!' I sighed. I leaned back in my easy chair and glanced round the room. There was a pile of chunky plastic toys in one corner with a little slide, kiddies for the use of. The place was starting to look grubby. That's the trouble with pastels.

I said: 'I'll leave you with Maggie and she'll ask you all the personal stuff we need to know. Meanwhile I'll see what I can find about Darryl. We might need you to point him out to us, if we go looking for him. Will that be OK?'

'Through the week,' Janet replied. 'I can get away anytime through the week. I have Dilly at weekends.'

'Fair enough. If we need more information would you prefer it if Maggie or PC Kent called to see you, or is it all right if I call? It's just that sometimes they're not available.'

'I don't mind who calls, if it helps catch him.'

'Right. Thanks. You're a brave lady, Janet, and you're doing the right thing. I'll say goodnight, and Maggie will take you home when you've finished.'

She thanked me, and I wandered off to set the wheels in motion. Except that I was the wheels, and I didn't have much motion in me. The happy gang were leaving the canteen in various states of jollity and I zig-zagged against the flow, shaking the occasional extended hand and returning seasonal compliments. Sparky and Nigel weren't among them.

I leaned on the bell push at the front desk and the duty sergeant came steaming out of the office with murder on his mind. He unclenched his fists when he saw me. Unfortunately, Darryl the Rapist didn't ring any bells in his memory. He just pursed his lips and shook his head. I half turned to leave, then said: 'Oh, one more thing, Arthur. WPC Kent helped with the interview. She seems very competent. What's her first name?'

The big sergeant, built like a mausoleum, looked over his left shoulder and then his right. When he was sure we were alone he leaned conspiratorially across the front counter. I put my ear close to his face.

'Roger Bannister,' he whispered.

It had started already.

Tomorrow I'd have a word about Darryl with our local intelligence officer and the regional rape squad. After that we'd have to go looking for him. I drifted up to the office and turned the lights off. Five minutes later the car started first time and I drove home on empty roads. There were no messages on my ansaphone. I flicked round the TV channels, didn't find anything worth the electricity and went to bed. Another Christmas gone.

It didn't take me long to deploy the troops next morning because DCI Makinson had commandeered most of them in his hunt for the doctor's killer. In the run-up to Christmas we put everyone we can afford out mingling with the shopping crowds, looking for pickpockets and fraudsters. It's amazing how many we catch. After Christmas it's back to burglaries. We'd had the usual spate and several victims were complaining about our lack of response. The front desk handles most of the grumblers, but if I can't find a reason to be out of the office the more persistent ones come through to me. I patiently explain how thinly we are stretched at times like these, but feel like screaming down the phone that this was the first Christmas I've had off since Bing Crosby was in short trousers and most of my staff can't remember when they last saw their children out of their pyjamas. The burglaries would go unsolved, or perhaps be Taken Into Consideration if we got lucky, and our rating in the public's eyes would sink even lower.

'Yes, Colonel,' I said into the phone for the tenth time as Maggie seated herself at the other side of my desk. 'We have a patrol car in that area, and we'll ask them to keep their eyes open.' I grimaced at her and nodded repeatedly at the earpiece. 'You're right, sir – horse-whipping is too good for them.' I put the phone halfway down and snatched it back again. 'Yes sir, . . . we will . . . thank you for calling.' This time it made it back to its cradle before he could ramble on some more.

'Colonel Blashford-Ormsby-Gridpipe,' I explained to Maggie. 'Someone has popped-off all his Christmas tree lights with an airgun.' I stretched my arms out as if aiming a rifle.

She said: 'A proper tree, out in the grounds, I presume.'

'*Perchow*!' I said. 'Got one. Good shot. No, I think he said it was standing on the piano.'

She gave me the resigned look I've seen so many times. 'Dare I ask you about Janet Saunders?' she wondered.

'Janet Saunders,' I told her, 'would come as a welcome relief. What else did she tell you?'

'Nothing useful. She said he didn't wear a condom, but she doesn't know if he was circumcised or not. She's started her period, so that's a relief. I had a word with her about AIDS and the availability of counselling, but she says she definitely wants a test.'

'Good for her. Let's go see Mr Wood and kill two birds with one well-aimed missile.'

Superintendent Gilbert Wood was spooning coffee into a mug as he shouted a *come in* to my knock.

'Ah, just in time,' I said as we entered. 'It must be at least six minutes since my last one.'

He dropped a teabag into another cup, saying: 'Maggie?'

'Ooh, coffee please,' she replied. 'I've just had one, but it's not often the super makes it for me.'

'Jesus washed his disciples' feet, Margaret,' he replied.

We sat down at his desk while the kettle boiled and small-talked about Christmas. When it clicked off, Maggie jumped to her feet. 'I'll do it,' she said. 'Don't want you scalding yourself.'

There were sounds of stirring behind me. 'Just two sweeteners for me,' Gilbert called to her. 'Oh, and don't put the teabag in the wastepaper bin.'

'Where do I put it?'

'Anywhere but the bin. The cleaning ladies have complained. They jam the shredder, or something. I don't know what we're supposed to do with them.'

'Those cleaning ladies are growing too big for their boots,' I grumbled.

Maggie placed three mugs on the table and we shuffled beer mats under them. 'I left the used bag on a saucer,' she said.

'When you have a few dry ones you could always put them in an envelope and post them to someone,' I suggested.

Gilbert took a sip and pulled a face. 'Anyone . . . ?' He made a pouring gesture over his coffee.

Maggie and I shook our heads and he looked disappointed.

'Or you could let them drop out of the bottoms of your trousers as you walked across the car park every evening.'

'Right,' Gilbert said. 'Having solved my problem of how to dispose of wet teabags, is that it, or is there something even more pressing?'

I looked at Maggie and spread my fingers, inviting her to talk. She told the super everything Janet Saunders had alleged the night before, and the little we knew about Darryl the Rapist.

Gilbert looked grave and gave a big sigh. 'Has anyone recognised him?' he asked.

I shook my head. 'No, but it's early doors. And if he's local he shouldn't be too hard to find. He seems to be a creature of habit.'

'So you want to fetch him in?'

'I think we should. We need to know who he is, at the very least.'

'OK, but don't waste too much time on it.'

There was a look of panic on Maggie's face as she looked from one of us to the other. 'What's the problem?' she demanded. 'He's a regular in the Tap and Spile. We'll get him.'

'It might be better, Maggie, if we didn't,' I suggested.

'And let him get away with rape!'

'Which would Mrs Saunders prefer: not catching him, or we arrest him and the CPS refuses to prosecute?'

Gilbert said: 'Darryl was right, Maggie. It'd be her word against his. The vast majority of rapists are known to their victims, and we have a less than thirty per cent conviction rate – if we go ahead with it. It looks as if he knows the score.'

'We can't just let him get away with it,' she protested.

'What would happend if it went to court?' I asked her. 'I liked Janet. I admire her courage and believe every word she said. But how would she look in the witness box?' I took hold of my thumb, as if counting. 'Her husband has the daughter through the week. That looks to me as if he has custody. Why is that? Was she the guilty party?' I moved to my index finger. 'Janet works in the pub three nights per week, but doesn't have a full-time job. Is she on benefits? Almost certainly. Does she declare her pub income?' I shrugged my shoulders. 'They're just for starters. What else might we find out about her that can be twisted by a barrister to destroy her character? She'd get torn to pieces, Maggie. It'd be worse than the rape.'

Poor Maggie looked shell-shocked. She'd heard of cases like this, heard of judges who still lived in the Stone Age and believed that 'she was asking for it' was a sound defence. But it's impossible to accept that there might be another point of view when you've dried the victim's tears, wiped the snot off her cheek and steadied her trembling shoulders. I didn't mention the final kick in the teeth: if the CPS decided that it wasn't worth pursuing, or if Janet decided not to give evidence, we regarded it as a clear-up.

'But,' Gilbert said, removing his half-moon spectacles and polishing them on a large handkerchief, 'as Charlie said, we need to know who he is. If he gets away with it once, he'll do it again. Let's have a look at him, eh?'

I turned to Maggie. 'How do you fancy a couple of nights on the town, with Mrs Saunders?'

'No problem,' she replied.

'Overtime?' I wondered, turning to the super.

He rolled his eyes. 'Two hours,' he said. 'Not a minute more.'

Chapter Two

I caught Annabelle on the telephone when I arrived home. It was rather late, but I was missing her, so I risked it. I'd been for a swift half with Dave and Nigel, and when Dave didn't invite the two of us home to share his evening meal we repaired to the Eastern Promise for something spicy to stimulate our jaded palates. The proprietor joined us and we lingered a while.

'It's me,' I said, recognising her voice, relieved it wasn't Rachel.

'Hello Charles. How are you?'

'Missing you.'

'Me too. Did you try to ring earlier?'

'Yes, I did.'

'Sorry about that. We were invited to a dinner party next door. Only came in a few minutes ago. Have you eaten?'

Annabelle takes a motherly interest in my diet. I said: 'Yes. I've just finished Dover sole, with jacket potato and seasonal vegetables.'

'No you haven't. Tell me the truth.'

I swivelled round in the easy chair and hung my legs over the arm. 'Er, chef's curry of the day,' I said.

'Look after yourself, Charles,' she sighed. 'You must start to eat properly. It's a pity you're not still here. We are going up to London tomorrow evening, to a brand new restaurant that has just been opened by one of George's clients, somewhere in the West End. He's recruited some chef from the television and it all sounds rather grand. Apparently he originates from Iran – that's George's client, not the TV chef – but he likes to call himself a Persian. Rachel says he's the wealthiest person she's ever met, and they know quite a few.' She lowered her voice as she told me about the Persian and his wealth.

'Sounds fascinating,' I said, my tone implying exactly the opposite. 'Let me know all about it.'

'Will do. And what about you? Did you arrive home in time for the social evening last night?'

'Mmm, no problem. The roads were quiet.'

'I'm so glad we could get away for Christmas, Charles. You deserved a break, after what happened last year.' She lowered her voice again. 'Even if we did have separate bedrooms.'

'That won't happen again,' I growled.

We chatted aimlessly for another twenty minutes. I'm not good at small talk, but this was no effort at all. I couldn't believe it was me saying these things, but it felt natural, comfortable. This was a second chance for both of us, and we were taking things very slowly, but it felt good.

We said our goodbyes. I hoped she would enjoy her posh meal and she told me to be careful. I watched the late news and went to bed, but I knew I wouldn't sleep. Too many people had reminded me about last Christmas, and I didn't need any reminding at all. I lay on my back, gazing at the ceiling, thinking about Annabelle, churning over all those emotions, imagined conversations and secret signals that I thought I'd grown out of at about the time my acne went away. It didn't work.

A car turned into the end of the street. A shaft of light

through a chink in the curtains swung slowly across the wall and over the ceiling, as if searching for something. I half hoped it was coming for me, but I heard a door slam several houses away, and the screech of a garage door that desperately needed a squirt of garage door oil. I sank back into my pillows and gave way to last year's memories.

Susan Crabtree threw herself off the multi-storey car park on the eve of the anniversary of the birth of Christ. No one saw her jump, so all we had was a dead body on the pavement, last week's paper blown against her leggings and a ribbon of blood gravitating towards the drain. I found a purse and a bunch of keys in the pocket of her anorak, and saw that she had brown eyes and a polyp near the corner of her mouth. A pair of shattered spectacles lay nearby and their indentations were visible on the sides of her nose. I couldn't be sure that she hadn't been hit by a car or even shot, so I checked for tell-tale marks as well as I knew how. We needed a head start on the pathologist, if possible. I gently lifted a strand of hair away from her ear and noticed that it wasn't pierced. One thing she wasn't was a fashion victim.

The doctor who pronounced her dead gave her a more thorough examination and concluded that she'd come from the fifth floor, the short way. The next question was all mine: was she pushed or did she jump? An ambulance took her to the hospital mortuary and fifteen minutes later myself and a uniformed PC were unlocking the door of Susan's bedsit.

He found the bundle, but from its shape we both had a good idea what might be in it. It was wrapped in newspaper and tightly bound with Sellotape, so it looked like something from an Egyptian tomb, except that they didn't have the *Guardian* in those days. I found a pair of scissors in a drawer next to the sink and the PC placed the bundle on a chest of drawers under the window, where the light was best. I started snipping. I get all the dirty jobs.

Inside, we found a tiny baby, wearing a blue romper suit with white and pink roses appliquéd to it. Blue for a boy. According to the dictionary infanticide is any killing of a child. In legal terms it means the killing of a baby while suffering from post-natal depression. Either way, it's a bummer.

I spent that Christmas Day morning in the post-mortem room of Heckley General Hospital. It's in the basement, adjoining the mortuary, and feels like you are deep in some nuclear bomb-proof bunker. All stainless steel, dripping taps and cold light. I took a chair to the farthest corner and settled down, praying that the professor wouldn't say: 'This is interesting, Charlie. Come and have a look.'

He didn't. I listened to his litany and said my amens silently, in my head. Miss Crabtree's injuries were massive, consistent with a fall from a high building, but death was probably instant, from the fractured skull. The shape of the fracture matched the flatness of the pavement. She was about twenty, and appeared to have been in good health. No operation scars other than a not fully healed episiotomy. The prof looked up at me after he'd droned that piece of information into the tape recorder and explained: 'She's given birth in the last three weeks.'

He opened her up, examined her organs and took his samples, to go away for analysis. Eventually he stepped back, saying: 'I think that's all we need,' and his assistant took over to do the tidying up.

I said: 'Does post-natal depression leave any signs, Professor?'

'I'm afraid not, Inspector,' he replied.

He changed his gloves and overalls and I saw him sneak a

look at the clock. It was eleven forty-five, and every kitchen in the country would be warming to the smell of roasting turkey. I wondered who did the carving at their house.

'Right,' he said, businesslike. 'Let's have the other one.'

This was the one I wasn't looking forward to. I swivelled the chair the wrong way round and sat with my chin on my folded arms, eyes focused on one perfect white tile on the far wall. The hard back of the plastic chair cut off the circulation to my hands and they became cramped, but it helped close my mind to an image that I didn't want to admit.

I worry about pathologists. More so about their assistants. I suppose they drift into their jobs, like most of us; but they could always drift out of them again, if they wanted, and they rarely do. Is an executioner just a serial killer who's learned how to avoid breaking the law? If so, what sort of a pervert does that make the pathologist?

I've always suspected these two were a pair of callous bastards, so it was a surprise when the Professor said: 'It's Christmas Day, and I need a drink. Let's have a snifter in the office, Charlie.' He'd done his job and we were walking along the corridor, away from the lab, the clatter of the heels of his assistant's shoes echoing off the antiseptic walls.

The Professor only had two heavy tumblers, hidden at the back of a filing cabinet, so he found a disposable cup for himself. It was Johnny Walker. I only had the one, but between us we drank nearly half the bottle before we wished each other a sardonic Merry Christmas and went our separate ways.

I'd telephoned Annabelle to suggest she put the turkey on a low light and had gone round to see Mr and Mrs Crabtree, Susan's parents. Someone else, thank God, had broken the news to them the night before.

Mrs Crabtree made me a cup of tea and sat me in an easy

chair with antimacassars on the back and arms. 'Would you like a piece of cake?' she asked in a soft girlish voice.

'No thank you,' I said. 'Come and sit down. Don't bother about me.'

She took a place on the settee, next to her husband. They were a few years older than me, so it looked as if they'd had Susan, their only child, when they were well past the first flush. That must have made her extra special to them.

After a long silence I told them about a note we'd found at the flat, and the pathologist's preliminary conclusions. Susan had almost certainly suffocated the baby and taken her own life while suffering from post-natal depression. There would be an inquest, but there was no reason why the coroner couldn't release the bodies immediately for a funeral.

Mrs Crabtree knew all about post-natal depression. She'd suffered badly from it herself after Susan's birth. 'Didn't I, William?' she'd prompted, turning to her husband. Ashen face, he nodded confirmation. There was an eloquence in his gesture that spoke volumes about his own ordeal.

I glanced round the room. It was stuffed with bric-à-brac, like a folk museum with too many exhibits and not enough space. Every picture frame was perfectly aligned with its neighbour, every polished surface shone like a millpond on a summer's evening. It was a SOCO's nightmare. I noticed that the feet of the three-piece suite stood in little cups so they wouldn't ruffle the pile, and wondered if I should have removed my shoes when I came in.

Mrs Crabtree had conquered her problem with the only therapy available to her at the time – housework – and poor old William had suffered in silence. I sat with my cup and saucer on my knee because I didn't know where else to put it, until Mrs Crabtree noticed and found me a little tray that clipped on the arm of the chair. She poured me a refill.

I asked a few questions about their daughter. She'd had a boyfriend, obviously, but they'd never met him. She left home shortly after becoming pregnant, because she wanted to be independent.

'Young people do, these days, don't they,' Mrs Crabtree said.

I nodded agreement and wondered how welcome a toddler would have been in that temple to hygiene. I didn't over-do the questions. There was no other crime to solve, and it's not my job to apportion blame or spread guilt. Three teas and an hour later I started to make leaving noises, but I needed to use the bathroom first. In there, everything that didn't hold water wore a fluffy cover, and when I washed my hands I noticed that the plug for the sink rested in a special little holder. Hey, that's a good idea, I thought, for a millisecond, and promptly changed my mind. There was a similar one for the bath plug.

Driving back to Annabelle's I composed my report in my head, for typing later. Typing and driving don't go together. I decided to say that Mrs Crabtree suffered from OTD – Obsessive Tidiness Disorder. I liked the sound of that, and had my first smile of the day. In this job you have to grab one when you can.

That was last Christmas. It was a good point to come out of the daydream, thinking about Annabelle. It was early, still fully dark outside, but I decided to get up. A shower and some breakfast would do me more good than a last desperate hour of snatched sleep. I don't need much sleep.

First bombshell of the day came when I made my customary visit to Gilbert's office. All the troops have been deployed and most villains are still in bed. That's when we relax for a few minutes with a cup in front of us and do the real policing.

'Have you heard about bloody Makinson?' Gilbert growled.

'Er, no.'

'How much do you know about the Dr Jordan job?'

'Next to nothing. Why, what's Makinson done?'

'Humph!' he snorted, tossing his head. 'Only gone and booked himself some leave to celebrate Hogmanay, hasn't he? Thought he'd grab a couple of days skiing in the Cairngorms while he was at it. Region have been on, asking what you're up to. Any chance of you looking after things while he slides up and down the side of a hill wearing a pink suit and make-up on his face?'

'Good for him,' I said. 'His priorities are right. I wish I could be more like that.'

'It doesn't catch villains, though, does it?'

'It probably does. So what's the state of play?'

'They know who did it, apparently, but he's gone away for a few days, too. If he's not done a complete bunk they're expecting him back anytime, so it's just a matter of keeping an eye on his usual address and picking him up. Can you take over tomorrow morning's meeting at HQ? Young Newley and Dave Sparkington are in the team, so they'll fill you in if you can't wait that long.'

'No problem,' I said. 'I've already had a bet with Sparky that they'd have to call me in to catch him.'

'Then it looks as if you won the bet. Now, how are you getting on with this rape job?'

The period after Christmas is harvest time for burglars. Garden sheds, bedrooms and hallways are bristling with new bicycles, power tools and electronic gadgetry. All desirable and highly portable. We'd raided three shops that claimed to 'Buy 'n' Sell Owt', and two of our cells were now stuffed with several thousand pounds worth of goodies, all still under guarantee.

'He said it was an unwanted present,' was the excuse of the week.

'What an ungrateful little sod he must be,' we'd respond, followed by, 'Get your coat.' There must be hundreds of fifteen-year-olds in Heckley who didn't really want another 21-speed, chrome moly-framed Muddy Fox mountain bike. Just think what they could buy with the thirty quid they'd get for it at the hock shop.

We contacted grandparents and favourite aunties and asked them to find the receipts and anything else that might bear a serial number, and a few lucky people had their presents returned. Some were still gift-wrapped.

The rape wasn't so straightforward. Maggie took Janet Saunders on a tour of the town's hostelries without finding Darryl. They had a quick look in the Tap and Spile on two evenings but avoided the landlord. We couldn't be sure how pally he was with Darryl and didn't want him scaring off. We dabble in something called sector policing. Certain officers are allocated areas of town and they try to familiarise themselves with the more visible characters who live there. Jeff Caton, one of my DCs, knew the landlord of the Tap, and gave him a reasonable character reference. He'd once alerted us to a drugs dealer who was using the pub to do business but was himself suspected of selling consignments of booze brought in cheaply from the Continent. That's the sort of villainy I can live with. I wasn't sure whether he'd finger one of his better customers for a rape, but in the absence of any other line of action decided that in the next day or two I'd better have a word with him myself.

At ten to nine on the morning of the thirtieth of December I ran up the front steps of City HQ and asked the WPC manning – personning? – the front desk to direct me to the Dr Jordan incident room. This was the big day, when I took over the enquiry. Walking down the corridor I contemplated Field Marshal Montgomery's pep talk to the Eighth Army prior to the battle of El Alamein. That should rouse them, I thought. Or should I make it Henry V's Agincourt speech? Then again, if I gave them a compilation from the two they might not recognise the sources. At the door to the incident room I paused and looked at my watch, other hand poised over the handle. I was four minutes early, but that was how I did business and they'd better get used to it. I turned the handle and marched in.

Sparky was sprawled in a chair, his feet on another, talking to Nigel who was sitting nearby. The only two others in the room were engrossed in the *Sun* crossword.

'Good morning,' I said.

'Morning, sir,' said the two City HQ detectives, brushing the tabloid to one side.

'Morning, Boss,' Nigel added. Sparky swung his legs to the floor and nodded.

'So, where's everybody else?' I demanded.

'We're it,' Nigel told me.

'Four of you?'

'There's another four on observations, sir,' one of the City DCs interjected. 'Well, two on duty and two off.'

Nigel did the introductions. I knew them by sight but had never worked with either. We shook hands and I gave them the bit about not calling me sir. Formalities over, I asked Nigel to fill me in with the story so far.

The last known person to see the doctor alive was a junky known as Ged Skinner. There was an entry in the doc's diary giving Skinner an appointment at six thirty p.m., about two hours before the estimated time of death. He had a drugs-related record nearly as long as the Duchess of York's last bank statement and DCI Makinson was convinced that he'd done the deed. Motive: possibly theft of a prescription pad. Or maybe just sheer wickedness because the doc wouldn't prescribe. I had to admit that it sounded likely.

'The trouble is,' Nigel continued, 'he's done a bunk. According to his common law wife he'd arranged a ride in a lorry down to London, straight after his appointment with the doctor. She said he had friends there that he was close to, someone he'd grown up with in care, and he tried to see them every Christmas. He'd be gone for about a week, definitely back for the New Year, she reckons, if he hasn't run away completely. We've alerted the Met, but it's like looking for a needle in a needle stack.'

'Do we know for sure why he was seeing the doctor?'

'Yes. He was on methadone. It's all in the doc's records.'

'So maybe he went round expecting to collect a week's supply.'

'That's what we thought.'

'And the doc wouldn't play ball?'

'Could be.'

When someone is on a heroin withdrawal programme they are often prescribed methadone as an alternative, to wean them through the bad times. Some people swear by it, others claim it is more pernicious than the heroin. Many junkies prefer it, as the high is more controllable and the quality is assured. Normal treatment is three doses a day, and the doctors often only issue a prescription for one day at a time. Ged Skinner was going away for a week. Maybe he got stroppy.

'Are these the reports?' I asked, pointing to a foot-high pile of papers.

They nodded.

'Great,' I sighed. 'So, where does Mr Skinner normally live?'

'In a squat in the Nansens,' one of the DCs told me.

The Nansens were a quarter-mile square block of terraced houses built at the turn of the century to house mill workers and named after the great Norwegian explorer and scientist. If only he could see them now.

'How many others live there?'

'About six adults, plus kids and dogs.'

I grimaced and nodded. 'Have you two been on all night?' I asked the City DCs.

They had.

'Right, then get yourselves off home, after you've told the others not to move if Skinner comes back unless they have some back-up. And to let me know. I wouldn't mind being there when we lift him. OK?'

When they'd gone Sparky said: 'I think they prefer working for you rather than Makinson.'

'Mr Makinson has his ways,' I replied, 'and I have mine. Sometimes I think I could learn a few things from him.'

Nigel started pulling his coat on. 'Short meeting,' he said. 'We can't do anything until he shows. Do you need me?'

'Yes. Do you have a warrant to search the squat when Skinner shows?'

'Er, no idea. You can do it, can't you?'

'If we arrest him. What else are you on with?'

'The Sylvan Fields burglaries. A few complications need sorting.'

'Fair enough. I'll have a couple of hours here reading

the file, see if anything jumps out at me. What're you doing, Dave?'

'Three or four scrotes to interview, see how well their stories have been rehearsed. Some stolen property to identify, and the dreaded paperwork, of course.'

'In other words, not much,' I said. 'In that case, meet me in the Tap and Spile at lunchtime, if you can. I think it's time to have a word with the landlord.'

'About the rape?'

'Yeah.'

'What time?'

I glanced at my watch and at the pile of reports. They'd grown since my last look. 'Oh, er, let's say twelve thirty, eh?'

'Right.'

Sparky was following Nigel out through the door when I shouted: 'Dave!'

He poked his head back round it.

'And don't forget,' I told him, 'knowledge catches crooks.'

He nodded and repeated my words. 'Knowledge catches crooks. I'll try to remember.'

It was the quietest incident room I'd ever been in. For two hours the phone never rang. It looked as if nobody knew I was there. Somewhere there should have been several other officers taking care of the assorted jobs that come with a murder enquiry: control staff, SOCO, liaison officer, correspondence diary, HOLMES expert, et cetera, et cetera. It looked as if Mr Makinson hadn't thought it necessary to tell them that I was taking over. Everything was tied up, and all I had to do was lift the culprit and keep him in cold storage until he returned. I thought about getting annoyed, but decided that life was too short.

I tore the grubby top sheet off a new A4 pad and attacked the pile of reports. Two hours later I decided that Makinson was right. The hot suspect for the doctor's murder was Ged Skinner. There were plenty of side alleys along the trail, and I like to think I'd have taken a longer look down them, but the right answer, as I'd learned at the quiz, is usually the obvious one.

From the reports I discovered that the doctor had been a bit of a laddo on the quiet. He had a girlfriend in every consulting room and a few others besides. There were going to be a lot of distraught females at the funeral, casting sideways looks at each other as they dabbed away the mascara. Then the recriminations would start. What's the collective noun for distraught females, I wondered? An anguish? A wail?

A jealous boyfriend or husband could have shot him, but it wasn't likely. The anger usually surfaces long before the violence does, and we'd have heard about it. There would have been public embarrassment and threats, but the doctor appeared to be as discreet as an undertaker's cough.

The White Rose Clinic was something else. I'd driven by many times, watched it being built. It was just another private hospital, as far as I knew, cashing in on the demise of the NHS. Now I learned that it specialised in cosmetic surgery. Why did the doctor, a Fellow of the Royal College of Gynaecologists, freelance one day per week at a clinic that specialised in cosmetic surgery? My mind went into freefall. Maybe I should have taken out that subscription for *Cosmopolitan* after all.

I found the answer in Nigel's next report. The clinic had a lucrative little sideline. They would, at special request, and only for certain valued clients who complied with their rigorous screening procedure, perform abortions. They didn't advertise this service, and relied on word of mouth to attract custom.

Once again, discretion was the name of the game. There'd been no hate mail, no letter bombs, no noisy protestors outside the gates. The anti-abortion lobby is fanatical and violent, but they didn't know the White Rose Clinic existed.

Ged Skinner was our man, no doubt about it.

I went upstairs and had five minutes with Les Isles, the superintendent in overall charge of the case. He was happy to wait another couple of days to see if Skinner surfaced. If he didn't we'd have a rethink. I was ten minutes late when I read the name of the Tap and Spile's landlord above the door and strolled in.

I'd been in the Tap before. I've been in most pubs at least once. The style was nineteen thirties Odeon: all big open rooms, dark wood and half-tiled walls. A drinking palace, nothing more. Back in the fifties they'd tried ballroom dancing, and the mirrored globe still hung in the middle of the ceiling. Pool tables and a juke box were an impoverished attempt at attracting a newer, younger, clientele. They had the money, these days, and were happy to pay two quid for a bottle of cheap foreign lager and not bother with a glass. Hopefully, it would be a long time before I came in again. I spotted Sparky in a corner contemplating a glass of orange juice and made a drinking gesture as I headed to the bar. He shook his head.

The place was nearly deserted. I ordered a glass of orange juice and soda and told the landlord who I was. 'We'd like a word,' I said, pointing to where I'd be sitting. He vanished for a few moments and returned with a female sumo wrestler who looked as if she'd been dragged out of hibernation. She stayed behind the bar and he came to join us.

'This is DC Sparkington,' I said, and launched straight

into it. 'We're looking for a man who is known to be a customer of yours. He's about five-six, five-seven, late twenties and a snappy dresser. Three piece suits and a tie. Close cropped hair. He comes in on Thursdays and Fridays and stands at the bar, but we don't think he's been in since before Christmas. Does he ring a bell?'

The landlord nodded. His shirt sleeves were rolled up and his forearms were black with tattoos. 'Yeah. I fink I know who you mean,' he said. ''Asn't been in for a while, though.'

'He was in on Christmas Eve,' I said.

'Might 'ave been,' he admitted. 'Can't be sure. It was 'eaving in 'ere.'

'Do you have a name for him?' Sparky asked.

'Nah. I chatted to 'im, like, now and again, if you know what I mean. You 'ave to, in this job. Never asked 'is name.'

'He's called Darryl,' I said.

He stroked his stubble with nicotine-stained fingers. 'Yeah, now you mention it, I did 'ear someone call 'im Darryl. What's 'e done?'

'Nothing, we hope. You know what we say: just want him to help us with our enquiries. So what can you tell us about Darryl? What did you find out when you had these little chats?'

He tapped the table with the edge of a beer mat, rotating it in his fingers, gathering his thoughts. How much did he ought to tell us? ''E was a good bloke,' he announced, when he was ready. 'I liked 'im. He 'adn't lived in 'Eckley long, 'e was finding 'is feet, if you know what I mean.'

'Any idea where he came from?' I asked.

'Nah. Never asked.'

'Or his second name?'

'Nah, sorry.'

'Did he come in a car?'

'Good question. I fink 'e did, sometimes, but now and again 'e'd ring for a taxi, if 'e'd 'ad a skinful, if you know what I mean.'

I turned to Dave. 'You know what he means by a skinful, don't you?'

'I've heard of it,' he said.

' 'E 'as some funny tastes in booze,' the landlord declared.

'Funny? In what way?'

' 'E kept asking if we 'ad any Benedictine. Said there was nowt like it with a drop of 'ot water for keeping t'cold out.'

'I'll remember that,' Sparky said. 'Anything else?'

'Nah, I don't fink so.' He studied for a few seconds, his brow furrowed with concentration until enlightenment brightened his face. 'Yeah, there is one fing. I know what 'e does for a living. 'E's an estate agent. 'E said that if I 'eard of anyone who wanted an 'ouse, or a mortgage, to let 'im know. 'E was their man, 'e reckoned.'

'An estate agent. That's useful,' I said, draining my glass and placing it carefully smack in the middle of its mat. It was time to move up a gear. 'According to our information,' I told him, 'on Christmas Eve he was chatting up one of your barmaids. Know anything about that?'

The frown returned briefly, but he'd evidently decided to play ball with us. In the balance of things keeping in with the police might be more profitable than Darryl's friendship. 'Yeah, that'd be Jan – Janet,' he replied. ' 'E asked me where she lived; said 'e might walk 'er 'ome, if you know what I mean.'

'So what did you tell him?' Sparky asked.

' 'Ow d'you mean?'

'Did you tell him where she lived?'

'No. Well, yeah. I don't know the number. It's the end 'ouse on Marsden Road, near the light, 'bout five minutes walk from 'ere.'

'And you told him that?'

'Yeah, I might 'ave done,' he admitted.

Sparky was about to speak again but I raised a finger to silence him. 'Has Janet been in lately?' I asked.

'No, not since that night.' He pondered on this, then said: ''Ere, they 'aven't run off together, 'ave they?'

'Not that we know of,' I told him. 'Now we know where she lives we might call on her. Sorry, Dave,' I added. 'What were you about to say?'

Sparky is as tall as me but about four stones heavier. He's probably my closest friend, and I'd hate him for an enemy. He's an archetypal Yorkshireman, with an attitude. He planted his elbows on the rickety table and leaned forward, towards the landlord. 'You told Darryl where Janet lived,' he stated.

The landlord nodded. 'Yeah, I fink I did.'

'What else did you tell him?'

'Nowt.'

'Nothing? Are you sure?'

'Yeah, 'course I'm sure.'

Sparky sat upright again. 'Have you ever been to Janet's house,' he asked.

The landlord cast a furtive glance at Godzilla behind the bar. She was engrossed in that morning's tabloid. 'Er, yeah, a couple o' times,' he confessed in a hushed voice.

'Were you invited?' Sparky asked.

'Yeah, well, not exactly.'

'You invited yourself round, was that it?'

'No, not exactly. She's all right, is Janet. I like 'er. It

was raining cats an' dogs one night, 'owling down, so I ran 'er 'ome in t'car. Then I called in a couple o' times on a Monday night. It's dead in 'ere, so I 'ave a night off, if you know what I mean.'

Sparky leaned forward again. 'Did you,' he asked, very slowly, 'ever have sex with her?'

The landlord shook his head. 'No.'

'But you would have liked to?'

'Yeah, well . . .' He cast another glance towards the bar. No other words were necessary.

Dave heaved a big sigh and sat up, looking at me. It was my turn. I said: 'But you tried? You offered your services?'

'Yeah, well, I fought, you know, she was on 'er own, like, an' I'm as good as, an' everyfing.'

'What did she say?'

'She weren't interested. She was good about it, though. Said she preferred to keep fings on a business footing, if you know what I mean.'

Good for you, Janet, I thought. 'And did you tell Darryl that?' I asked.

The landlord shuffled in his seat, uncomfortable.

'Or,' I continued, 'did you just tell him that you'd been round to her house a couple of times and that she'd made you welcome, *If you know what I mean?* Is that what you did, eh? Make him think that Janet was available for any fucking deadbeat who fancies a screw! Was that it?'

I wanted to take him by the throat and shake him until his eyeballs turned to cheese. I wanted to tell him that thanks to him and his pathetic inadequacies Darryl went round and raped Janet with a Kitchen Devil carver held to her throat, while she was wrapping her daughter's Christmas presents. But I didn't, because I wasn't allowed to.

I felt Sparky's hand on my arm. 'Let's go,' he said. 'We've got all we can here.'

Our cars were side by side in the car park. I leaned on the side of mine while Sparky unlocked his door. 'Thanks for your help, Dave,' I said. 'You did well.'

'I thought you were going to plant him.'

'I meant before that. I think we know a bit more about our friend Darryl, now.'

'Except the important stuff, like his surname and his address.'

'Yeah, well, maybe Maggie will come up with something.'

Dave swung into the driving seat and pulled the belt over his stomach. 'It's odd we don't know him,' he said. 'I wonder where he comes from?'

'Who? Darryl?'

'Mmm.'

'Oh, I know where he comes from.'

'You know? How?'

I tapped the side of my head with a forefinger and asked: 'Remember the office motto: knowledge is power?'

'I thought it was knowledge catches crooks.'

'Sorry, you're right. Knowledge catches crooks.'

'So where does he come from?'

'Burnley.'

'Burnley!'

'Burnley. As sure as God made Wallace Arnold buses.'

Chapter Three

Annabelle rang me that evening. 'Before you ask,' I told her, 'I've had a piece of cod from the market, grilled to perfection – mmm! – with some melted cheese over it, and a few vegetables.' Actually it was boil-in-the-bag, but what you don't know can't give you indigestion.

'Well done,' she replied. 'I'm glad you are eating sensibly, if you are telling the truth.'

'Scout's honour. Followed by a big cream bun from the bakery. What about you? How did your evening with Farouk go?'

'Farouk? Who's Farouk?'

'This Egyptian carpet dealer who took you to his restaurant.'

'He's Persian, and he's called Xav. I imagine it is short for Xavier. Actually he's very nice. Older than I expected, but ever so charming.'

'I'm jealous already. How was the meal?'

'The meal itself was fine, but I think I may have upset George and Rachel.'

'Go on,' I laughed.

'Blame it on your Yorkshire forthrightness rubbing off on me . . .'

'Bluntness,' I interrupted. 'We call it bluntness.'

'Bluntness, then. Poor old Xav asked me what I thought of

his lovely new restaurant, so I told him. George looked ever so embarrassed and if looks could kill you'd have an APW out for Rachel. Did I get that right?'

'Ha ha! That's my girl. What did you say?'

'Well, the restaurant is called Omar Khayyam's, rather predictably, and Xav has the contract for a chain of them, attached to something called Luxotel Hotel and Conference Centres. It is supposed to be an alternative dining experience, more upmarket than the hotel restaurants, to give top businessmen somewhere to impress their more affluent clients.'

'I'm impressed already,' I said, 'and I haven't even been.'

'You would have seen it for what it was,' Annabelle assured me. 'For a start, I told him that the name was naff. I said it sounded like a takeaway.' She giggled at the memory. 'Then I criticised the decor. It was all done in pale green and lilacs, what you would describe as a puff's boudoir. I told him that I would have chosen something bolder; perhaps largely white, with black and red panels and gold borders; something with a more Eastern feel.'

'Sounds good to me. What did he say?'

'That was the surprising thing. He had a good look around and said he agreed. He wished that he had consulted me earlier. I wondered if he was just being polite, or patronising me.'

'Don't be silly,' I said. 'I've told you before, you have a flair for that kind of thing.'

'Then he asked me to suggest another name, before it was too late and he'd had all the signs made. After some thought I said I'd call it Jamshyd's.'

'Jamshyds?'

'That's right. He was a Persian king, fabulously wealthy, mentioned in the Rubaiyat.'

I said: 'As in: "The wild ass stamps o'er his head, and he lies fast asleep"?'

'Mmm, not quite, that was another king. "The lion and the lizard keep the courts where Jamshyd gloried and drank deep," but I'm still impressed.'

'Don't be – it's the only poem I know. Your version sounds much more appropriate. I'm glad you enjoyed yourself, Annabelle, and it sounds as if you gave them something to think about. So when are you coming home? You know I'll be extremely happy to come and fetch you.'

'Ah. That's why I rang.' her voice had dropped several tones. 'Would you be very disappointed if I stayed down here for the New Year, Charles? Xav rang me earlier today and said he would like to show me the designs for the next restaurant. Apparently it is nearly at the decoration stage and he needs to move fast if he's changing things. He says he will even pay me consultancy fees, would you believe? Do you mind, love? I'll come back if you insist.'

What do you say? Do you insist? The words *no win situation* are not usually anywhere near the tip of my tongue, but right then I couldn't think of a better expression.

'Oh,' I said.

'It's only a couple of days. I'll come back on the train, the day after New Year's day.'

That was three days. 'Er, right,' I mumbled. 'You've, er, caught me off balance. I was looking forward to coming to collect you.'

'Oh, I'm sorry if I've upset your plans, Charles, but I really would like to have a go at this. It's a wonderful opportunity.'

Bugger my plans, I thought, it's me that's upset. 'Yes,

I can see that,' I told her. 'Don't worry about me. You show those experts a thing or two that they couldn't learn at college, and tell me all about it when you come home, eh?'

'I knew you would understand, and you know what they say?'

'What's that?'

'Absence makes the heart grow fonder, of course.'

'Of course.' And so does lying in each other's arms under a duvet, with the rain blowing soundlessly against the double glazing and Rimsky's *Sheherazade* playing very low on the CD. And I know which I prefer.

You don't see a suspect for weeks, then two come along at the same time. I was listening to *Today* on Radio 4, mug of tea in hand, feet on the gas fire, when the phone rang. The Prime Minister was on the radio, delivering his New Year message. Law and Order was high on the priority list again. He was determined to make Britain a safer place for young and old alike. Measures would be announced to curb the increasing tendency towards violence and he promised five thousand more policemen on the beat by the end of next year. I yawned and reached for the phone.

A refrigerated van had drawn up at the end of Ged Skinner's street and a figure answering to his description had leaped down from it, carrying a sports bag, and entered the squat.

'I'll be with you in about twenty minutes,' I said.

I was pulling my coat on when the phone rang again.

'Priest.'

'It's Maggie, Boss. I didn't want to ring you last night, but I went for a look-round with Janet Saunders and we found Darryl.'

'Brilliant! Well done.'

'He's called Darryl Buxton, but we've nothing on him.'

'Great. Look, Maggie, I'm sorry to cut you off in your finest hour, but I'm on my way to lift the bloke we think did the doctor. You stay with it today, see what else you can find, and I'll have a word with you later. OK?'

'Will do. Good luck.'

'Cheers.'

The unseasonable weather was changing; the sky clearing and the breeze swinging to the North. I pulled my down-filled jacket out of the closet and swapped the contents of my pockets round. Once I wore it up mountains, but now it was just another winter coat. Outside, the fieldfares were stuffing themselves with my cotoneaster berries, as if they knew something we didn't.

A panda car was parked two streets away from the squat, with Sparky's Escort behind it. I pulled in behind them and spoke to the crew of the panda.

'Let's get on with it,' I said.

One of them lifted a radio. 'Mr Priest is here. Ready when you are.'

'OK,' came the reply. 'Let's go go go!'

We didn't make a fuss. Just drove to the front and back of the house and marched into the yard. I hammered on the door.

Sparky nodded at my jacket. 'Expecting bad weather?'

I nodded and sniffed. 'Smell that breeze,' I said. 'That's ice, straight from the Arctic.'

He looked up at the sky and sniffed audibly. 'And polar bear shit,' he confirmed.

A bleary-eyed woman in a pink candlewick housecoat came to the door. It was only seven a.m. but she'd no doubt still be wearing it at noon. She had a ring through her nose and on her throat was the biggest ripe blackhead I've ever seen. I could hardly take my eyes off it. The nearest she got to soap was on TV five evenings per week.

'Police,' I said. 'We believe Ged Skinner is here. Could you find him, please.'

'I'll, er, go look,' she mumbled, and tried to close the door. I put my arm out to hold it open and went in. Sparky and a City DC followed me.

'Ged!' the woman shouted. 'It's the police, for you!'

We were standing in a dismal passage with brown walls and lino on the floor. A pram and a bike took up most of the room and several kid's toys lay around. Doors opened and inquisitive faces, mainly children's, poked round them. A little girl appeared, wearing a short vest and no knickers. She stared up at us, fingers in her mouth. Sparky spoke to her. He's good with kids and I'm grateful.

Skinner came bouncing down the stairs wearing a T-shirt with the Nike logo on the front and shell suit bottoms with don't-I-look-stupid stripes under one knee. He was about five foot nine, with longish hair and a little wisp of a beard. His complexion looked as if it came with extra mozzarella. 'What's up?' he asked.

'Ged Skinner?'

'Yeah. What of it?'

'We'd like a word with you, somewhere more private. How about coming out to the car?'

'What's it about?'

'We'll tell you there.'

'I'm having my breakfast,' he protested. 'I've just come in.'

'We won't keep you long,' I said. Fifteen years was the time I had in mind. The passage was filling with people of assorted ages and states of dress.

''E's only just come in,' a spotty youth in what looked

like a Dodgers nightshirt confirmed. I didn't know they did nightshirts.

'Look,' I told Skinner. 'We need to talk to you. It can either be here or down at the station, the choice is yours.'

'I'm not going anywhere 'less you tell me what it's about.'

The woman with the blackhead had adopted a protective stance alongside him. 'Why don't you leave us alone?' she ranted. 'We 'aven't done nothing.'

I was waiting for the next line: 'Why aren't you out catching murderers,' but she said: ''Aven't you anything better to do?'

'Are you coming out to the car?' I demanded.

'I'm not going nowhere unless you tell me what it's about.'

'OK, have it your way. Ged Skinner, I am arresting you on suspicion of being involved in the death of Dr Clive Jordan. You do not have to say anything but it may harm your defence if you do not mention, when questioned, something that you later rely on in court. Anything you do say may be given in evidence. Do you understand? Good, let's go.'

The spectators were stunned into silence, except for the little girl who started to cry. 'The doctor?' Skinner said, shaken. 'You think it was me what did the doctor?'

'Take him in,' I told Sparky, 'and let's have this place searched.'

'Let's see your warrant,' Skinner insisted.

'I'm all the warrant we need,' I told him. 'Let's go.'

'Hang on,' Skinner protested. 'I haven't got any shoes on.'

I looked down and saw his bare feet for the first time. 'For God's sake, someone fetch his shoes,' I yelled.

'Where do you want him taking, guv,' the City DC asked.

'Heckley. We're still allowed to make our own tea there.'

While Skinner was being processed I had a toasted tea cake in the canteen then ran upstairs to see if anything was happening in the office that I needed to know about. Maggie was hanging her coat up.

'Did you get him?' she asked.

'Bet your ass,' I replied with a wink and a jerk of the head. 'But we had to arrest him. We'll let him settle in, have a word with the duty solicitor, then I'll put the thumbscrews on him.'

It had worked out well. The evidence was a bit weak, all circumstantial, and the custody sergeant might have thrown it out, so I'd normally have done an initial interview and hoped something would have come from that. We'd arrested him because he wouldn't cooperate, and that meant that I could now authorise a property search.

'Have you time to hear about Darryl?'

'You may not believe it, Maggie,' I told her, 'but Darryl is my number one priority. I'm just Makinson's running dog in this murder case. Fire away – what have you got?'

She tucked her blouse into her skirt and sat down opposite me. Her hair was wet, several strands clinging to her forehead. 'We went looking for him last night,' she began. 'Janet and me, that is. Found him in a town-centre pub. The Huntsman. It was fifties night – you'd have been at home. Darryl was leaning on the bar, chatting to anyone who came to be served. Got the impression that was his technique. It was early, about eight thirty. Looked like we'd have a long wait and Janet was upset, so I phoned for a taxi and sent her home. Hope that's all right?'

'No problem. Go on.'

'Darryl stayed until chucking-out time. He drove home

alone and I followed him to a flat in that posh new block near the canal. The address matched the one on record for the owner of the Mondeo he was driving. He's called Darryl Buxton and he's clean, I'm afraid. All the other details are on your desk.'

'Brilliant, Maggie. We'll make a detective of you yet. Looks as if you'd better take an afternoon off when things settle down – you heard what Mr Wood said about overtime.'

'That's OK. There's more. This morning I followed him to his place of employment. He works in the town centre, for someone called Homes 4U. That's number 4, capital U. Snappy, eh?'

'Speaks volumes about their clientele,' I said.

'Quite. They're some sort of estate agents, specialising in cheap rentals, DHSS work, that sort of stuff. They're big around Manchester and are just expanding to this side of the Pennines. I rang them up and had a girl-to-girl chat with their receptionist. She sounded a bit dim. Darryl is the local manager.'

We were sitting at Nigel's desk and I'd straightened most of his paper clips as I listened to Maggie. I pulled at his middle drawer to find some more and saw the *Guardian*, open at the crossword. My proudest achievement is that I've created the only department in the force where officers dare to be seen reading the *Guardian*. I slid the drawer shut again.

'Now you've sorted that out,' I said, 'I don't suppose you'd like to have a go at this murder case would you? Sort that out, too?'

Maggie smiled and her cheeks flushed, just a little. 'If you need me, but what I'd really like is a bacon sandwich in the canteen, if you don't mind.'

I nodded my approval and she asked me if I was joining her. 'No, I've just come from there,' I said.

When she'd gone I pulled the crossword out and read through the clues. They might as well have been written in Mandarin Chinese. One across was 'Editor rejected ruse set out (6).' Possibly an anagram of *set out*, but nothing flashed into my brain. I put potato. Two lines below was nine across: 'Comes down, about to fix forest in grand planned development (9,9).' The second nine referred to twelve across. I wrote apple pies and crocodile in the appropriate squares. For fifteen, nineteen, twenty-two and twenty-seven across I put: haddock, ruminant, frogspawn and Zatopek.

Then, with a blunt black fibre-tipped pen, I carefully drew a line through all the clues for the lines that I'd filled in. You need inspiration like that for the *Guardian* crossword.

I was admiring my work when a pair of hands fell on my shoulders. 'Need any help?' Sparky asked.

'Er, n-no thanks,' I stuttered, guiltily, 'I, er, think that's as far as I can go.'

'Read the clue out,' he invited.

'Clue!' I gasped. 'Clue! Since when did we bother with clues?'

He'd come to tell me that the interview room was set up and Skinner and the duty solicitor were waiting for us. We discussed tactics for ten minutes and went downstairs.

Skinner was smoking. We, the employees, are not allowed to smoke in the nick, but stopping our clients doing so would be to violate their civil liberties. I found him an ashtray. Sparky switched the tape recorder on and did the introductions. It was ten thirty a.m. and we had him for another twenty-three hours. I verified that he was Ged Skinner and his main place of residence was the squat.

'Did you know Dr Clive Jordan?' I asked.

'Yeah,' he grunted.

'How did you know him?'

''Cos he was prescribing methadone for me.'

'Why?'

He looked straight into my eyes and said: ''Cos I'm a fucking dope-head, ain't I?'

I said: 'I know why you were taking methadone. What I want to know is why was Dr Jordan prescribing it for you? He wasn't your GP, was he? And as far as we know he wasn't attached to any programme.'

Skinner galloped his fingertips on the table. 'Yeah,' he said. 'Sorry. I, er, met him about five weeks ago, at the General. The wife was sent to see him, by her doctor. Women's problems. She was worried – scared – so I went in with her. He was good about it. Brilliant. Said she was pregnant but there was nothing to worry about, if she was careful with herself. Gave her some pills and told her to come back in a month. Then he looked at me and said: "That's her fixed up, now what are we going to do about you?" I said "How do you mean?" and he told me that if I didn't get off drugs I might not live to see my kid.'

'Who told him you were on drugs?'

'Nobody, I don't think. He could see from the state I was in.' He raised his arms and said: 'This is sound, for me.'

'Go on,' I invited.

He folded his arms and sat for a few moments with his chin on his chest. 'I've done all the cures,' he began. 'All the do-gooders have had a go at me. St Hilda's, Project 2000, the City Limits Trust. You name it, I've done it. But nobody talked to me like he did. They're all sympathy and encouragement and "I know what you're going through."' He raised the pitch of his voice for the last bit and affected a posh accent. 'There was none of that with the doc. He said:

"Get off it now or you're dead. D-E-A-D fucking dead!" He said he'd help me as much as he could, but he couldn't do it for me. It was up to me. I said right. Let's give it a go.'

'So he started prescribing methadone for you.'

'That's right. One day at a time. He'd leave a script for me either at the hospital or, later, I'd collect one from his flat. I'm down to twenty milligrams.'

'From what?'

'From whatever I could get. 'Bout hundred milligrams, plus horse.'

'And you were doing OK?'

'Yeah. You don't gouch out on it, but it helps you through the bad times, which is all the H does, when you've been using it as long as me.'

'So when did you last see him?'

'Day before Christmas Eve, 'bout half past six.'

'At his house?'

'That's right.'

'How long were you with him?'

'Not long. Two minutes. We just stood on the doorstep chatting for a while. He gave me a script for two days and a letter to take to this GP in London.'

He was anticipating my questions. I sat back and let Sparky take over.

'What GP in London?' he asked.

'A GP in London. When I told him that I wanted to go there he persuaded me that a script for a week wasn't a good idea.'

'Where were you going in London?'

'Wandsworth.'

Sparky made an encouraging gesture with one hand. 'You're allowed to elaborate,' he said. The new caution has been a big help. Suspects now know that silence, or being obstructionist, might ruin their defence, so they usually give an answer of sorts, but Skinner was almost being helpful.

'Right,' he said. 'I have some good friends in Wandsworth. Jim and Mary. We was in care together, from being about ten. We split up when we were sixteen, but we've always kept in touch. I go see them every Christmas, if I can. I told the doctor and he asked me to find out the name of a GP down there. He rang him and did me a letter of introduction, so I got my scripts no problem.'

'We need Jim and Mary's address, and the doctor's,' Sparky told him. Skinner recited them from memory and I wrote them down to save time waiting for the tape to be transcribed.

'So where were you at eight o'clock that night,' Sparky went on.

'Easy. In a van on my way down south.'

'Can you prove it?'

'My brother-in-law was driving it. Well, he's not really my brother-in-law. He picked me up at home just after six. We went round to the doc's and then set off. Will that do?'

'No.'

'I don't want to drag him into it, if I can. He's not supposed to take passengers.'

I chipped in with: 'Did you stop anywhere?'

'Yeah. We stopped for a fry-up.'

'Where?'

'Don't know the name of the place. It's on the Peterborough road, just after the long red wall, after you pass the airfield.'

Sparky and I looked blank. There's a whole culture of travellers who never use a map, never remember a road number; they navigate by landmarks, like the early fliers did.

'Near the greenhouses,' he explained.

'Right,' I said. 'And did you save the receipt?'

'No.'

'What a pity.'

'The brother-in-law claimed it. He insisted on separate receipts and kept them both. For his expenses. He'll have it.'

We were supposed to be tying him up and he was doing it to us. 'Two fry-ups in one day,' I said. 'He'll clog his arteries.'

'No, he didn't eat them both,' Skinner told me, earnestly. 'I had one of them. He just told his firm that he had, for the money.' Now he was taking the piss.

Sparky said: 'How did you learn of the doctor's death?'

'Jim and Mary have a phone. The wife – she's not really the wife – rang me, Christmas Day. Said it'd been on Radio Leeds.'

'What did you think?'

He shrugged his shoulders. 'What am I going to do for my scripts? That's what drugs do to you.'

'Who did you get your drugs off before the methadone?' I asked.

A look of panic flashed across his face. 'I can't tell you that. I'd be a dead man.'

'OK. If you didn't kill the doctor, who did? Were you in with anyone heavy? Had you told your supplier about him? Was he losing a good customer because of the doc?'

'No. I didn't tell a soul, except the wife. And I bought my H casual, like. Nothing regular. Half a gram, when I had the money. That's all. It's all the other stuff they put in it that fucks you up.'

'Are you all right for today?' I asked.

'Yeah, but I haven't got it with me.'

'And tomorrow?'

'I need to fix something for tomorrow.'

'Want our doctor to see you?'

He hesitated. 'I don't know. Maybe now's the time to break with it.'

'OK,' I said. 'We'll leave it at that, for now.'

He was taken to one of the cells. Judging by his trousers, the duty solicitor went for a round of golf and Sparky and I trudged up the stairs to the CID office.

'What do you reckon?' Sparky asked. Someone always asks it. I knew what I reckoned, but I wasn't admitting it, yet.

'Check it all out,' I said. 'Let's see what they turn up at the squat – a gun would be nice. Talk to the brother-in-law, get the receipts. Then let's have a look at Jim and Mary in Wandsworth and the doctor down there. Have a word with traffic. Try to arrange for someone local to get a receipt for a breakfast from the cafe-near-the-wall-by-the-silver-stream-under-the-trees-by-the-flyover. Could be worse. It could have been in Welsh.'

Maggie was in the office. 'It's on your desk,' she said.

'That was quick.'

'We don't mess about. When are we going to have a word with him?'

'Darryl?'

'Mmm.'

'Not yet,' I told her. 'I want to concentrate on the doctor job, if you don't mind. Makinson will be back on the second, and I've a feeling he's not going to be pleased with what I have to say. Maybe we'll go for Mr Buxton when the debris has fallen to the ground, eh?'

'What about tomorrow? We could get him then.'

'Tomorrow, Maggie, is a bank holiday. I suggest we all

have the day off. What's good enough for Mr Makinson is good enough for the rest of us.'

'Blimey!' she exclaimed. 'I don't believe what I'm hearing.'

'Well just keep your fingers crossed that our Darryl doesn't strike again.'

'I never thought of that. Do you think he might?'

'I doubt it. Hopefully this was a one-off.' I wondered if I was making a mistake. Maybe we should put the scarers on him as soon as possible. 'Have you an Almanac handy?' I asked. 'There is one avenue we can try.'

Maggie fetched it from where it hung on a piece of string from a nail in the notice board. I thumbed through it after studying the map and dialled a number.

'Pendle Police Headquarters,' a voice sang in my ear.

'Good morning,' I said. 'Could you please put me through to DI Drago at Burnley Padiham Road CID.'

'Putting you through.'

After the usual beeping and clicking a voice said: 'Padiham Road CID. DI Smith speaking.'

'I said: 'Hello. This is DI Charlie Priest at Heckley CID. Is DI Drago available, please?'

'Drago? DI Drago? Sorry, Mr Priest, I've never heard of him.'

I looked at the date on the front of the Almanac. It was eight years old. 'Oh,' I said. 'He must have moved on. Doesn't time fly? Peter Drago owed me a favour and I was calling it in. We were at the Academy together a long time ago, and one night I saved him from a six-foot bald-headed nymphomaniac. I wonder if you can help me. How's your local knowledge?'

'Not brilliant, I'm afraid. Only been here three weeks. I was at Chester before that.'

'Right. Well, I'd be very grateful if you could make a few enquiries on my behalf with your intelligence officer or any other local men.'

'I'll see what we can do, Mr Priest.'

'Good. Thanks. We are about to have a talk with a character called Darryl Buxton, about an alleged rape on Christmas Eve. He has no form, but we think he may have come from Burnley. If I give you his description do you think you could see if he's known to anyone, please?'

'You mean, informally?'

I winked at Maggie. 'Yes, informally. Just between ourselves.'

He told me that I wouldn't be able to use it and I said yes, I was aware that I wouldn't be able to use it, and he eventually said he would, so I gave him the description. Computers are good for storing information, but there are some things you just daren't put on them. I wanted to know if there was anything like that for Darryl Buxton. All's fair in love and law.

'What was all that about?' Maggie asked as I replaced the handset. 'What's Burnley got to do with it?'

'It's a long story,' I replied, settling back in the chair. 'It all started in the First World War.'

The East Lancashire Regiment was in the thick of it. In 1914 they recruited locally: men from one town, or one street, enlisting together to form what were known as Pals Battalions. Brother trained and fought side by side with brother, father with son. They escaped the drudgery of mill or coalmine to take the King's shilling and fight to make the world a better place. They yelled blood-curdling war-cries as they stabbed bags of straw with their bayonets and imagined they were killing Germans. The only difference, they were assured, was that the real thing would be running away from them. Nobody told them that their enemy was probably a blond-haired Adonis who'd grown up in the fields and mountains of Bavaria, not stooped over loom or shovel breathing foul air for twelve hours per day.

Nobody told them about machine guns.

Nobody told them about the Military Police who followed behind and shot anyone who turned to run, even though their comrades were falling around them like over-ripe plums in the first autumn gale.

And nobody ever mentioned the firing squads that were waiting for the frightened or the feeble or the ones who simply saw more suffering than anyone could bear.

When it was over, when the politicians saw the opportunity to *save face*, when Satan himself was sickened by the carnage, those that remained limped their way back towards the Channel, towards home. They left behind their friends, their sight, their youth and, some of them, their sanity.

For the East Lancs, a ragged remnant of their former selves, luck changed. They regrouped and billeted at Fecamp, in Normandy. Centuries before, the Benedictine monks who lived there had devised the medicinal brew of grape and herbs that now bears their name. It was offered to the soldiers of the East Lancs to soothe the pain, and, being fifty per cent proof, it worked. They asked for more. To men who were still young enough to remember every pint of weak beer they'd had, it had a kick like a field gun.

They brought the pestle-shaped bottles home with them, to stand on the sideboard alongside the shell cases, the uniformed photograph and the framed message from the King. And they brought a taste for the contents with them, too.

Like the gene for brown eyes, or cystic fibrosis, or the belief in God, it passed down the generations. Eighty years later a handful of pubs and clubs around Burnley still do a thriving trade in Benedictine, serving it to the great-great-grandchildren of that ragtaggle army that left its dreams 'hanging on the old barbed wire'.

Sparky had joined us. 'You know some stuff,' he said, when I'd finished.

'It doesn't win quizzes,' I admitted.

'So you reckon he comes from Burnley,' Maggie said.

'I'd bet on it.'

She was picking at her fingernails, absent-mindedly removing imaginary dirt from under them with her thumbnail, a faraway expression on her face. 'It'd be nice if they could come up with something,' she said. She wanted Darryl behind bars.

'Day after tomorrow,' I told her. 'We'll have a word with him then. Put it in your new diary.'

Sparky was pulling his coat on. 'I'll get down to the squat, Boss,' he said. 'See if they need any help.'

'OK. I'll probably be here if you want me, but try not to.' I didn't envy them, having to cope with all the residents, plus children and animals. It'd be a pantomime.

'What are you doing tonight?' he asked.

'Not sure. Haven't thought about it.'

'In that case, come round. See the New Year in with us.'

'Aren't you going out?'

'No. Sophie's going to a party, so Daniel would be left on his own. We'll stay in with him.'

'Right, thanks. I'll come round late on, if that's OK?'

'See you then. I might have to tear myself away to fetch Sophie. The joys of fatherhood,' he added, making a face.

A copy of the *Sun* was lying on Jeff Caton's desk, with the headline '5,000 New Cops'. I picked it up and read the story.

It didn't take long. The streets were about to be reclaimed for the people. The PM's new initiative would meet the muggers and vandals and drug pushers head-on, make them realise that they had no future in the New Society. Suddenly, we had Society again. They made it sound as if our towns and villages would be flooded with policemen. You'd be able to walk your dog at two in the morning, safe in the knowledge that a friendly bobby would be standing on every street corner.

I pulled out my calculator and typed 5,000 into it. Divide by forty-three forces, except that the Met would get the lion's share, then by the seventeen divisions in East Pennine and the number of stations in Heckley. We cover twenty-four hours per day, seven days per week, but each officer only works five eight-hour shifts. I tapped the appropriate keys. Then there's holidays, training courses and sick leave. I hit the equals button and watched as minute electrical forces shuffled molecules into new locations, spelling out a number. It said that at any given time the citizens of Heckley would have the benefit of an extra 0.49 of a policeman on duty. Allowing for meal breaks, paperwork and time in court, it worked out as the equivalent of a rooky wolf cub. Halle-flipping-lujah.

I did a report for Makinson and caught up with the burglaries. Lunch was a mug of tea. The doctor in Wandsworth was on his rounds, I was told, but I'd catch him about ten to four. Sparky rang to say that they'd found nothing of interest at the squat and Nigel told me that Skinner's brother-in-law had been traced. He'd be having a word with him shortly.

It had never looked good, and then it all fell to pieces. Nigel came in with the till receipts and they sounded just like the one a Traffic officer from Cambridgeshire described to me. The doctor in Wandsworth verified that he had been contacted by Dr Jordan, and Skinner had collected his prescriptions from him like a good little boy. Jim and Mary were stalwarts of the local church and supported Skinner's story, and finally, we didn't have a weapon.

'Let him go,' Superintendent Wood said.

'Let him go,' Chief Superintendent Isles concurred.

'You can go,' I told Skinner. The only bright spot was the thought of the look on Makinson's sunburnt face when he learned the news, and I wondered how I could wangle being there at the time.

I hung around in the office until I knew the Bamboo Curtain would be open and had my favourite, duck in plum sauce, for tea, washed down with a pint of lager. There was no reason why I shouldn't have a little celebration of my own. The place was almost empty, so early in the evening, and the proprietor came and shared a pot of Chinese tea with me, on the house. Later, it would be rowdy with drunks, but the staff would serve them with patience and courtesy, their contempt suppressed by ten thousand years of oppression.

There were no messages on my ansaphone but the postman had made a delivery. The various financial organisations that knew my address were suggesting that now was the time to reorganise my lifestyle and the house insurance was due. I binned most of it and had a shower.

I had no clean shirts. Well, no decent ones. I don't wear designer clothes and automatically reject anything with the label on the outside. If they want me to advertise their wares they should pay me, or at least bring their prices down. All jeans are made from the same material on the same machines to the same measurements. Only the labels vary, with perhaps an odd row of decorative stitching. I buy mine in the market at half price. I pulled on a pair that had that washed-once look, when the colour is at its brightest.

There is one exception to my aversion to style. Wrangler

do a shirt that has a row of mother-of-pearl press-studs down the front instead of buttons, and the first time I saw one I thought that one day all shirts would be like that. Harold Wilson was at Number Ten at the time, but Scott McKenzie was at number one. I found a faded example in the recesses of the wardrobe and put it on. I was only going to Sparky's; I'd do.

Once upon a time I thought I was trendy, at art school, when I was competing with the other young blokes, like a stag at rutting time. I had an Afghan coat. I gave it to the Oxfam shop, and a couple of years ago I'm sure I saw it on telly, when Kabul fell. What goes around comes around.

I made a mug of tea and relaxed for a while to a Dire Straits CD, hoping Annabelle would call me. It was ten o'clock when the phone rang, as I was opening my front door, leather jacket half on, half off.

'Priest!' I snapped into it, with faked authority.

'Hi, Charlie. Pete Drago. How are you?'

'Hiya, Dragon,' I replied. 'This is a pleasant surprise. I'm fine, how are you?'

'I'm OK, thanks. Counting the days, of course, like you, I suppose.'

'Time flies, don't remind me.'

'It doesn't seem like fifteen years since I rescued you from that big nympho when we were at the Academy.'

'Your memory's playing tricks. It was me rescued you.'

'No it wasn't. I was knocking her off for the rest of the course.'

'So were most of the others.'

'Then everyone was happy. I wonder what happened to her?'

'I married her. So where are you, these days?'

'Ha ha! Good one. I'm at Penrith, back in uniform.'

'Penrith? What took you there?'

'It was either move up here and go back into uniform or have my buttons cut off in front of the massed troops of the division. It's not too bad.'

'I get the message. It sounds as if you haven't changed much.'

'It was a long time ago. Listen, I rang Padiham Road for a chat with a couple of old pals and they said you'd been after me.'

'That's right. We have a suspected rapist called Darryl Buxton who may have originated in Burnley. There's nothing on the PNC for him, so I was hoping for some local knowledge.'

'That's what I was told. When I heard the name the hairs on the back of my neck stood on end, except that it's not quite right. The bloke I'm thinking of is called Darryl *Burton*.'

'Burton?' I repeated. 'No, this is definitely Buxton. What did your man do?'

'He raped a sixteen-year-old schoolgirl, eight years ago. Invited two of them to his flat one bank holiday Monday and plied them with cheap wine. One of them passed out and he raped the other. He pleaded not guilty and just before the trial the girl's parents withdrew the charges. It had been made plain to them that he intended destroying her credibility in court. I think she knew what it was all about.'

'It sounds like our man. What does he look like?'

The description could have been read from Maggie's report. 'Yuppy meets football hooligan' was his final assessment.

'It's him,' I said. 'He's moved away from Burnley and changed his name.'

'If it is the same bloke he's a nasty piece of work. He was

only about twenty, but he worked as a heavy – a repo man – for a firm of bailiffs, or something.'

'This one works for an estate agency called Homes 4U. He's a branch manager.'

'That's them! Homes 4U. Estate agency is putting it a bit high, I'd say. They're not above calling round to slow payers with the baseball bats.'

'Great. You've been a big help, Pete. We're bringing him in after the New Year, so it'll be good to have some background on him.'

'I haven't finished yet,' he said. 'I left a few months later, but I've a feeling that he pulled something similar after I'd gone. The man to talk to is called Herbert Mathews. He was our collator but he retired on ill health about a year ago. I'll give you his address. If it breathed in Burnley, Herbert knew about it.'

We chatted for a while, agreeing that we ought to get together, knowing we wouldn't. We'd said our farewells when a thought struck him. 'Charlie!' he shouted as I was replacing the phone.

'Yeah.'

'I just thought of something. I believe you told Padiham Road that this rape was on Christmas Eve?'

'That's right.'

'Well, the one I investigated was on a bank holiday Monday.'

'So?'

'So you know what tonight is? Maybe there's a pattern.'

'Shit!'

'Quite.'

'Happy New Year.'

'Thanks. And you.'

Chapter Four

We rang off and I sat thinking for a while. Sparky's wife, Shirley, answered when I dialled their number.

'Hi, Shirl,' I said. 'Would you be terribly disappointed if I didn't come round? I'm falling asleep and don't think I'll be very good company.'

'I'll be a teeny bit disappointed,' she replied, 'but my teenage daughter will be devastated.'

'Sophie? I thought she was at a party.'

'She just rang to say it was boring, so Dave's gone to fetch her. At least, that was her excuse. She'll be upset when you're not here.'

'I doubt it,' I said.

'Charlie,' Shirley began, 'don't tell me you haven't noticed that your goddaughter has an almighty crush on you.'

'Er, no, can't say I have.'

'Well she has.'

'Oh heck. What do we do about it?'

'Nothing. We're hoping she'll see the light. Are you sure you can't come round?'

I wanted to. These days invitations are rarer than apprenticeships at the Job Centre. I nearly made a joke about having me for a son-in-law, but decided not to. It was a delicate subject. 'Listen, Shirley,' I said. 'Don't tell Sparky – Dave

– but something's cropped up. I'm going to the nick for an hour, see if I can help, that's all.'

'Oh, right. So what shall I say when they come in?'

'Tell Sophie that I'm curled up in front of the fire with a mug of cocoa and the latest Jeffrey Archer. That should do it.'

'Aversion therapy.'

'Precisely.'

'Charlie?'

'Mmm.'

'Thanks, love. And be careful.'

The town centre was crowded with groups of young people, singing and swaying, spilling into the road as they toured the pubs. Some wore funny hats or strands of streamers round their necks. Nobody wore a coat. They breed 'em tough, these days. The wind had swung again, away from the Pole, but it was still thinner than orphanage custard. Fortunately, alcohol is a good antidote. Tests have shown that vast quantities of it slopping around in the stomach are equivalent to wearing two vests and a jumper.

I eased the car through the crowd, towards the Tap and Spile. The sexes were still segregated, but the time for mass pairing-off was rapidly approaching. A group of giggling girls sharing hardly enough clothes for one staggered into the road. I stopped and waved them across, and the one who got the blouse blew me a kiss. A party of young men in T-shirts shouted at them. Love was in the air, empathy was running high, but it could all change at the drop of a lager bottle or a misunderstood come-on. It was just a matter of time.

Darryl's silver Mondeo wasn't in the Tap's car park. If he had any sense he'd have used a taxi, tonight of all nights. I eased out into the street again and worked my way round most of the town-centre pubs, without finding him. Uniform branch were out in force, but I didn't speak with them.

Once I was clear of the throng I hot-wheeled it to the fancy canal-side development where Darryl lived. It had started life as a wool warehouse, a century and a half ago, when buildings were made to last but there was still something in the budget for ornamentation. It escaped the vandals in the town hall by the thickness of a small bundle of tenners and was now a highly desirable block of upmarket apartments, complete with security gates and private moorings. Most of the parking spots were occupied, but not by Darryl's car. I noticed that some of his neighbours were doing a lot better than he was.

I telephoned the nick and asked for all cars to look out for him. If anyone radioed in with a contact, tell them, I said, to check if he was with a woman. If he was, they had to ruin his chances. I can be a heartless so-and-so. If Charlie's not getting it, nobody gets it.

I drove back to the Tap. The streets were quieter, with everybody inside the pubs, pouring the last desperate drinks down their throats, as if prohibition came in on the chime of midnight. A minibus of women pulled out, leaving a big parking space for me.

I'd forgotten how crowded pubs could be. Did I once enjoy this? I couldn't believe I ever had. It was shoulder to shoulder, with a pall of smoke hugging the ceiling. At my height I was getting a superdose. I looked around and started to fight my way to one of the anterooms that branched off the main saloon, in search of a drink, or some air.

The landlord was behind the main bar, serving drinks to the four-deep throng like a robot. An order would be shouted at him or one of his staff and a tenner passed across. Pints were pulled and a handful of coins given back. Then on to the next customer. Nobody checked their change. The sumo wrestler was dressed in red, her hair piled impossibly high. She looked as if she should have been standing at the far end of a bowling alley.

It was marginally quieter in the far room, except for the constant procession to the toilets. I yelled an order for a pint of lager over someone's head. He turned indignantly, found himself staring at my chest and decided to wait. The barman passed me a can.

'We've no glasses,' he shouted.

'Does that make it cheaper?'

'No.'

I handed him a pound coin and said: 'Call it right.'

'It's eighty pence short,' he replied.

'They're only seventy-five pence in Safeway's,' I protested.

'Then go do your drinking there,' he told me.

I gave him another pound and turned away.

A bunch of women were filing into the ladies', handbags at the ready. I stood back for them and found a piece of wall to lean on. Darryl might have been there, but I couldn't see anyone who fitted the picture I'd formed of him in my mind. Sometimes, that's a misleading thing to do. I wiped the top of the can with my shirt cuff and took a swig. It was warm.

The first of the women emerged from the loo and stood waiting for her friends, so they could form a united assault on the wall of bodies they had to negotiate. I looked, then looked again. She had the kind of figure and face that turn brave men into quiche eaters. I sidled towards her, noting that she looked nervous, out of her natural habitat, in that crowded place.

'Anyone would think it was New Year's Eve,' I said,

pulling up alongside her. Might as well go straight into the clever stuff.

She gave me a little smile. 'I saw you come in,' she replied. 'How did you manage to get served so quickly?'

'Influence,' I replied. I waved my free hand expansively and glanced around. 'I, er, just happen to own the place.'

'Don't tell me,' she laughed. 'You're Pete Stringfellow.'

She had a large face, with shoulder-length wavy hair, streaked with blond. Her eyes, nose and lips were all extravagant, giving her an earthy appearance, but her shoulders, bare apart from the thin straps of her dress, were narrow and delicate. It wasn't really a dress, more like an underslip, in a silken material that clung to her curves as if by static electricity.

'His son, actually,' I said. 'If you'll let me buy you a drink I could demonstrate how I did it.'

'Thanks, but I'm all right. We're just leaving.'

'That's life,' I said, resignedly.

'We're going to a party. Well, it's not really a party. Just a few girls having a laugh, sort of thing.' After a pause she added: 'You could always come to let the New Year in . . .'

It was tempting, but I heard myself saying: 'Thanks all the same, but I'd probably spoil your evening.'

'Yes, you probably would,' she replied, smiling.

'Is this your local?' I asked, choosing my words carefully to avoid the oldest chat-up line in the world.

'No. First time I've ever been in. Is it yours?'

'Similar. My third time in about twenty years. Probably my last, too.'

One of her friends came out of the loo, retrieved a champagne glass with a cherry in it that she'd left on a table, and joined us. She had wild frizzy hair and spectacles with luminous green frames. 'You're a dark horse,

Jackie,' she said. 'So who's this you've been keeping a secret, hey?'

Jackie of the generous lips stared into my eyes with a pair that looked as if they'd been sculpted from porcelain and glass by a mad scientist. Eyes like that are not just windows to the soul, they are an expression of the glory of creation – like the first buds of spring, or the Milky Way seen through a telescope. The lashes that framed them were long and heavily mascaraed, but they were all her own.

'Oh,' she said, 'he's just an old friend. He's called, er, Hugo.'

'Hello, Hugo,' Green Specs said. 'I don't suppose you've another friend for me, have you?'

I decided to play it strong and silent. I said: 'No.'

There was a crash and a scream from the other room, and we all turned to look. A youth came barging towards us, chased by several others, fighting their way through the crowd that was parting like the Red Sea. They dragged him down and fists and feet started going in. The first youth's buddies rallied to his support with chairs and bottles and soon the air was filled with flying missiles and the screams of women.

Jackie's friends coming out of the ladies' came up against another bunch trying to get in, away from the violence. I pushed open the door to the gents' and said: 'In here,' propelling Green Specs and Jackie through it. I held it open until all the women were inside and followed them.

The blokes shaking the drops off were bemused by the sudden influx of talent into their sacrosanct space. 'Come to help me, luv?' one of them said.

'Who do you think I am,' a girl replied, 'Tinkerbelle?'

I leaned on the door, holding it closed against the hammering on the other side. A toilet flushed and a big chap, about six-six, came out of one of the stalls, stuffing his shirt into his waistband. His first thought when he saw the women was that he'd been in the wrong toilets, and his expression of panic reduced us all to a mass fit of helpless giggling. Jackie fell shaking against me and I wrapped my arms around her and sobbed with laughter into her hair. I enjoyed that bit.

When the thunder of war had rolled away I took a tentative peek out, then pulled the door wide open. The place looked as if it had been hit by a pre-emptive strike by the Sandinistas. Every table and chair was overturned and people stood around dazed by the suddenness of it all. Girls wept and boyfriends comforted them with cuddles and braggadocio. Smoke pressed against the ceiling, as if from cannon fire, and the clock behind the bar showed one minute past midnight. We'd missed it.

A small crowd stooped around a figure sitting on the floor near the bar, so I walked over, feet crunching on broken glass, to see if assistance was required. It was the landlord, bleeding profusely from a head wound. There is a God, I thought.

'Got 'it by a can,' a youth explained.

'Not light ale, I hope,' I replied.

'No, it looked like Webster's to me.' I was obviously in the presence of an aficionado.

A hand slipped into mine and I turned to find Jackie with me. 'We're going,' she said. 'Our taxi's here. I just wanted to say goodnight. And Happy New Year.'

She tipped her head back and stood on tiptoe, for a kiss. I planted one smack on those gorgeous lips, like I'd wanted to do ever since I'd first met her, sometime last year. Her eyes were sparkling, literally – a million fireflies whirling and spiralling in them in some ritual dance of passion. I pulled her closer and revelled in my newly acquired power over women. The floor was sparkling, too. I looked up and saw that we were standing under the globe of mirrors, which had been turned on for extra atmosphere.

'Happy New Year,' I sighed, stealing an extra squeeze. 'I'll come out with you. Where's your coat?'

'I haven't brought one.'

'You'll freeze to death. And mind your feet on the glass.' As we reached the door a pair of bobbies in flak jackets strolled in, big and intimidating. I winked and received a brief nod of recognition. In the car park I said: 'It's Charlie, by the way. Hugo's identical twin.'

'Hello, Charlie. And goodbye. I'm Jacqueline. Are you sure you won't come to this party?'

'No. I'd better not.'

'Are you married?'

'No.'

'But you have a girlfriend?'

'Yes.'

'I bet she's rather special, isn't she?'

Her friends were squeezing themselves into the back of a white Granada. 'This is ours, Jackie,' one of them called to her.

'Yes, she is,' I said.

'Ah, well,' she sighed.

Jackie was shivering with cold. My jacket was unzipped and I enfolded her in it as we kissed for the last time. Her lips parted ever so slightly before she took them away. The curve of her back, the silken material under my hands, and the smell of her reached parts of me that no fizzy lager ever did.

'Either put him down or bring him with you,' Green Specs was saying. We disengaged reluctantly and Green Specs gave me a cherry brandy peck. She was still holding the champagne glass. I reached out and took it from her.

'Jackie!' I called as she moved towards the taxi.

She turned back to me. 'Be careful,' I said, quietly. 'There's some nasty people about.'

'Are you a policeman?' she asked.

I stooped until my lips were next to her ear. 'No,' I whispered. 'I'm a police*woman* in disguise.'

Her laugh was every bit as generous as the rest of her. 'I thought so,' she said. 'They knew you.'

'Listen,' I went on. 'If you ever come across a man called Darryl, run away, drop him, fast as you can. Understand?'

She looked concerned and nodded.

'And tell your friends.'

'Darryl. Right. And you be careful, too, Charlie.'

As the taxi drove away three faces turned in the back seat, pale in the street lights, and hands waved. I waved back and cursed myself for being fifty kinds of fool. There was a footfall beside me, and one of the PCs said: 'Trust the CID to get all the perks.'

'Life's a bitch,' I said, planting the champagne glass in his gloved hand. 'Here, have one on me.'

Next morning I awoke with a hangover. At first I blamed the monosodium glutamate in the Chinese, until I remembered the large gin and tonic I'd taken to bed with me. I've never done that before, and it didn't start out as a large one. It was just that some adjusting of quantities was required after the initial sip, and before I knew it the tumbler was full. Annabelle had left greetings on the ansaphone, and I was missing her. The g and t was compensation.

After breakfast and a shower I rang the number that Pete Drago had given me for Herbert Mathews, and Mrs Mathews answered. After the introductions and explanations I asked: 'Do you think he'll be well enough to talk to me?'

'Oh, he'll be delighted,' she said. 'What he's missing most

of all is shop talk. He's been a bit better over Christmas, but he's still in bed at the moment. We had a late night, last night. When would you like to come?'

'This afternoon, about two?' I asked, tentatively.

They'd moved house, after Herbert's retirement, to the bungalow in the country. Now they lived halfway between Burnley and Keighley, on the edge of Bronte country. The little brick cottage stood in a quarter of an acre and would have had long views if it hadn't been for the neighbours' cypress trees. I'd have chainsawed the lot the first time they went on holiday.

When I saw Herbert he reminded me of my father. He'd made an effort, bless him, and wore a shirt and tie, with a fawn cardigan over them. But there was no disguising the sunken cheeks and the claw-like hand he extended, or the plastic pipe that ran across his face, bleeding oxygen under his nose to enrich the air, because his lungs were down to twenty-five per cent. I'd seen it all before. The muscles of my jaw tightened as I shook his hand, and hardly any sound came out as I tried to say hello. I sank into an easy chair opposite his shrunken figure and Mrs Mathews went to put the kettle on.

I said: 'Welcome to Yorkshire, Herbert. Was it a lifetime's ambition to live this side of the border?'

'Property prices are lower,' he retaliated. 'And now I know why. Coming here gave me this.' He tapped his chest, trying to smile and cough at the same time.

'I'd have thought all this fresh air would be good for you.'

'You would, wouldn't you? But it's too late for that, even if it were so simple.'

We chatted about the weather and the job for a while and his wife brought the tea. I told him that Pete Drago sent his regards. He wasn't impressed.

'How long have you to go, Charlie?' he asked.

'Couple of years. A bit less.'

'Are you married?'

'No.'

'I never rated Drago,' he said. 'Thought he was a waster. But now I'm prepared to admit I might have been wrong. He knew what he wanted from life and he went for it. Didn't care who he hurt. I don't agree with that, but I wish I'd been a bit more like him. If there's anything you want to do, Charlie, do it now. Don't put it off or wait for it to happen.' He reached out and put a hand over his wife's and I raised the teacup to my lips, to hide behind.

'And another thing,' he went on. 'Choose your friends carefully. How many from the job do you think have visited me since I finished? Go on, have a guess.'

'Not many, I don't suppose.'

'None. Not one.'

He became agitated and started to cough. Mrs Mathews passed him a handkerchief and told him not to upset himself.

When he'd recovered I said, lamely: 'It's a bit out of the way, up here.'

'We haven't always lived up here, Charlie. Believe me, once you leave, you're history. Nobody wants to know you.'

I had another cup and enjoyed a piece of Christmas cake with Lancashire cheese. It was nearly as good as Wensleydale. When we'd finished I said: 'Down to business, Herbert. What can you tell me about a character called Darryl Burton, or Buxton?'

His eyes widened and his body stiffened. 'Darryl Burton,' he repeated. 'Darryl Burton. Don't tell me you've managed to pin something on him?'

'No, I'm afraid not. But with your help I'm hoping to.'

'What's he done?'

I related the story of the Christmas Eve attack and told him what we knew about the mysterious Darryl.

'It's Burton all right,' he asserted. 'He's changed his name. It's him, as sure as God made little green apples.'

'Drago said he'd done something similar a few years ago. Is there anything else we ought to know?'

'Five times,' he said. 'He's done it five times, that we know of. Yours makes it six.'

'*Five times!*' I gasped. 'Are you telling me he's been accused of rape *five* times?'

Herbert's breathing became laboured and his wife looked concerned. 'Do you mind if he has a little rest,' she said. His panting was shallow and rapid, hardly giving each fresh charge of oxygen time to get past his Adam's apple.

'Of course not,' I replied. 'Tell you what, I'll have a little walk round your garden, if you don't mind. It looks as if one of you has green fingers.'

Herbert cleared his throat with a noise like a Sammy Ledgard bus changing gear on Blue Bank. I was glad to get out of there, into the fresh air. I'd had enough of sickness. I recognised the signs: the bottles of pills on the sideboard; the get-well cards with ready-written messages to save the sender the trouble; the bucket hiding behind the settee, where it could be grabbed in an emergency.

Nature was reclaiming the garden, too. Herbert was a vegetables man, and orderly rows of sprouts, turnips, broccoli and onions were long past their best, overgrown and straggly, losing the battle against the local competition. I found a colander in the kitchen and filled it with sprouts and a few other things.

'Oh, you shouldn't have bothered,' Mrs Mathews told me, obviously pleased.

'It's no bother, and there's nothing like home-grown. How is he?'

'He's all right now. He just has these bad spells. They don't last long. Would you like some sprouts for yourself? It's a shame to waste them.'

'I can't stand them,' I confided. 'I'd like to ask Herbert a few more questions, but I can always come back, if you'd prefer it.'

'No,' she assured me. 'He's all right for a while. Talking to you is the best tonic he's had in a long time.'

I went through into the sitting room and asked Herbert to tell me all about it.

Darryl Burton, as he was then, had stood in the dock accused of rape on three occasions. Each time the victim had been interrogated by Burton's barrister and reduced to hysterical weeping as he harangued her in ways that would have had the police hauled before the Council for Civil Liberties. She had led his client on, he accused her. She had been with many men before. He'd puffed and pouted, pleaded and pointed, spittle flying from his lips as he turned victim into villain and guilt into innocence. She had admitted that she liked a good time and regarded herself as 'fun loving'. She knew what to expect. And the judge went along with it and directed the jury to acquit.

On one other occasion the CPS had refused to prosecute, and the first victim, sixteen years old, had withdrawn the charges. How many women had failed to report an attack was anybody's guess, but it was almost certainly the hidden portion of the iceberg.

'Do you know this barrister's name?' I asked.

'No, sorry,' Herbert told me, shaking his head.

'What about the instructing solicitor?'

Herbert pressed his knuckles against his lips. 'Sorry,' he said, after a while. 'I can't remember. My memory's going. It was a fancy foreign name. He was from Manchester – they said he'd never lost an important case.'

'I know the type,' I said. It's the instructing solicitor who loads the gun and dumdums the bullets. The barrister just pulls the trigger in court. 'What about Burton's juvenile record. Did he have one?'

'Mmm. He was a classic. We should have predicted how he'd turn out, except that there's thousands like him who mend their ways. He was cautioned for burglary when he was fifteen and should have been cautioned again for another, but he refused to be. We had no evidence so we had to NFA it. Later, he was suspected of an aggravated burglary and indecent assault, but we couldn't make it stick.'

NFA. No further action, but we still count it as a clear-up. Accepting a caution is an admission of guilt, but if the culprit refuses to accept it the ball bounces straight back at us. We have to put up or shut up. And even if he is cautioned, when he reaches the age of eighteen his slate is wiped clean and he can start again. Then we have to rely on the memory of men like Herbert, but strictly off the record, of course.

Rapists who ply their trade indoors usually started on a life of crime as burglars. They break into empty houses at first, but as their skills and bravado increase they turn to houses with sleeping occupants, preferably lone females or single mothers. The adrenalin level is high and one thing leads to another, or maybe the victim wakes, and suddenly there's an escalation in the offence. That's what Herbert meant when he called Darryl a classic.

Muggers, who rely on speed and opportunity rather than stealth and cunning, are different. They evolve into the rapists who drag their victims into the bushes or a handy back alley. Both types are just as dangerous. The next step on the ladder of infamy is murder, and Darryl was pulling his way up the rungs.

'You've been a big help, Herbert,' I said, standing up. 'I'm glad I called.' I placed my cup and saucer on the table and picked up my coat.

'Glad to be useful, for once. I was wondering where he'd gone. There was a bit of a local campaign against him after the last acquittal. Someone did some posters with his name on them and stuck them on lampposts all around the town, and the local paper was threatening to expose him. It was enough to drive him away from Burnley, but it looks as if he washed up in Heckley. Sorry about that. Do you think you'll get him?'

'Thanks a lot. We'll get him, sooner or later. Let's just hope it's sooner.'

I shook his bony hand and thanked Mrs Mathews for the tea. 'I'll show you out,' she said.

I'd turned to leave when Herbert said: 'Charlie.'

'Mmm.'

'Don't ring Padiham Road, will you?'

'How do you mean?'

'Don't ring them, to tell them to visit me.'

He'd read my mind. 'Why not?' I asked.

'I don't want them coming to see me. Not now. It's too late.'

'If you say so.'

'I do.'

'What about me. Do you want to know how we get on?'

'You can come anytime.'

'Thanks.'

'Good luck with it.'

'And you, Herbert. And you.'

As Mrs Mathews opened the door from the room for me I turned back to him again. 'This solicitor from Manchester,' I said.

Herbert looked at me.

'I've met his type before. And beat them. And I'll move heaven and earth to beat this one, too.'

January 2 was the day I'd promised Maggie we'd bring Darryl in. It was also the day Annabelle was coming home. I didn't know if I was up to such excitement, but I'd do my best. I thought I'd slept in when I looked at the curtains and saw how bright it was outside, but when I opened them there was a thin dusting of snow over everything. That meant traffic chaos in the town so I set off early. I welcomed the troops back, gave a stirring address about fighting crime in the last years of the millennium and sent them out into the bleak streets.

All except Maggie. I said: 'Come and sit down.' When she was comfortable I said: 'On second thoughts, do you fancy a bacon sandwich?'

She looked down at her figure and pulled a face. 'I'd rather not, Boss. I've been overdoing them, lately.'

'Fancy watching me eat one, then?'

'Oh, go on then.'

We repaired to the canteen and I told her about my journey to see Herbert Mathews. Maggie listened, her face a mask of disbelief.

'*Six times!*' she exclaimed when I'd finished. 'He's done it six times?'

'Six that we know of.'

'Oh, Charlie, we've got to stop him. He'll kill someone, one day.'

'That's what we're being paid for, Maggie. Question is, how do we do it?'

'Do we know who the other girls are?'

'Herbert gave me a list of names. Go over there, first chance you have, and see what you can find from the court histories and their intelligence files. Try the Crime Information System with both his names. Have a word with Herbert – he'll be pleased to see you. Look at anything else you can think of. When we hit Darryl for real I want it to be with everything we have.'

'Right. But what are we doing about him meanwhile?'

I popped the last corner of sandwich into my mouth and washed it down with a swig of tea. Our canteen bacon sandwiches are the best in the Western hemisphere. Rumour has it that a sheep station near Alice Springs does better ones, but it's unconfirmed. When I'd replaced my mug on the formica table, dead equidistant between the yellow squiggles, I said: 'Let's go ruin his day.'

Chapter Five

The snow had vanished but I was grateful for my big jacket. Science has failed to improve on the properties of good quality duck down. Or wool and cotton, come to that. Polyester is OK for ties – gravy stains wipe straight off. Maggie was wearing a smart suit with trousers and a raincoat.

Homes 4U were in a single-fronted shop on the edge of the town centre, where rents are cheaper. There was an alley alongside, so I drove down the back street and saw his silver Mondeo parked in a tiny yard with a big notice on the wall that claimed the space for D. Buxton, Manager. I left my Vauxhall blocking him in and we walked through the alley to the front entrance.

The gum-chewing girl at the front desk had more rings through her facial features than a Masai dance troupe. Her bleached hair was dragged together and held by a rubber band, like a horse's tail sprouting from the side of her head. I'd heard Maggie call it the slag's cut. She can be very uncomplimentary about her sisters.

'Police,' Maggie said. 'Will you please tell Mr Buxton that we'd like a word with him?'

The girl recovered quickly, sliding her magazine under the table and reaching for the telephone. 'I'll, er, see if Mr Buxton is in,' she said.

'No, love,' Maggie insisted, leaning over the desk. 'You'll tell him we'd like a word with him.'

I examined the notices on the walls. Several desirable properties were available for rental and DSS giros were only accepted with ID.

'There's two police people here to see you, Mr Buxton,' the girl was saying.

I smiled at her. 'I've never been called a police person before,' I said.

'He says he'll be down in a moment.'

The moment dragged into three minutes and I was beginning to eye the stairs when he arrived, full of bluff cheeriness.

'Gentlemen – I mean officers!' he blustered, taken aback by Maggie's presence. 'Sorry to keep you waiting. Spend 'alf my life on the old dog and bone, these days – you know how it is. So what can I do for you? Is it a problem with one of my tenants?'

He was exactly as I'd imagined him. I must be getting better at it. 'This is DC Madison and I'm DI Priest,' I said. 'From Heckley CID. We'd like a word with you, in private.'

The bonhomie slipped from his face. 'Go do some shopping, Samantha,' he told the girl, nodding towards the door. She grabbed her coat and scuttled out like a startled rabbit.

I dropped the latch and turned the sign to closed. Samantha was crossing the road, her thin white legs spanning the gap between miniskirt and Caterpillar boots like a pair of rugby goalposts. She reminded me of Popeye's girlfriend, Olive Oyl, but I doubted if she'd ever been extra virgin.

'Where were you on Christmas Day?' I demanded, turning back to face Buxton.

'Christmas Day?'

'Mmm. Only eight days ago. Turkey for dinner, Queen on the telly, if that helps.'

'I was at my parents'. Why?'

'All day?'

'No. I left home about twelve, got there about one. Had lunch, stayed for tea. Got back to Heckley about eleven. I go see them every Christmas. What's this all about?'

'We're investigating a rape. What about the night before? Where were you on Christmas Eve?'

'Christmas Eve?'

'That's what I said.'

'I went round a few pubs in the town. What of it?'

'Name me them.'

'I don't know their names. They're just pubs. I 'aven't lived in Heckley all that long.'

'Do you know the Tap and Spile?'

'Yeah. I know the Tap.'

'Did you go there?'

'What if I did?'

'Do you know the barmaid there?'

'Janet? Yeah. I know Janet.'

'How well do you know her?'

He gave a little cock-eyed smile, his lips pursed. 'Very well,' he said. 'I fink I can say I know her very well.'

'She says you followed her home and raped her at knifepoint. Did you?'

'She said that?'

'Mmm.'

'Janet?'

'Mmm.'

'The cow! The friggin' little cow!'

'Are you denying it?'

'Course I'm friggin denying it! And I'm not saying anuvver word until I've spoken to my brief.'

'Fair enough. We want to do a formal interview with you at Heckley nick. Ring your brief and tell him to be there, soon as pos.'

'You bet I'll ring 'im. I'm sick o' this. You're not gonna pin this on me.' He picked up the phone and tapped a number into it. Most of our clients have at least to consult their Filofaxes.

'Sick of what?' I asked, but he didn't answer.

'Simon, please,' he said into the phone after a moment. 'He's what?' His face was a picture. 'Well, who else is there?' He was quiet for a while, then told the listener that he was being hauled off to the station for a formal interview. 'Some bird's saying I raped her,' he told them, glancing up at me. 'No, I'm not under arrest.'

He ummmed and said: 'Right,' several times, his displeasure plain to see.

When he put the phone down I said: 'Simon wouldn't be Simon Mingeles, would he?' We'd crossed paths before.

'Yeah, matter of fact he would.'

'And he's not available?'

'No.' He bit his lip. 'He, er, went off for a fortnight's skiing, yesterday.'

'How disappointing for you. And me, too. It's a long time since I met Simon. As a matter of fact one of our DCIs is away skiing at the moment. I don't suppose Mr Mingeles has gone to the Cairngorms, has he?'

'No. Klosters.'

'Yes, he would, wouldn't he? Ah, well, have you thought of trying Gareth Pierce? She specialises in defending the indefensible.'

He looked confused. Gareth Pierce has that effect on me,

too. 'Mr Turner's coming over,' he said. 'But he's told me not to go wiv you unless you arrest me.'

'What time is he coming?' I demanded.

'Free o'clock.'

Whatever happened to the *th* sound? I blame it on drinking too much cold lager. It paralyses the tongue. 'OK,' I said. 'You be in the station at two thirty and we'll arrest you then. If we have to come for you I'll use it to have you remanded. Understand?'

He probably understood better than I did. 'Right,' he said.

In the car I said: 'Sorry, Maggie. I know you'd like to have taken him in, but this way the clock doesn't start until the brief arrives. We'll play them at their own game.'

'It's all right,' she replied. 'I guessed that was it. Do you want him in custody?'

'Not bothered.'

We were on the High Street, waiting for the lights to change, when I said: 'Presiley . . . Baxendale.'

'Presiley Baxendale? What about her?'

'That's who I want defending me if ever I'm up before the court.'

'Why her?'

'Dunno. It's just a nice name.'

'You're starved of affection,' she responded. 'When does Annabelle come home?'

'Today. I'd like to meet her at Leeds station, if I can get away.'

'What time?'

'I'm not sure. I'll give them a ring.'

She'd come home via London, and trains from there arrived at regular intervals. She could have been on any one. If I missed her it would have meant her waiting for the connection to Huddersfield and then a taxi. She could have left a message on my ansaphone, but she wouldn't expect me to collect her. That was one of the million little reasons that made me love her. There were some big reasons, too.

I tried ringing Rachel, but nobody was in. They were probably having a round of golf. Ah, well, back to work. I went to see the custody sergeant and told him about the prisoner I'd invited in to be arrested. He heaved a big sigh and closed his eyes, as if in prayer.

They must have done some further colluding, because they arrived together. Turner was older than I expected and didn't look the type to be associated with Mingeles. Maybe he was the firm's last remnant of the old school. Buxton looked happy enough with him. When we were settled in the interview room I switched the tapes on and recited the caution. It was twenty minutes past three.

'Mr Priest,' Turner began. 'My client strenuously denies these charges. We suggest that if you have any evidence then you present it so we can refute it. Otherwise, you must let him go. The word of a woman with a known reputation for sleeping around who is disappointed at my client's lack of commitment towards her is hardly grounds for making such serious allegations.'

So that was it. Straight out with the big guns. Maggie's chin was resting on her arms, folded across her bosom. A muscle in her cheek was twitching.

'Tell me about Christmas Eve,' I said.

'What's to tell?' Buxton replied. 'I took her home and we had it away. That's all. She consented to everything that took place.'

'Who do we mean by she?'

'Janet, the barmaid at the Tap and Spile.'

'How well did you know her?'

'Only to talk to, up to then.'

'What did you talk about?' I invited.

He took a few breaths, sorting his thoughts, wondering how much he ought to say. Turner was sitting askew, facing him, rotating a pencil in his fingers, ready to pounce should Buxton overstep the mark and give too much away.

'We'd chatted, that's all. I could tell she fancied me, but, to tell the troof, she wasn't my sort. I knew she'd been about a bit . . .'

'How did you know that?' I asked.

'It's common knowledge. The landlord of the Tap was knocking her off, for one.'

I felt Maggie flinch. 'Anybody else?'

'Well, no, no one I could name.'

Turner chipped in with: 'My client already said it was common knowledge, Inspector.'

'We don't accept common knowledge in any court I've ever attended, Mr Turner,' I told him, tersely. 'Let's stay with the so-called facts, however fanciful. Go on, please.'

Buxton said: 'I bought her a couple of drinks. Like I said, I didn't fancy her, but any port in a storm, eh? I'd had a few myself and she was getting better all the time. Know what I mean? So I asked her if she wanted a lift home.'

'And she accepted?'

'No, not exactly. She didn't want it to look obvious. She told me where she lived and said come down in a few minutes, so I did.'

'Where did she say she lived?'

'Marsden Road, at the end. There was a light outside, she said.'

'What number?'

'She didn't tell me no number.'

'That's a bit odd, don't you think?'

Turner jumped straight in with: 'It seems perfectly sensible to me, Inspector. The street light might be more easily located than the house number.'

'Perhaps,' I admitted. 'We'll have it checked.'

I sat back and looked at Maggie. She unfolded her arms and placed her fibre-tipped pen neatly on her pad. So far she hadn't written anything. 'Tell us what happened when you got there,' she said.

'What's to tell? We had it away, that's all. Twice.'

'Twice?'

'Yeah,' he smirked.

'Before that,' Maggie said. 'Didn't you have a coffee?'

'No, we didn't bovver.'

'So what happened? You're not telling me that you and this woman you hardly knew simply took your clothes off and got on with it, are you? There must have been some preliminaries.'

'Yeah, well, just a few. We had a bit of a snog and suddenly she said she needed a shower. I asked her if she wanted her back scrubbing and she said: "Why not?" So we went upstairs and that's where we had it the first time.'

'In the shower?' I asked.

'Yeah.'

'How?'

'How? How d'yer fink?'

'I'm asking you. Did you have it standing up or lying down? I'm a novice about these things.'

'Standing up, of course.'

'Against the wall?'

'Yeah.'

'Isn't that uncomfortable?'

'Uncomfortable! 'Course not.'

We let the image solidify in our minds for a moment before Maggie took up the questioning again.

'So where did you have it the second time?' she asked.

'On the bed.'

'On it or in it?'

'On top of it.'

'Wasn't that a bit . . . wet?'

'No. We got dry first. We dried each other, then went to the bedroom. One thing led to anuvver and we did it again. She was lapping it up, and I was past caring what she was like. It was bloody good.'

'So you dried her and she dried you,' Maggie stated.

'Yeah, that's right.'

'One towel each or did you share it?'

'Er, one each, I fink.'

Turner stopped twiddling his pencil.

'What colour were they?' Maggie asked.

'Inspector,' Turner said, ignoring Maggie. 'In a moment of such high passion I think it unlikely that any man would remember the colour of the towels, don't you agree?'

I ignored him and when his words had settled out of the air Maggie repeated the question. 'What colour were the towels, Darryl?'

'White,' Buxton said, defiantly. 'They was white.'

We tried to pin him down with other details, but it was like trying to lasso the clouds. Janet, he'd claimed, had asked him to stay the night with her. When he refused she wanted to know when he would see her again, and what his phone number was. He'd made it plain that this was just a one-night stand, whereupon she'd demanded money. Darryl, as we already guessed, had 'never paid for it in his life'.

Crying 'Rape!' Turner told us, was the last resort of an unscrupulous rejected woman.

We bailed him to report back in twenty-eight days but we were only posturing. As we hadn't charged him we couldn't even apply conditions. We suggested that it might be a good idea for him to stay away from Mrs Saunders and the Tap and Spile and Turner nodded wisely. It wasn't much to offer Janet but it was the best we could do.

We watched them leave, Turner holding the door wide for his client, ushering him away to safety.

'The boss wants you,' the custody sergeant said as he closed his book.

'Since when?'

'He rang down about an hour ago.'

I looked up at the clock. 'Is he still here?'

'Yep.'

'Right. I'm on my way.'

Maggie said: 'What do you want me to tell Janet, Boss?'

'The truth?' I suggested, after a few seconds' thought. 'But break it gently. Tomorrow will do, Maggie. Have a think about it overnight.'

The superintendent was up to his elbows in paperwork when I breezed into his office. 'Just the man,' he said. 'What would you prefer: body armour for everyone; three police dogs; or new tyres on the pandas?'

'Decisions, decisions, decisions,' I replied. 'I wouldn't have your job for all the tea in Greenland.'

He replaced the cap on his fountain pen. 'I suppose that's why they pay me such vast amounts of money. So, how did it go?'

'Like trying to kill a pig by stuffing butter up its bum with a hot knitting needle.'

'Slippery, eh?'

''Fraid so. He has us over a barrel and he knows it.' I gave him the gist of the interview.

'In which case,' Gilbert said, with that self-satisfied expression on his face that means he's found an easy way to break bad news, 'you should have some time on your hands.'

'I wouldn't go that far. What is it?'

'Your friend Chief Superintendent Isles has been on the phone. Apparently DCI Makinson has broken his leg while attempting a double-back flip-flop, with pike, and is now lying in Invercock-a-leekie hospital, tucking into copious supplies of grapes and chocolates sent to him by concerned colleagues. Isles wants you to take over the murder enquiry.'

'Oh no!' I gasped, burying my head in my hands.

'I'm sorry, Charlie,' Gilbert said, reaching across the desk and placing a sympathetic hand on my shoulder. 'I didn't realise you and Makinson were so close.'

'It should have been his bloody neck!' I hissed.

'Now now, Charlie. That's not a nice thing to say.'

I sat back and blew my nose. 'I don't need this, Gilbert,' I said. 'And I definitely don't want it.'

'Why not? You're my murder specialist. I'd have thought a nice little society killing like this would be a welcome change to an up-and-coming detective like you.'

'I was up-and-coming when you were, Gilbert. About the same time as the Wright brothers. The trail's gone cold. We were up a gum tree with Skinner. I'd probably have come to the same conclusions as Makinson, but I like to think I'd have kept an open mind.'

'And you wouldn't have gone gallivanting off on holiday in the middle of an enquiry.'

'No? Well, maybe all that's changing. From now on I'm going to be a bit more like him.'

'But not yet, eh?'

I scowled at him. 'Can I use your phone?'

Nigel was still in the office. I told him the news and asked him to organise a big meeting at City HQ for the following morning, with everybody there who'd been on the original enquiry. The first step towards becoming like Makinson was delegation.

'Great!' Nigel said. 'Great! But it's a bit short notice, isn't it?'

'They've all got telephones, haven't they?'

'Er, yes.'

'Right, then.'

Mr Wood and I walked out of the building together. At his car I said: 'Listen, Gilbert. This Darryl Buxton character might get away with this rape, but it's only a matter of time before he does something really bad. I want his prints and DNA on record. He does a lot of drinking around town – I'd like to target him, if you've no objections.' In theory, we can take DNA samples from anyone convicted of a reportable offence, but because of the cost we generally limit it to sex offenders, crimes of violence and maybe burglary. If we could do Buxton for drink-driving we'd splash out for him.

Gilbert slammed the door and wound down the window. 'What will you suggest next, Charlie?' he said. 'OK, but make it swift and subtle. Don't forget he has some clever allies.'

'Swift and subtle. I like that. Goodnight.'

'Goodnight.'

I was unlocking my car door as Gilbert drew alongside. 'One thing I forgot to mention,' he said through the open window.

'Mmm.'

'Makinson's leg. Apparently it's his fibia and tibia. Just thought you'd like to know.'

'I don't think it's amusing,' I told him, but I couldn't help smiling as I said it.

Before driving off, I tried Annabelle's number, but she wasn't at home. I knew that trains from London arrived at Leeds at about twenty to seven and twenty past; if I dashed straight over there I had a sporting chance of meeting her.

I missed the station turning and had to go on a city tour round the one-way system before I approached it again. This time I made it. The parking arrangements were obscure, but I eventually deduced that the first thirty minutes were free. I bought a platform ticket and ran down the steps. The 1839 had arrived, but Annabelle wasn't waiting for the Huddersfield connection. I rang her at home again, but she still wasn't there.

When my half hour was up I went out of the concourse and moved the car to a different space, to fool the attendant, if there was one. Annabelle wasn't on the 1918, either. I rang her number and after two rings she picked up the phone.

'Ah, you're home,' I said.

'Hello, Charles. This is a pleasant surprise. Yes, I came up on the ten to four from Kings Cross.'

'Was it a good trip?'

'No problems. Where are you?'

'I'm, er, in Leeds. Had to come, on business. I was thinking of going to the station, see if I could catch you.'

The tannoy immediately burst into life, warning passengers not to leave luggage unattended and ruining my story.

'It sounds as if you are already there,' Annabelle observed.

'Yes. Just arrived. Can I pop round to see you?'

'Of course you can. Have you eaten?'

'I'm OK. See you in about forty-five minutes.'

I did it in thirty-eight.

As soon as I saw her any gloom that was lingering around me evaporated like desert dew. We hugged and kissed and I told her I'd missed her.

'I made you a sandwich,' she said as we broke free.

'That's not what I've missed,' I said.

Annabelle brought me up to date with Rachel and George. They thought I was 'very amusing' but otherwise were not quite sure what to make of me.

'That's probably the best I could expect,' I said, tucking into a huge salad sandwich in home-made bread. Don't ask me how she does it.

'So,' I said, when I'd finished. 'How did you get on with Zorba the Greek?'

Her cheeks flushed slightly and she frowned. For a moment I thought it was from an unpleasant memory, but I quickly realised I was wrong.

'He's called Xav,' she told me. 'Short for Xavier Audish, and he's Iranian, not Greek.'

'Oops, sorry,' I said. 'I didn't realise you were on such good terms. Did he show you his . . . *designs*?' I lingered over the final word.

'Yes. We spent quite a bit of time together, and with the architect. One day we went to a fabric supplier. It was wonderful. I never imagined you could buy such exotic materials. It looks as if they might use my ideas, which is very exciting, don't you think?' Her face was animated as she spoke.

'Wonderful,' I agreed. 'I'm really pleased for you. Tell me about Xav. I'm a little worried that I may have a rival.'

A little smile flickered across her eyes. I hoped it was

mischievous, but I wasn't sure. 'Well,' she began, 'he's tall, and handsome . . .'

'Taller than me?'

'Umm, as tall as you. Well, nearly.'

'Handsomer than me?'

'He's older than I thought he'd be.'

'And rich?'

'He's a very charming man, Charles. He was very proper and appeared to value my opinions. If you must know, I like him. He has offered to pay me a consultancy fee and I am grateful, but that is as far as it goes.'

After a silence I said: 'I was only teasing you.'

'I'm sorry, Charles,' she said, taking my hand. 'It has been a long day and I'm tired. Xav is very nice, but for all I know he has four wives and twenty children. I think you are safe.'

Somehow, I didn't find her words reassuring. We played a CD and I told her about the rape and how I'd been lumbered with the murder. I try to involve her as much as possible, so she might understand when I'm late for our appointment or fall asleep over dinner.

At eleven thirty I said: 'Are you sending me home to my cold and lonely house?'

She nodded. 'If you don't mind, Charles. I just want to curl up in my own bed and sleep for ten hours.'

'I mind like hell,' I said.

'You will get over it.'

As we said our goodnights I put my arms around her. 'I missed having you to myself over Christmas,' I told her.

'Me too.'

'Friday night,' I said. 'How about if I book a table at the Wool Exchange? And then let's spend all weekend together, just the two of us. How does that sound?'

'What about the enquiries?'

'Nigel can handle them.'

She snuggled closer and said it sounded very nice.

The incident room at City HQ had been taken over by a fraud enquiry, so we held our meeting in their small lecture theatre. Nigel had rallied the original team and the room slowly filled with uniformed and plain clothes officers wondering what the fuss was about.

At dead on nine I told them the news about Makinson and introduced myself as the new officer in charge of the murder enquiry. '"What about Ged Skinner?" you are all wondering,' I said. 'Sadly for us, ladies and gentlemen, Mr Skinner's alibi is as watertight as a coot's rectum. More importantly, he convinced me that he didn't do it, which leaves us with an unsolved murder and twelve wasted days.' I made it pretty plain that I wasn't impressed. 'I know that you have all been reassigned to other duties, and I have your reports, but I want you all to give some more thought to what you saw and heard while making your enquiries. If you have anything at all to offer please see me or DS Newley.'

I told them that operations would be conducted from Heckley and dismissed them all except the ones who'd had special tasks.

'Tell me about the gun,' I said to a DS who'd taken the bullet to our firearms people at Huntingdon.

'It was very interesting,' he began. 'According to them the bullet was a thirty-eight, fired from a revolver with seven right-handed grooves. That made it a service issue Webley, or an Enfield, probably a relic from World War Two.'

'Mmm. Anything else?'

'Yes sir. The bullet was lead, and not jacketed.'

'So what can we deduce from that?'

'It was pre-war vintage. We started making them jacketed in about 1938, but they were only gradually introduced.'

'Somebody must have decided that shooting Germans with unjacketed bullets wasn't very sporting.'

'Probably. The doctor was shot in the side of the head, at very close range. According to the powder marks the barrel must have been in contact with his head. Analysis of the residue confirms that the bullet was pre-war, with the original powder in it.'

'So now we're looking for an old soldier who kept his ammunition dry.'

'Unless he got rid of it or it was stolen.'

'Don't make it difficult,' I sighed. People rarely report losing an illegally held gun.

The SOCO had a full catalogue of prints and fibres, but nothing to match them to. The best – the only – piece of information we had was that the doctor almost certainly knew his killer. There were security doors on the block of apartments where he lived, with a speaker system for visitors to ask admittance. He must have let him, or her, in.

There aren't too many blocks of flats like that in Heckley. I said: 'Wait a minute. Wait a minute. Where exactly did the doctor live?'

'Canalside Mews,' the SOCO replied. 'Number eight, top floor.'

'Really!' I said, sitting back with a jolt. Darryl Buxton lived at number one, ground floor.

There were two messages on my desk when I arrived back at Heckley. The first one read:

Boss,

The towels are white. Buxton saw Janet wrapped in one when he went into the bathroom. The street lamp is right outside the house. The number is marked on the door but it would still be difficult to read after dark.

Sorry. Maggie.

The next one was slightly briefer:

Dear Inspector,

Will you please stop leaving used teabags in your wastepaper bin.

And oblige, the Cleaners.

I screwed one up and threw it into the aforementioned bin and put the other in my drawer just as Sparky and Nigel wandered in, carrying a cardboard box each.

'More reports,' Sparky explained, placing his box on the end of my desk.

'Associated property,' Nigel told me.

'Why,' I began, 'did nobody think it worthwhile to bring to my notice the fact that our dead doctor and our serial rapist lived in the same block of flats?'

'Do they?' Nigel answered, wide-eyed.

'We didn't know,' Sparky replied, on the defensive.

'I thought Mr Makinson *kept you fully informed*,' I told them. 'I thought he was *very professional*.'

'Oh, we knew where the doctor lived,' Nigel countered. 'It was where your rapist lived that we had no idea.'

I felt my cheeks pull back into my sickly grin. 'Love – forty,' I conceded, deciding to change the subject. 'What's in here?'

Nigel flicked open the lid of his box and read from the inventory that was inside. 'Not much worth talking about:

contents of his pockets; his mail, diary, address book; one bullet, used; and his door keys.'

I turned to Sparky. 'Any photographs of the body?' I asked. 'We might as well start again, from the beginning.'

He spread the ten-by-eights on my desk. The doctor was laid more or less in the recovery position, with a halo of blood around his head, soaking into the pale carpet. I pulled a close-up towards me.

'He was a good looking so-and-so,' I said, quietly. With a good brain, too, until someone drilled a hole through it. I pushed the pictures around, re-arranging them, absorbing their message.

'There's the SOCO's video of the flat here,' Sparky said. 'Do you want to watch it?'

'Umm, no, I don't think so. Did you mention the keys to the flat, Nigel?'

'Yes, they're here.'

'I think I'll have a look for myself, then. Have you two seen it?'

They both shook their heads.

'OK. Well, let's not move about in a pack. I'll have a ride over there now while you two have another look through this lot. Draw up a table. You know the score: motive, opportunity, evidence; that sort of thing. Sort out a list of acquaintances for us to interview. Then maybe you can have a look at the scene later, if you think it worthwhile. We've been lumbered with this, good and proper, so let's show them how a murder enquiry should be conducted, eh?'

'Right, Boss,' they replied in unison. They looked pleased.

Mews is agent-speak for upmarket. There was no central courtyard, no alley where horse-drawn delivery carts used to clatter over the cobbles. The Canalside development was a rectangular block of a building, in newly-cleaned Yorkshire stone that had been carved and crafted when skills were cheap and the best materials could be dug straight out of the ground. It backed on to the canal, with the old lifting beam still jutting out like a witch's nose. The building was preserved for posterity and earning a bob or two for the owners. That was fair enough. For once, the word pretentious didn't spring to mind.

Most of the parking places were empty, apart from a couple of small but newish cars and a Suzuki four-wheel drive with silly coloured splashes on the sides. The front door of the flats was made of wood but free from the jemmy marks and metal plates screwed next to the lock that you always see on the council-owned blocks. To one side was the communications system, with a button for each of the eight apartments and a digital display; to the other was a bank of mail boxes. I put the appropriate key in the lock and turned it.

The central hallway reached the full height of the building. Once, bales of wool or finished cloth would have been swung and raised and lowered here. Labourers would have manhandled them, clerks in stiff collars registered them and bowler-hatted buyers cast knowledgeable eyes over them. This had been Heckley's gateway to the world. Now it housed the staircase and the lift shaft. The floor was quarry-tiled and there were framed prints by a failed impressionist on the walls. In the middle of the floor was a water feature whose photograph had probably graced the cover of the brochure, with a small fountain but no fish.

The first door on the left was number one. I'd half expected it to bear a plaque saying 'D. Buxton, Branch Manager, Homes 4U', but it didn't. He had the good sense to realise that anonymity is sometimes preferable to advertising. It all depends on the line of work you are in. I ignored the open lift door and attacked the stairs.

The rooms must have had high ceilings, for I was puffing by the second floor. There was one flat on each side of the stairwell, eight in all. The doctor had what the agent no doubt called the penthouse. I gathered my breath as I examined his door. It told me nothing, so I went in.

It was love at first sight. The doc had furnished the place from scratch with a generous budget, whereas I'd inherited my house and its contents from my parents. His tastes were not exactly mine, but his mark, his stamp, had been on it from day one. My house is slowly evolving to something more my style. Meanwhile, it looks as if it were furnished by a committee.

I'd have gone for something more up-to-date. This was strictly art deco, which looked dated, in my opinion, and conflicted with the building as a whole, but he'd done a good job. The kitchen was custom made with neatly integrated Neff appliances and the carpets were off-white throughout. In his sitting room I flicked a row of switches just inside the door and several wrought iron standard lamps came on but did little to dispel the gloom. Romantic but impractical. A thin coating of aluminium powder on everything, left by the SOCOs, reminded me that this was a murder scene. The pool of congealed blood, defiling the centre of the carpet like a stigmata, confirmed it.

All his Christmas cards had been gathered up and left in a pile. I read through them although I'd seen a list of the senders in the reports. He'd received about five times as many as me. From patients, I told myself. Our clients rarely send us greetings cards. It was a small consolation.

The pictures on his walls were black and white prints

of film stars. Humphrey Bogart in *Casablanca*, squinting through wreaths of smoke. Greta Garbo. Dorothy Lamour. Not my taste at all. I love the cinema, but not the people in it. Bogie is held up as an icon of the twentieth century. For what? About ten hours' work and an ability to talk without moving his lips while blowing smoke down his nose.

I didn't stay long. I knew before I came that there was nothing useful for me to see – it was just a starting point. To find the person who killed him I first needed to know the man. I studied the view from his windows, across the town with the hills looming up like a wall across the valley, and wondered how much the flat would sell for. Probably more than I'd want to pay, unless they had to bring the price down because of its recent history. Then I remembered the neighbours and decided that it wasn't for me, after all. Who wants to live next door to someone who drives a Suzuki with red and yellow splatters on the sides?

I was on my way out when I saw it, on the worktop in the kitchen. Tucked in a corner, next to his electric kettle, was a plastic container about six inches high, like a miniature swingbin. Exactly what I wanted for putting used teabags in, I thought. I pushed the top open with a finger and saw that it contained . . . teabags. Great minds, and all that.

I considered stealing it, but its presence would have been recorded on the video of the crime scene, and besides, I'm supposed to be fighting that sort of thing. I'd look out for one in the shops, and one for Gilbert, too. Anything to please the cleaning ladies. After a last lingering look at the place where the doctor's life had leaked away I switched off all the lights and carefully locked the door behind me. Outside, I emptied his mailbox and took the contents back to the station.

* * *

My mobile rang as I pulled into the station car park. 'It's me, Charlie,' Sparky said. 'Do you want some fish and chips bringing in?'

'Ooh, yes please. What about Nigel?'

'He's here with me. 'Bout fifteen minutes.'

'I'll put the kettle on.'

I had a quick look through the thick pile of mail I'd brought in. The only proper letter was from someone called George, probably an old college friend. It was a résumé of the past year, as if they kept their friendship alive with an annual report but rarely met. There was a bank statement, the usual quota of junk, and reminders that the doctor's subscriptions to the RSPB and the *British Medical Journal* were due. A Christmas card from a lady called Melissa, who was still thinking about him, had been redirected from an address in Chesterfield. I dumped the junk and put a rubber band round the other stuff.

My desk was as clear as it ever gets. Nigel had left a list of people he thought we ought to interview again. I pushed everything to one end and covered the rest of it with used sheets of paper from the flip board, held down by strips of Sellotape. That's the nearest we have to table covers in CID. I fetched an extra chair out of the main office and the salt and vinegar from Sparky's bottom drawer. The kettle was just coming to the boil as they breezed in, closely followed by the familiar aroma.

We ate the fish and chips with our fingers, out of the paper. The first ones after Christmas always taste especially good. Nigel and Sparky had been to the General Hospital, to talk to the doc's former colleagues. 'One bloke's a bit cagey,' Sparky said. 'A registrar. That's one below a consultant, isn't it?'

Nigel confirmed that it was.

'How do you mean, cagey?' I asked.

'He wasn't as fulsome in his praise as most of the others. I got the impression he didn't like him.' He screwed his paper up and put it back in the plastic bag the fish and chips came in. Nigel produced a roll of kitchen towel for him to wipe his hands on.

'That's because our dead doctor was having an affair with his wife,' Nigel told us.

'Oh,' I said. 'Go on.'

He wiped his own hands and took a drink of tea. 'I enjoyed those. One of the ward sisters took great relish in telling me about the doc's sexual exploits. Actually, he wasn't a doc. Being a consultant made him a mister. She went all misty-eyed at the memory. She said there was a story going round that he was doing a bit for the registrar's wife, who knew all about it but turned a blind eye.'

'Is this in the reports?' I asked.

'No. She thought it wasn't important and it didn't seem right to mention it so soon after his murder.'

'How jolly considerate of her,' I said.

When we'd finished the currant squares Nigel had brought in from the bakery over the road I reached out for the list he had compiled. 'We'll talk to all these again,' I said. 'No doubt they have all remembered something new, or there's a little titbit they didn't like mentioning earlier.' I studied the list.

'I wouldn't mind going back to the General,' Sparky said. 'One or two who worked with him don't come on until one.'

'OK. That's you sorted. Nigel, how do you feel about going to York to see his parents?'

He nodded. 'Mmm. No problem.'

'Fine. This is his mail, collected from the flat. Take it

over there, ask them if they want to let people know before they learn it from us. Keep copies of anything that might be useful. And that leaves me. Now let me see . . .' I held the list at arm's length and studied it. 'I think I'll have a word with, oh . . .' I gave them a big smile. '. . . The girlfriend, Natasha Wilde, whoever she is.'

Chapter Six

I knew Natasha Wilde was an actress in a soap, I'd read it in the reports. I washed my hands in the smelly stuff that comes out of the dispenser and cleaned my teeth. I wasn't swayed by her fame – I'd have done the same for any royalty.

Appletreewick is a neat little village in Wharfedale. It's a proper working dales village, hardly touched by 'offcomers'. I've done plenty of walking around there, when scenery and a decent pub for lunch were more important than packing the miles in. Most of my walking is like that, these days. She lived outside the village, towards Burnsall, in Apple Tree Cottage. 'You can't miss it,' she'd told me on the phone when I arranged to see her. 'It's the last cottage on the right, with the lovely crooked chimneys.'

It took me nearly an hour and a half to get there, and although it was still only mid-afternoon the light had nearly gone as I left the main street behind and cast my eyes chimney-wards. The sky was heavy with snow and I realised that I had a sporting chance of being snowed in with her. Who'd be a cop? I found the cottage first time and walked up the long path to the front door. There was a parcel on the doorstep. I picked it up and pressed the bell. The parcel was addressed to Miss N. Wilde and came from Star & Media Photography of London.

The door was opened by a vision in pink. The pants were tight enough to protect the wearer from a ten G turn and the blouse shone and shimmered like a mirage.

'Hello,' he said. 'Can I help you?'

'My name's Priest,' I told him. 'Miss Wilde is expecting me.' I thrust the parcel forward. 'And your postman's been.'

He studied the parcel for a moment, then turned and shouted: 'Natasha! Your policeman has arrived, and your photos are here.' He looked back at me, smiled as if he meant it, and invited me in.

For a so-called cottage the rooms were huge. The frontage appeared reasonable, but it must have stretched back for ever. The walls were stone and a big fire blazed in the hearth. I've been in smaller saloon bars. At the far end of the room was a baby grand piano with the lid propped open, as if someone had just stopped playing it. Mr Pink invited me to sit down on a spindly easy chair with Laura Ashley loose cushions and said Natasha wouldn't be a moment. He started to open the parcel.

She made her entrance just as he pulled the first photograph out. She was about five foot tall and not much less from front to back. It's a fact of life that actresses are on average two cup sizes larger than their non-thespian sisters.

'Inspector!' she gushed, approaching like an attacking shark. I stood up and held a hand out, wondering if I should kiss her on the cheeks or curtsey. We settled for a simple shake.

Her hair was ash blond, in a style that I last saw on Doris Day. The complexion was perfect and her teeth looked as if they had been precision machined from a billet of the finest marble. They were small and regular and could have inflicted serious damage on small animals. She was good looking – beautiful, even – but I found her curiously sexless. It's something I've been experiencing more and more, recently. Maybe I should have a word with someone.

'Sit down, please, Inspector,' she insisted, graciously, and sat opposite me, with the fire between us.

'Your pictures are here,' Mr Pink said again, handing one to her.

'Ooh, that's just lovely,' she replied, after examining it, and passed it across to me.

'Very nice,' I concurred.

She was wearing exactly the same oufit as in the photograph – skin-coloured jodhpurs and a white polo-necked sweater. The jodhpurs on the real thing were so tight they left nothing to my imagination. I could have done a reasonably accurate anatomical drawing right there and then. In the photo the camera angle was chosen to show off her other physical charms.

'Can I keep this?' I asked.

'Of course you can.'

I placed it on the floor alongside my chair. 'Right. Thank you. First of all, can I introduce myself? I'm DI Charlie Priest from Heckley CID . . .'

'Oh, what must you think of me?' she interrupted, putting a hand to her head. 'I'm Natasha Wilde and this is Peter Khan, but everybody calls him Genghis.'

I nodded towards him. 'How do you do.'

'Genghis is an arranger,' Natasha went on. 'One of the best in the business, and a very good friend of mine.'

'Flowers or furniture,' I asked.

'Music,' he replied, as if everybody made the same mistake.

'Genghis did the score for the Pedro Wallis commercial,' Natasha said.

'Really.'

'You won't have seen it,' he said. 'It hasn't been released yet.'

'I'll look out for it. Now, no doubt you realise that I'm here in connection with the death of Dr Jordan. I'd like to go over a few things with you, if you don't mind, Miss Wilde.'

'Please, Natasha,' she insisted.

'Thanks, and I'm Charlie. First of all can I say how sorry I am. It must have been a shock to you.'

'Oh, we were all devastated, weren't we, Genghis? We'll help all we can, Charlie, but we told that Mr Makinson everything we know. He was ever so kind.'

Genghis nodded his agreement.

'I know, and I've read his reports. Unfortunately he's broken his leg, skiing . . .'

'Oh no!' she exclaimed, and Genghis looked stricken.

'. . . and I've taken over the investigation.'

'What about that drugs man?' she asked. 'Haven't you found him yet?'

'Yes, we've found him, but he has an alibi. We've eliminated him from enquiries. He's called Ged Skinner – I don't suppose the doctor ever mentioned him, did he?'

'No, I'm afraid not.'

'When did you last see the doctor?'

'The weekend before. He stayed here, and was supposed to be coming over on Christmas Eve. We were having a house party. When we heard that poor Clive was dead it ruined the whole thing.'

Natasha had known Dr Jordan about three years. She met him at the clinic when, she said, she was having her nose fixed. Since then they'd been very close but she knew little about his other acquaintances or his work. It looked as if the doc lived in parallel universes: one at weekends with his showbiz friends, and in the real world from Monday to Friday.

A mobile phone warbled on a bookshelf. Genghis picked it up and took it out of the room. I don't know whether it was for privacy or because he was well-mannered, but I suspected the latter and warmed a little towards him. I was asking Natasha if Dr Jordan had ever told her about any problems with the anti-abortionists when Genghis returned. He hovered close to her, like a humming bird, as she said: 'No, I'm afraid he never mentioned anything like that.'

When she finished speaking he said: 'Shall I make us all some coffee? How do you like it, Charlie?'

'Black please,' I replied, 'with nothing in it.' I was trying to cut down on the sugar, so I might as well impress them with my sophistication.

'That was Curtis,' he told Natasha. 'They can't come this weekend. Ewan has lost a filling. He's had a temporary one done but he's to see his orthodontist on Saturday.'

'Oh, the poor darling,' Natasha sympathised.

'Did you notice,' I began, trying to drag the conversation away from Ewan's molars and back to my murder enquiry, 'any changes in the doctor's moods or behaviour at any time? Was anybody putting any pressure on him in any way?'

'Who, for instance?'

'Well, were any ex-girlfriends causing him aggro? Then there's the drugs thing. Do you think he was under any pressure to supply anyone? Did he have any worries that he wouldn't discuss with you?'

She was silent for a few seconds, looking passably

thoughtful. 'He was screwing someone at the clinic,' she declared, as indifferent as if she were disclosing the colour of his eyes.

'Who?'

'I don't know. I told him I didn't want to know.'

'Someone single or someone's wife?'

'I think she was married.'

'Well, that's something for us to look at. Anything else?'

'There was something. I remembered after Mr Makinson called and wondered if I ought to mention it, but he said you were looking for this drugs man and we were fairly certain it was him, so I didn't.'

'And what was it?'

'I think someone must have reported Clive for mal—, er, mal—'

'Malpractice?' I suggested.

'That's it – malpractice – sometime in the past. I hadn't known him very long – a few months – and Ewan was doing the pilot for *Emergency Doctor*. Did you see it?'

'No, I'm afraid I didn't.'

'It was ever so good. I can't think why they didn't go ahead with the series. Well, apparently, he'd been reported to the General Medical whatsit, for doing a really dangerous operation on the captain of this boat, during a storm. He'd had a heart attack, and the doctor revived him by giving him an electric shock from a table lamp. It was terribly dramatic.'

'It sounds it,' I said. 'And was he all right?'

'Who?'

'The captain.'

'Oh, him. Yes. And they were all saved. We've a copy of the video somewhere, if you'd like to borrow it.'

'Video? Oh, I see. Er, some other time, perhaps, when we've solved this, er, case. So what had this to do with Clive?'

Genghis came in with the coffees and a plate of biscuits and stood near me. 'I brought the cream and sugar,' he said, 'so you can put your own in.' His crotch was level with my face and it was impossible not to notice his preferred side for dressing. The right, just for the record. But he knew how to make good coffee. I told him so and he blushed.

'He's a darling,' Natasha said. 'He's been very good to me since . . . since poor Clive was murdered.'

For a second or two I thought she was going to show some emotion. 'You were telling me about this video,' I said, reaching for a biscuit.

'Oh, yes. Well, Ewan asked Clive about how a doctor would feel if he was charged with mal—, er, mal—'

'Malpractice.'

'Malpractice. Clive threw his hands up and said: "Tell me all about it!"'

'As if he'd been through it himself?'

'That's right. He was a big help to Ewan, first-hand experience and all that, but you'd have to ask him about it. I was rehearsing for *Humpty Dumpty* and didn't need the distraction.'

'Of course not.'

I was hungry so I had another biscuit and finished my coffee. 'That's been very useful, Natasha,' I said. 'I'd better be on my way before I'm snowed in with you. Was there anything else?'

'No, except . . .'

'Go on.'

'No, it's nothing.'

'Now you'll have to tell me.'

'Well, I thought of all sorts of things at first. You do, don't you, when someone's been murdered. Who could have done it? And all that. Should we have noticed something and perhaps prevented it happening? And then, when Mr Makinson told us about this drugs man, it all seemed so obvious.'

'I see what you mean,' I said. 'So what was it?'

'It's just that . . . he used to play squash. He was mad about it. Even took me, once. I was hopeless!' She giggled at the memory of it.

'And what happened?'

'He just stopped going. One weekend I asked him if he'd played at all through the week and he said he'd stopped. Didn't want to play anymore.'

'When was this?'

'About a year ago. No, more than that. Summer before last, if I'm not mistaken.'

'Where did he play?'

'In Heckley. It must have been near the hospital because he used to play after work or at lunchtime or something.'

'Right,' I said.

'Do you think it's important?'

I shook my head and smiled. 'No, but this malpractice charge might be.'

'I'm sorry. We really would like to help you catch whoever did this to poor Clive. He was a lovely man.'

I asked a few questions about *Dales Diary* and the music business. It was interesting, and I was reluctant to leave that fire. Before I was in danger of overstaying my welcome I said: 'I'd better go, but there's just one last question I'd like to ask.' She looked at me as I picked her photo from the floor. 'Will you sign this for me, please?'

There was a thin layer of snow over everything, like

a dust sheet over furniture, waiting for the decorators to arrive, but the wipers swept it aside easily enough. Genghis advised me to go the long way, through Burnsall, where the hills were less steep, and to come back if I had any problems. A few cars had preceded me and the snow on the main road had already turned to slush, but the traffic was crawling. We must be the worst winter drivers in the world. It was nearly ten when I arrived home. Annabelle had left a message to call her on the ansaphone.

'You haven't been working until now, have you, Charles?' she asked.

'Yes,' I replied, 'but you could hardly call it work.'

'Why is that?'

'I've been to interview an actress called Natasha Wilde. She's the leading lady in *Dales Diary*, on television.'

'Really! And what has she done?'

'Nothing. She was supposed to be the girlfriend of our dead consultant, but she hardly played the devastated fiancée. I've seen greater expressions of sorrow over a spilt drink.'

'Perhaps she was acting being brave.'

'Perhaps.'

'Charles,' Annabelle said, hesitantly. 'About this weekend.'

'I've booked a table at the Wool Exchange, for eight on Friday,' I told her.

'Oh.'

'Is there a problem?'

'No. No. But Xav rang me earlier tonight and said he'd like to introduce me to a designer that he's thinking of engaging. Apparently he's sacked the others – they were taking advantage of him and their suggestions were second rate, as you know. He wants me to be there when he talks to these other people. He says he respects my opinion.'

'Well he's right about that. But I thought you were going to do the designs.'

'Umm, well, I thought so, but perhaps it's all a bit too ambitious for someone with my little experience.'

'Nonsense,' I assured her. 'You can do it. The only thing these so-called experts have is confidence.'

'The problem is, he wants me to go up to London, first thing on Saturday, on the early train, so I wouldn't want to be too late.'

'Oh. So do you want me to cancel the table?'

'No, of course not, as long as we are not too late.'

'Do you want me to take you down?'

'That's kind of you, but I'm not sure when I will be coming back.'

'Why? How long are you thinking of staying?'

'Only until Sunday or Monday.'

'So where will you stay?'

'I'm not sure, at the moment. At Xav's, perhaps, or he'll find an hotel for me. He's paying my expenses and a fee.'

There must have been something in the way I said: 'Oh.'

'Charles, what are you suggesting?' she demanded.

'Nothing. Nothing at all. I'm just missing you, Annabelle. Xav knows he's found someone special, and he's got me worried, that's all.'

'Don't be silly, Charles,' she replied. 'I'll look forward to seeing you on Friday.'

I put the phone down and prayed for the biggest blizzard to hit the North since the Great Ice Age. I had a sandwich – banana, honey and a sprinkling of cocoa – and caught up with the news on TV. They were having it bad down South, but they always are.

I took a shower and went to bed reasonably early. Then I remembered that I had no ironed shirts. I got up and hung a couple over the shower head, in the hope that the creases would drop out overnight. I dreamed about operating on Genghis to remove a piano from his brain, on the deck of an open boat with only an electric iron for a scalpel and big waves crashing over us.

'What have we got?' I asked. We were seating ourselves around my desk again. Nigel carefully lowered three steaming mugs and sat down.

'Custard creams,' Sparky replied.

'Pass 'em over, then, please.'

'Wait a minute,' Nigel said. 'Wait a minute. Where did that come from?'

Sparky followed his gaze to the wall behind my desk and smiled. Natasha had written: 'To Charlie, with lots of love, Natasha Wilde', on her photograph, with four kisses, and I'd pinned her on the wall next to my new calendar from the Bamboo Curtain.

'She's dotted that last i in an unfortunate place,' he observed.

'I hadn't noticed,' I said.

'I take it you had a succesful meeting,' Nigel declared.

'She's a very nice lady.'

'Find anything useful,' Sparky asked, 'apart from her telephone number and her favourite tipple?'

'Mmm. She confirmed that the doc was knocking somebody off at the clinic, presumably the registrar's wife that we already know about; about eighteen months ago he mysteriously stopped playing squash; and, sometime in the past, he's been accused of malpractice.'

'Malpractice?' Nigel said. 'What was that about?'

'She didn't know. Can you look into it, please? Try the General Medical Council.'

'Right. And what's so special about giving up squash?'

'Nothing. She was just trying to be helpful. One minute he was a keen player, then he stopped, that's all.'

'Perhaps he had a recurring injury. It happens all the time.'

'Yep.'

Sparky chipped in with: 'You said he was knocking someone off at the clinic.'

'Mmm.'

'The registrar works at the General. Was this a different one?'

'Sugar! I don't know. I'm certain she said the clinic. Maybe she meant the hospital. What's the difference between a clinic and a hospital?'

'I think your mind wasn't on the job,' Sparky said.

'You could be right,' I admitted. 'Let's try to check it from this end. What did you two find?'

Nigel said the parents were bearing up remarkably well. Doctoring was the family business – they were both GPs. He'd come away with the names of a few friends and had promised to have a word with the coroner about releasing the body for a funeral.

'And at the hospital?' I asked, turning to Sparky.

'Nothing worthwhile. To be honest, there seems to have been a great deal of affection for the doctor, from both sexes. Everybody agrees that he was a fine doctor and a good bloke. He had his flings, but he was a gentleman with it.'

'Sounds a bit like me,' I said.

'Just what I thought, Charlie. So I collared the registrar and asked him if he knew that the doctor, or consultant, to be precise, had been shagging his wife.'

'I hope you weren't so circumspect,' I said. 'The first rule of good interviewing is to be unambiguous.'

'Well, actually, I told him that I'd heard rumours. He said he'd heard the same rumours, but as he and his good lady were leading separate lives and just keeping up appearances until the kids went to college, he wasn't bothered.'

'Mmm. Interesting. Did you push it?'

'You bet. I asked him where he was on the night in question. He and his wife threw a dinner party for eight neighbours. It's something they do monthly, or thereabouts, rotating round each other's houses.'

'Keeping up appearances.'

'Quite. He's given me a list of names.'

'Let's have 'em checked. Anything else, either of you?'

'Yes, there is,' Nigel replied, blushing like a schoolboy about to present his parents with a favourable report. 'I took Dr Jordan's letters and cards to his parents, but copied most of it. His bank statement made interesting reading. Apart from his salaries there were deposits of three hundred, three hundred and fifty, and another three hundred, at monthly intervals. I checked his previous statements and it's been going on for nearly two years. The amounts vary, but it's usually three hundred, three hundred and fifty, or occasionally four hundred, at the end of the month.'

'Maybe he does some other work,' I suggested. 'He could be on a retainer, or something.'

'And doesn't pay tax on it?'

'How do you know he doesn't pay tax on it?'

'Because if he declared it it wouldn't come out at such a round figure.'

I said: 'I don't know who you've been mixing with, lately, Nigel, but you're developing a terribly suspicious mind.'

'There was one exception. Last September the payment was missed, but there was a double payment in October. In the doctor's diary,' he went on, 'I came across an entry at the appropriate time that said: "AJKW not paid, ring him." That's all.'

'So you reckon that these payments are coming from someone called AJKW.'

'Yes.'

'Any ideas who it is?'

'Yes,' he declared with undisguised triumph.

'Go on.'

'Last night, in the absence of a better offer, I took the telephone directory to bed with me.'

'I have nights like that,' Sparky interrupted.

'Shut up,' I told him.

'I worked my way through the Ws and found an entry for A.J.K. Weatherall. It only took a couple of minutes. It's got to be the same person. Odds of it not being are about equal to your chances of winning the lottery. And he's a chemist in Heckley, which clinches it, I'd say.'

'You mean . . . a pharmacist chemist?'

'That's right.'

'Sheest!' I sat back and whistled through my teeth.

Nigel bit into a custard cream and had a sip of his tea. I popped one in whole and took a swig. Sparky dunked.

When we'd swallowed the biscuits and digested the information, Sparky said: 'So what do you reckon? They were scamming the NHS?'

Long time ago, when the Earth was young and sex came

before marriage only in very cheap dictionaries, prescriptions were free and professional people were assumed to be honest. Things have changed since then. The price of a prescription is now often four or five times the cost of the medicine it procures. 'Ah!' says the Health Minister, gleefully. 'But sixty per cent of patients are exempt from paying the charges.' They draw perverse satisfaction from the fact that most of the nation's sick fall below some arbitrary poverty level. Their logic escapes me.

Pharmacists recognise the injustice. Some of the more unscrupulous ones tear up the prescriptions and pocket the difference for themselves. Others just sell the medicine to the customer at the market price and are happy with the profit on that. Either way, it's called fraud. It is OK for the Government to rip us off, but not enterprising individuals.

But that wasn't what was happening here. A chemist could do that in the privacy of his own shop. No collusion was required with a sympathetic general practitioner. If Nigel had stumbled on something, it was much more serious.

'Fake prescriptions,' I said. 'Do you think we're talking fake prescriptions?'

'I'd say it's a strong possibility,' Nigel replied.

'You mean,' Sparky began, 'some friendly doctor makes out a few hundred prescriptions for patients who haven't been anywhere near his surgery, and the chemist claims the fees for not dispensing any drugs?'

'A very succinct summary, I'd say, David,' Nigel agreed.

'And they share the proceeds,' I added.

'Four hundred quid a month. That's eight hundred if they're sharing equally. How many prescriptions is that?'

'Haven't a clue,' Nigel admitted. 'I've considered having a word with Fraud. What do you think, Charlie?'

'Yeah, good idea,' I said. 'They're bound to know more about it than we do.' I thought about it for a second, then decided: 'No. Bugger Fraud – they'll take for ever. Let's have a word with A.J.K. Weatherall ourselves and ask him what it's all about. After lunch. First of all let's have it all down on paper and tagged for the computer.'

For the first time I felt optimistic. Something of the thrill of the chase was welling up inside me, like I always get when an investigation turns the corner. You gather the facts and they don't make sense, until, hopefully, a simple piece of information comes along and everything starts to fall into place. We hadn't reached that stage, yet, but things were moving.

Maggie knocked on the door and popped her head round it, which was the cue for Sparky to jump up and gather our mugs together.

'Private party or can anyone join in?' she asked.

'Have a warm seat,' Sparky told her as he sidled past in the doorway.

'Don't drop the teabags in the bin,' she called after him.

'We've finished, come in, Maggie,' I said.

She sat down and sniffed. 'It stinks of fish and chips in here,' she declared.

'It's that lot,' I said, vaguely waving towards the main office.

'Good grief, where did she come from?'

I turned round and met Natasha Wilde's ample charms, captured on Kodak paper. 'Present from a grateful customer,' I boasted.

'Did you dot that i?'

'No I didn't! What do you think I am?'

'Hurrumph! Did you get my message? I missed you yesterday.'

'I'm sorry, Maggie. I never realised you cared so much.'

'I meant . . . You know what I mean.'

'Right. About the white towels and the street light.'

'Mmm.'

'Doesn't help us much, does it? How is she?'

'She's a brave lady. I told her the score, how he'd play his defence. She realises that the chances of a prosecution are slim. She was washing sheets and blankets when I went round. Said it was the tenth time. She's too scared to have little Dilly with her for the time being and says she now sleeps in Dilly's bed with the light on.'

'Did you tell her that he'd done it before?'

'I said we had suspicions.'

'What was her reaction?'

'She wasn't surprised. Said it was only a matter of time before he killed someone.'

'If he hasn't already,' I said, and told her about the doctor living in the same block of flats.

'Really?' she said, leaning forward. 'And apart from that, have you found anything else to link them?'

I shook my head. 'Not a sausage. I've asked all the mobiles to keep an eye out for him, and Jeff Caton's arranging for some casual observations to be done. If we can't get him for rape we might be able to clip his wings for a while.'

'It's more than his wings I'd like to clip. He went out in a taxi last night.'

'Damn! He's reading our minds. Give her plenty of attention, Maggie,' I said. 'Until she starts to feel more secure. Ask her if a panic button would help. That's about all we can offer.'

'It's not much, is it?'

'No.'

The pharmacy was in a parade of shops on the Sweetwater side of town. Better class council houses give way to a posh estate where the roses grow up pergolas and they have tit boxes on the walls instead of satellite dishes. The sad irony is that the birds prefer nesting in the satellite dishes. It was sandwiched between a unisex hair salon and a wine store, or a barber's and an off-licence if you came from the council estate.

'Why do they call themselves unisex hairdresser's when they do both sexes?' Nigel wondered as he swung into the layby that fronted the shops.

'Because bisexual hairdresser would have other connotations,' I told him.

'Why?'

'I don't know. Do you want to go round the back while I kick the front door in, or do you want to kick it in while I cover the back?'

A woman came out of the pharmacy fiddling with her handbag.

'They're open,' Nigel said.

'This job's not what it used to be,' I grumbled. 'Come on, let's have a walk round.'

We passed the fronts of a greengrocer's and an all-purpose store that had baby clothes and model cars in the window. A poster said the local dramatic society wanted players for their next production – *Iolanthe* – and someone had lost a dog. Cars and four-wheel-drives driven by women were coming and going, buying something for tea after picking up the kids. What a life. We turned the corner, into the service road that ran behind the shops.

There were the usual dumpsters and piles of empty boxes. The greengrocer had taken a delivery of Cape oranges and still had a few Christmas trees left. At the far end of the parade a butcher's van was unloading a carcass. Across the lane was a row of garages-cum-storerooms, one per shop. The door to A.J.K. Weatherall's was wide open and his car was inside.

He owned a Lotus.

'Well, well,' I said. 'What's that worth?'

'Six years old . . . Oh, about twelve or fifteen thousand, at a guess.'

'And about thirty thousand new?'

'Something like that.'

'Let's go talk to him.'

We completed our circuit of the block. Passing the back of the butcher's I tried not to inhale and wished I had the willpower to go vegetarian. Trouble is, I like my steaks.

The grey-haired lady behind the pharmacy counter said she'd tell Mr Weatherall we were here. She slipped into the back room, behind a partition made of striped glass that we could be seen through, and we heard her say that two reps were asking for him.

'Mr Weatherall won't be a moment,' she told us with a smile when she returned.

I studied the goods on offer. Half of the front counter was dedicated to the prevention of pregnancy, with a variety of choice that was bewildering. Colour, shape, size and flavour had all to be considered. I feigned shock and turned away.

Apart from the usual flu and indigestion remedies, the rest of the shop was filled with all the stuff you needed after the things on the counter failed. Perhaps abstention was the best way after all, I decided.

'Sorry to keep you waiting, gentlemen,' Weatherall blustered as he came into the shop. He looked expectantly from one of us to the other, as if he ought to recognise us. He was about thirty-five, seriously thinning on top, with cherubic features and rimless spectacles.

'That's all right, sir,' Nigel said, showing his ID. 'I'm DS Newley from Heckley CID and this is DI Priest. Do you think we could go somewhere private for a chat? It shouldn't take more than a few minutes.'

'Oh, er, right. I thought you were company representatives. Sorry about that.'

'That's OK, sir.'

'We'll be upstairs, Monica, if you need me. This way, please, gentlemen.'

He lived above the shop. We sat on easy chairs that had seen better days and he lit the gas fire. He adjusted the vertical blind on the window to admit more light and apologised for the mess. 'We're in the middle of moving out,' he explained.

'Going far, sir?' I asked.

'No. We've bought a house on Sweetwater Lane, not too far away.'

'So you're not leaving the shop?'

'No. No. Just the opposite. Thinking of buying another, in fact.'

'Business must be good, sir.'

He smiled. 'Yes, I suppose it is. We just happen to be in a good location, with a decent catchment area and no big national nearer than the town centre. We're doing well.'

'I'm glad to hear it,' I said.

Nigel broke in with: 'We're looking into the death of

Dr Clive Jordan, Mr Weatherall. We believe you knew him.'

'I wondered if that was it.' He looked worried. Or sad, it's hard to tell the difference. 'Yes,' he continued, 'I knew him, but not very well.'

'How well?'

He studied his fingernails for a moment, realised he was fidgeting and placed his hands on his thighs. 'We met about three years ago, at the Lord Mayor's Ball in the town hall. I heard someone say his name and introduced myself. I see his prescriptions now and again, but not very often, so I made a joke about his handwriting.' He chuckled at the memory. 'I remembered him from school but he was a year above me and almost certainly didn't know I existed. We both went to Heckley Grammar, and he was school captain. I'm afraid I wasn't very good at sports.'

'And when did you last see him?'

'About a year after that.'

'What was the occasion?'

A fingernail went to his mouth for a moment before he thrust his hands into his pockets. 'That first time,' he began, 'at the town hall – we bumped into each other again, waiting for the ladies' coats, and walked out together. I was with my wife and he was with a girlfriend. She looked extremely young. When we reached the cars he was in a beautiful little Lotus. We were admiring it, me saying I'd always wanted one, and he said he'd probably be selling it in about a year, might I be interested? We said yes, and the following summer he rang me and I bought it. I haven't seen him since then.'

Nigel glanced at me, his face sagging like a melting cake. I pursed my lips and looked up at the ceiling.

'Did you pay cash for the car, sir?' Nigel asked. The enthusiasm had gone from his voice.

'No,' the pharmacist replied. 'We drew up a contract and I pay him monthly. It was actually his idea – said there was no point in paying exorbitant interest charges. He was terribly decent about the whole thing. And trusting. To tell the truth, I was a bit taken aback by him. If I'd been in his shoes I wouldn't have been so trusting, I can tell you.'

I said: 'Maybe he was a good judge of character, Mr Weatherall.'

The chemist nodded and said: 'Presumably I'll have to keep making the payments into his estate.'

'I would imagine so.'

'Ah, well.'

'The trustees will probably be in touch with you.'

'We did find some regular deposits in the doctor's bank account that we couldn't explain,' Nigel told him. 'Presumably they were from you?'

'Probably,' he replied. 'I transfer three hundred pounds a month to him, sometimes a bit more, if I can afford it.'

'Right, well, I think that clears that up nicely,' Nigel conceded. He turned to me. 'Do you have any further questions, Mr Priest?'

'No.' I shook my head. 'As you said, I think that clears things up, er, very nicely, thank you.'

'In that case, thank you for your assistance, Mr Weatherall.'

On the stairs I casually asked him where he'd been at eight thirty on the night in question, 'Just to complete our record of the interview, sir.' He and his wife had been working at the new house all evening. I resisted slamming Nigel's car door but yanked the seat belt tight. Nigel rattled numbers into his mobile phone as I watched two young girls walk by. They looked about fifteen but must have been twenty and had six kids between them: two infants in buggies, two toddlers pulled along by hand and two older ones following behind.

Nigel folded the phone and started the car engine.

'Tell me the news,' I invited.

'It's a white Lotus Elan, owned by A.J.K. Weatherall of Sweetwater, Heckley. Previous owner: Dr C.D. Jordan, also of Heckley. Shit!'

'And botheration,' I added. 'Back to the station, please, driver, let's have an early night.'

'Sorry, Boss,' he said.

'Nothing to apologize for, my young friend. It had to be investigated.'

I closed my eyes and dozed as we drove back, the heater blowing on to my legs and the weak winter sunshine flickering across my eyes. It was my antidote for disappointment. I pretended I was lying on a sunbed on a Caribbean beach and felt curiously content. I went to Heckley Grammar School. I was school captain, too, about fifteen years before the doctor had that honour.

'What's making you smile?' I heard Nigel say, above the whisper of the breeze in the palm trees.

'Oh, I'm just daydreaming.'

'What about?'

'I was wondering what toffee-flavoured condoms are like.'

been twenty and had six kids between them. [illegible] two soldiers, pulled along [illegible] and two [illegible] ones following behind.

[illegible] into the phone and [illegible]

[illegible]

[illegible]

[illegible] of [illegible]

[illegible] I looked. There is no [illegible]

[illegible]

[illegible] my [illegible] friend. [illegible] collapsed.

[illegible]

[illegible] had [illegible]

[illegible] whispers of the breeze in the palm trees.

"Oh, [illegible]

"What [illegible]

[illegible]

Chapter Seven

On my way home I called in at Marks and Spencer's and bought two new shirts – it was easier than ironing – and stocked up with ready meals. The travel agent next door was still open, so I collected brochures for Italy, Kenyan safaris and, as an afterthought, cruises.

Annabelle and I needed a holiday. I'd love to have taken her to Kenya, but the memories might be too bittersweet for her. She married a missionary worker there when she was still very young, but he couldn't resist the temptations of the Happy Valley set. They made a fresh start back over here and found happiness of a sort, until he died of cancer.

A week in Florence doing the galleries, followed by a walking tour in the Dolomites, sounded just perfect, but would mean waiting until the weather was warmer. I'd leave the brochures with her on Friday, see what she thought.

Sparky interviewed the residents of Canalside Mews and came away with lots of ideas about salt-water aquariums and integrated hi-fi systems but nothing that helped in the hunt for the doctor's killer. He even talked to Darryl Buxton, but managed to keep the two cases isolated from each other. Darryl had been out at the time of the shooting, he said, with his secretary. They had, Darryl told him, 'Something going, know what I mean?'

Two residents had heard a bump or a bang that could have been a gunshot, which gave us an accurate time of death. We place great importance on knowing the exact time of death. In the absence of the name of the trigger-puller, knowing the precise moment that the trigger was pulled is a small victory over ignorance. The doctor kept himself to himself, everybody said, and no strangers had been seen hanging around. It was all in the original reports and now we had it twice.

I talked to the staff at the White Rose Clinic. When I first started grammar school my father had just been made sergeant and we moved to Leeds for a while. I used to come home via the city centre and would often make a diversion through the various department stores. More and more often I found my route taking me past the perfumery counters. The ladies who sold Clinique, in their high-collared white tunics and immaculate make-up, were my favourites. I remembered all this when I first saw the White Rose's receptionist.

Her hair was pulled tightly back, but she had the features to carry it. The eyelashes looked like two black widow spiders and her teeth out-dazzled the uniform. I pulled my stomach in and flashed my ID like there was an intruder on the premises and I had a .357 Magnum in my belt that hadn't been used for two days and I was scared of it growing rusty.

'My name's Priest,' I said, 'from Heckley CID. I have an appointment with Dr Barraclough.'

She smiled and tapped a number into a state-of-the-art communications system. I mentally filled in an MFH report on her: five-three, forty-five, hundred and twenty pounds, and stunning with it, in spite of the heavy make-up. She could have saved herself fifty minutes in front of the mirror every morning and still given the odd cardiac arrest to the clinic's male visitors. Her shoulders were like an American footballer's, but they may have come with the uniform. The name badge said: 'Cicely Henderson, Receptionist'.

'There's Mr Priest to see you, Dr Barraclough,' she said into a microphone the size of a toothbrush.

The foyer of the clinic was all exposed brickwork, but it looked good. Chinese rugs were scattered around and a huge shaggy collage hung on a wall, depicting a stylised moorland scene, with mill chimneys in the valleys with smoke streaming from them. The artist must have done that bit from memory. The heating was high, which is always a sign of prosperity.

'Would you like to take a seat, Mr Priest,' she said. 'Dr Barraclough will be with you in a moment.'

I preferred to lean on her desk. 'How many reception staff are there, Mrs Henderson?' I asked.

'Two of us full-time, and two part-timers who cover the weekends,' she replied.

'So do you and the other person work different shifts?'

'Yes. We cover from eight in the morning to ten at night.'

I was about to say that I'd like a word with her later when a door opened and Dr Barraclough, Medical Director, swept into the foyer.

'Inspector . . .' he greeted me, hand extended.

He was wearing a suit that was just a tone too blue, white shirt and complementary striped tie. His hair was a fraction longer than respectable and greying to order at the temples. He could have stepped straight off the set of a Northern Upholstery commercial.

The hand might have been a musician's or a surgeon's, with long, perfectly manicured fingers. I tried not to crush them, although I suspected his livelihood had long-since ceased to depend on them.

'Dr Barraclough,' I said. 'Thanks for seeing me at such short notice.'

He led me to his office after asking Cicely to make us two coffees, if she didn't mind. 'The decent stuff,' he added, with a wink.

Her look said that for him she'd gladly have fetched it herself from Brazil, walking all the way with one stiletto heel missing.

The office was tidy and hi-tech, as I'd expected. A photo frame stood on his desk but I could only see the back of it. No doubt it helped him resist the temptations of his position and gave off a signal to predators. His window looked up the moor, towards Blea Fell, our local hill.

'Nice view,' I said, accepting his invitation to sit down.

'It is, isn't it? Some of us jog to the top three times a week.'

'Really? I'm impressed.'

'But I'm not one of them,' he added, smiling at his own joke.

'Oh.'

'I believe you said your predecessor had broken his leg while skiing, Inspector.'

'Yes, I'm afraid so. I've read his reports but I find the personal approach more useful.'

'I can understand that. We were all devastated by Clive's – Mr Jordan's – death. He was one of the best obs and gynae surgeons in the business and one of the finest human beings I've ever known. The Lord truly moves in mysterious ways. How can I help you, Inspector?'

I'd just noticed the tiny crucifix in his lapel. 'I believe,' I said, 'that you perform abortions here?'

'We do, Inspector, but do not confuse that by assuming we approve of them. Nobody *approves* of abortion. It is wrong, full stop. However, the issue is not as simple as that. I'm sure you know the arguments, but to fast forward to the bottom line, the attitude of the White Rose Clinic is to be in favour of giving the prospective mother the informed choice of either continuing with the pregnancy or having a termination. Ultimately, it is between her and God, or her conscience. We create a safe, non-judgemental environment in which she can reach a decision, and supply all the counselling and medical support she needs. We consider this to be a responsible approach to a very difficult situation.'

Perhaps, I thought. 'And Dr Jordan actually performed the terminations?' I suggested.

'Yes, he did.'

'So how many would he do?'

'Most of our other clients are with us for two, sometimes three, days. We work to a cycle which means most beds are available on Wednesdays and Saturdays, which is when we perform the terminations. The usual figure is somewhere between a dozen and . . . oh, as many as twenty on a Wednesday, with perhaps six or eight on a Saturday.'

Cicely came in with the coffee and returned the smile I gave her. This time I decided to indulge myself, and used the cream and sugar.

I quizzed the doctor about the workings of a private clinic. He was helpful and completely at ease with the situation. The cosmetic surgery was usually done on Mondays and Thursdays, by surgeons moonlighting from other hospitals, although he didn't use that word. He'd moved into administration early in his career, after finding that other people's varicose veins and bowel troubles were more than he could take.

'And you've never had any problems with the pro-life people?' I asked.

'The only problem I have with them is that title,' he said. 'I like to think that we are pro-life at the clinic.'

'No threatening letters? No demonstrations outside? Nothing like that?'

'No, Inspector, not at all. We pride ourselves in our discretion. All our referrals come by personal recommendation and we never advertise. A lady might come in to have a blephorectomy, for example. Some time later the daughter of a friend – at university, perhaps – confides in her that she is pregnant and doesn't want to marry the father. Our client tells her that she knows a very nice clinic where she can obtain all the support and attention she needs. It's amazing how the word spreads, Inspector.'

And the same would be true, I thought, if it just happened to be the *au pair* confiding in the lady's husband.

'Doesn't the father need to give his consent?' I asked.

'We consider it desirable, especially if she's married, but it's not a requirement. And it's only a signature on the bottom of a form. We don't check it.' He smiled and flapped a hand.

'Right,' I said. My ex-wife had an abortion after she left me, without my consent. I hadn't known she was pregnant until it was too late. The top of Blea Fell had vanished in the mist and a squall was dashing sleet against the window.

'. . . anything else?' Dr Barraclough was saying.

'Er, no. I mean, yes,' I stumbled out. 'Dr, er, Mr Jordan's private life. I get the impression that he led quite a colourful one. What can you tell me about that?'

'Nothing, Inspector. He was a fine doctor and that's all

I cared about. He was a single man, I believe: young and handsome. The surprise would be if he wasn't breaking a few hearts, here and there, don't you think?'

'But whose? That's what I want to know. Was he, can you say, having a relationship with anyone from the clinic?'

'I really have no idea.'

'A married woman, perhaps?'

'I'm afraid gossip of that sort never reaches me, Inspector. The nursing staff may be able to help you with that, but I hope you will be discreet. Many of us were very fond of Clive, in our own ways. Please try not to cause any further upset.'

'Thank you. I was going to ask you if you minded me having a word with some of the staff.' I had a printout of all their names that Nigel had obtained. 'If possible I'd like to interview the ones I've highlighted,' I said, sliding it across his desk.

'No problem. We want to see someone behind bars for this dreadful crime as much as you do. Feel free to talk to anyone you care to, but please appreciate that this is a working hospital and time is money, as with your job. If you show the list to Mrs Henderson she'll be able to tell you when they are available.'

'Smashing. I'll try to be brief with them. There is one last thing that you may be able to help me with. We have received a suggestion from other quarters that Dr Jordan may have been cited for malpractice, sometime in the past. Possibly about five years ago. Were you aware of this?'

He looked puzzled and fiddled with his shirt cuffs, adjusting them to the optimum fifteen millimetres. 'Ye-es,' he said, after a while. 'There was something . . .'

'Can you remember what, Doctor? We could go to the Medical Council, but, as you said, time is money.'

'It was all something over nothing,' he said, his brow furrowed with concentration, 'but I can't remember the details. It was completely unfounded, I can assure you of that. We'd just opened, and Clive had been highly recommended to us, then this happened, at the General. It put a bit of a cloud over him for a few weeks, but it all blew over. Your best bet will be to ask at the General – they'll tell you all about it.'

'If I can find someone to ask,' I said. 'If I can cut through all the red tape. If I can find someone who doesn't start telling me about confidentiality. There are ways of extracting information from institutions like the General, Dr Barraclough, but like I said, I prefer the personal approach. I'd be very grateful if you could give me a head start.'

'Yes, I know what you mean, but I'm sure it was all a storm in a teacup.'

'It might not have been a storm in a teacup to the complainant.'

'You mean someone might have borne him a grudge?'

'Something like that.'

'Could you leave it with me, Inspector? You're quite right, there was something, a few days after he joined us, but it all blew over. I'd forgotten all about it but it should be in there, somewhere. My secretary is off today, but I'll ask her to dig out Clive's file, first thing in the morning, if that's OK?'

'That will be fine. I'll look forward to hearing from you and thanks for your cooperation.'

I went down the short corridor that led back to the foyer. I thought about standing there and yelling: 'Step forward everybody that Clive Jordan was shagging!' but decided it might be against Dr Barraclough's guidelines, and I didn't want anyone killed in the stampede. I'd have to do it the hard way.

Mrs Cicely Henderson was not one of the names I'd highlighted, but I decided to start with her. I like to keep my methods flexible.

'Thanks for the coffee,' I said.

'You're welcome,' she replied. 'Was Dr Barraclough able to help you?'

'Yes, he was. And he's given me permission to talk to all the staff, so I've decided to start with you.' I gave her my lopsided grin and just knew her legs were turning to jelly. Some of her make-up had rubbed off on to the edge of her tunic's mandarin collar. She'd have to have a fresh clean one every day, eye-squinting white and crisp as an iceberg lettuce. I wondered what she was like at ironing shirts.

I told her about Makinson's broken leg, just to be friendly, and explained that I was doing follow-up interviews. Someone had spoken to her early in the enquiry, but she'd said that she rarely saw the doctor and had heard no scurrilous gossip about him.

'How often did you see him?' I asked.

'Just once a week, when he came in on a Wednesday.'

'Did you speak to him?'

'He'd stop here for a moment and ask me how I was, that's all.'

'I get the impression that he was a bit of a charmer.'

'Yes, he was, if you like that sort of thing.'

'A ladies' man?'

'Yes, I'd say so.'

'You're an attractive woman,' I stated. 'Did he ever approach you? Chat you up? Invite you out?' I gave myself a small pat on the back for slipping the compliment in and making it sound like a professional observation. She looked uncomfortable and might even have blushed under the make-up.

'N-No,' she stuttered, meaning yes.

'You don't seem sure.'

'Well, it doesn't seem right, talking about the dead when they can't defend themselves.'

'The doctor was murdered, Mrs Henderson,' I reminded her. 'It's my job to defend him, by tracking down his killer. If you know something that isn't in your previous statement you'd better tell me right now.'

She sighed and said: 'Right.'

I was standing at her desk and there was no handy chair for me to pull closer. 'Come and sit over here,' I said, and walked across to a small sofa.

She sat down next to me and crossed her legs. Her tights were the same shade as the pancake mix on her face. 'That's better,' I said. 'Now what do you want to tell me?'

'About four years ago,' she began. 'Clive – Mr Jordan – invited me out. I'd left my husband about three years earlier and was still off men. He was very persistent but I kept saying no. Then he stopped asking me.'

'Right,' I said. 'Right. Thank you. He must have been very disappointed.'

'There's more.'

'Oh. Go on, then.'

'As I said earlier, two of us work full-time on reception. This week I'm covering from eight a.m. to four p.m. My opposite number is called Josephine Farrier. She comes on at three and stays until ten. Josie – Mrs Farrier – was having an affair with Clive.'

'Are you sure?'

'She told me herself. He must have approached her after I turned him down. Last summer she poured her heart out to me – said she loved him, wanted to leave Eric, her husband, and the two children. Unfortunately for her, that was the last thing on Clive's mind. It was all a bit pathetic – real Marj Proops stuff. It had been going on for years, she said, after work. When she was on early she was supposed to be at a pottery class, would you believe?'

'It happens,' I said. 'People in love do desperate things. Do you think her husband – Eric – knew?'

'I don't know. I told her not to be so stupid. Men only wanted one thing, I told her, and Clive was no different to the rest of them.'

For a moment I felt . . . invisible. 'You weren't very sympathetic,' I said.

'It wasn't sympathy she needed, it was a good shaking.'

'Right. Did you tell her that she'd been the doc's second choice, after you?'

'No. I couldn't be so cruel.'

'And she never mentioned that her husband knew?'

'No, but do you think it's possible to keep something like that secret?'

'I don't know,' I replied, untruthfully. I'd discovered the answer the hard way, a long time ago. I didn't have a highlighter pen, so I underlined Mrs Josephine Farrier's name on my printout. She had some questions to answer.

I interviewed the ward sister, two enrolled nurses and the finance manager without coming to any conclusions, other than agreeing with Nigel's statement about them all being good-looking. I couldn't help contrasting the accommodation – every bed in a private room, wallpaper on the walls, no hospital smell – with Heckley General where my father spent his final days. As a visitor, I'd definitely prefer to come here. As a patient, I wasn't so sure.

Hunger's clammy tentacles, clutching at my innards, drove me away. I had hoped to last out until Mrs Farrier came to work, at three o'clock, but I'd hardly eaten for twenty-four hours. As I strolled into the foyer for the last time, after seeing one of the nurses, Mrs Henderson looked up from a keyboard and smiled expectantly, awaiting the next name on my list.

'I think that's it for today,' I said. 'I need to be in the station, shortly.'

'Will you be coming back, Mr Priest?' she asked.

'Yes, I think I'll have to, but thanks for your help today.'

'You're welcome.'

I turned to leave, then stopped, hand to head as if deep in thought. 'There was one final question I'd like to ask you,' I said, turning back to her.

'Yes?'

'Now, what was it?' I tapped my cheek with a fingertip. 'Ah, yes,' I said. 'I remember. You said you were off men, Mrs Henderson. I was wondering: are you still off them?'

'Yes,' she said, but her smile was so broad her make-up did well to contain it. A little flirting can go a long way.

I called in a cafe in the town centre that did steak and kidney pies you could trust, with apple pie and custard to follow. Maggie came in a few minutes after I arrived back at the station. She'd been to see Herbert Mathews, who sent his regards, and to consult the court histories at Burnley. We now had a clear picture of Buxton's career as a serial rapist – allegedly – but nothing that helped much. All it did was harden our resolve to nail him.

I let Sparky finish the interviews at the clinic. 'I'll tell you what,' he said when he returned.

'What?'

'We're mixing with a higher class of woman on this enquiry.'

'You mean Mrs Farrier was a good-looker?'

'And the other one. All of them, in fact.'

I said: 'Maybe it's us. Perhaps we're growing old, beginning to see women in a new light.'

'If it is, then yippity-di-doo. Let's have more of it.'

'What else did you discover?'

'She admitted that they were lovers, right to the end. On the night in question she was out with her husband at a choral festival at the local church. Lots of people there that they knew. I've got some names, one of which is Dr Barraclough. He sold them the tickets.'

'Check them out just the same,' I said. 'Let's not have another Ged Skinner.'

'Right. So what do you reckon?' Sparky asked.

'I reckon,' I told him, 'that so far we've caught more red herrings than a Russian trawler. Do you know what we need?'

'Er, no. What do we need?'

'A chart. That's what we need. When in doubt, draw a chart. And there's nothing like one for impressing the top brass when they start asking questions.' I pulled the flip-board easel from the corner and turned over to a clean page.

'Why not do it on the computer,' Sparky suggested.

'Because I wouldn't know where to start,' I confessed. 'Would you?'

'Er, no.'

'I've only just mastered the flip-board. And besides, this way I get to use coloured pens. Let's start with the doctor.'

I wrote his name at the top of the sheet, drew a black

square around it to signify deceased and put the date, December 23.

'Supplying drugs to Ged Skinner,' Sparky suggested.

I wrote the exact words and drew a little box. 'That's his alibi box. Number one means he claims to have one, two means we've checked it, three, it's foolproof. Two, would you say?'

'Yeah. Two.'

'Next?'

'The registrar. And his wife.'

I wrote them in and put 'sexual' along the connecting line to suggest possible motives. 'Alibis?'

'Only one.'

'We haven't spoken to her yet, have we?'

'No.'

'We'd better put that right, soon as pos.'

'Noted.'

'But presumably she was at the same dinner party?'

'That's right. She did the cooking.'

'Unless they had a takeaway,' I suggested, 'and while she was waiting in the shop for eight portions of spare ribs, Peking duck and sweet and sour dogs' bollocks to be prepared she nipped out to the doctor's and bumped him off.'

'Brilliant, Holmes,' Sparky said. 'Let's bring her in.'

'Maybe not. Who's next?'

'The chemist.'

'A.J.K. Weatherall. Motive?'

'Money?'

'He'll still have to pay for the car, into the doc's estate.'

'In that case, maybe they really were on the fiddle.'

'OK.' I put a 1 in his alibi box. 'He and his wife were fitting curtain rails at the new house,' I explained.

'How pleasant. And that brings us to the bag of worms at the clinic.'

'Mr and Mrs Farrier.'

'Right.'

'Motive?'

'Sex, again.'

'Alibi?'

'Yes, but not checked.'

'One.'

'Yep.'

'Barraclough?' I had to bend the word downwards because I was running off the edge of the page.

'Barraclough? What's his motive?'

'Sex, jealousy, anything. We can't rule him out.'

'OK. Alibi?'

'You said he was at the same carol concert as the Farriers.'

'Of course. So that's a one, again.'

'Yep.'

'What about Jordan's acting friends?'

I pulled a face and sighed. 'I don't think so. We'll have to keep a weather eye on them, though. Can't rule them out completely.'

'Next?'

I wrote 'Malpractice?' at the bottom of the page.

'What are we doing about that?' Sparky asked.

'Dr Barraclough is supposed to be ringing me. I'll give him a reminder.'

'So, is that it?'

I shook my head. 'No, there's one last group.' I wrote 'Abortions' in the last bit of clear space.

'I thought Barraclough was convinced that the pro-lifers didn't know the clinic existed,' Sparky said.

'That's what he said, but we can't be sure. I'm not thinking of just the pro-lifers. Mr Jordan performed between four and five thousand terminations in his short but eventful career. Including fathers, that's ten thousand potential dissatisfied customers.' I wrote 'X 10,000' next to 'Abortions' and clicked the top back on the pen.

We were both silent for several minutes, pretending to be studying the chart. I was thinking about the five thousand foetuses that Jordan had been instrumental in destroying. I imagined ten schools, side by side. Filing into them was a long line of boys and girls, smart in their grey uniforms. They carried satchels and sports bags and jostled and teased each other. For as far as the eye could see. I'm in favour of choice, but I couldn't do it.

Sparky leaned his chair back on two legs and flipped his notebook shut. 'You know your comment about the Russian trawler?' he said.

'Mmm.'

'I think you'd better make it the whole bleedin' fishing fleet.'

Chapter Eight

Sparky was right. We were no nearer narrowing the field down than when Ged Skinner walked out of the station. We hadn't even considered Darryl Buxton. Much as I'd have loved to have pinned it on him, living in the same block of flats as the dead man was hardly grounds for suspicion. Monday, I'd have a word with Mr Wood and Mr Isles. We needed more manpower. Every alibi would have to be checked, every interview re-done. Maybe somebody's guard would drop, or their story wouldn't tally with the first one they'd given. They'd embroider it, add bits that contradicted what they'd said earlier, and talk themselves into a murder charge. And Mother Teresa might buy a Harley for nipping to mass on. I told Sparky that I'd see him Monday and went home.

I had a luxurious shower and smothered myself in smelly gunge that Annabelle had given me for Christmas. Tonight we would eat in style; the Wool Exchange was the best restaurant in Heckley. There wasn't much competition – the second best was the Bamboo Curtain – but it had a certain class that no amount of new money can re-create. I pulled the last of the new shirts from its box and carefully unfolded it. It was dark blue, with a thin grey check. It would look good with my dark suit and the red silk tie, which was another present from Annabelle.

I pulled the knot tight and slipped my jacket on, studying myself in the mirror. I looked good, even if it was archetypal detective. The face was pale and I had a few more wrinkles, but they were all in the places where I smile, and I smile a lot. I picked up the holiday brochures and drove round to the Old Vicarage, next to St Bidulph's, where Annabelle lived.

She was wearing a fawn suit that I'd never seen before and a red blouse. The suit wasn't her colour – she's at her best in something really bold – but she still looked stunning. She looks good in one of my old sweaters when she's helping me with emergency maintenance in my garden. I stood watching her as she moved around the rooms, checking windows and switches. When she was ready I led her to the front door and held it open. As she passed me she gave me a kiss on the cheek.

'What did I do to deserve that?' I asked, pleased but slightly surprised.

'You look very handsome,' she said, rather gravely, and gave me a squeeze.

'And you look very beautiful,' I replied, but she turned away, and my kiss fell on her cheek.

'Tell me about the Wool Exchange,' she said, in the car.

'Right,' I replied. 'Here comes a rather vague history lesson. The present building was built by the wool barons in the eighteenth century, although there was something there long before that. It was where they auctioned their produce and conducted their other businesses. It was in use well into this century, but I'm not very good at dates. At other times they used it as an exclusive club and entertained their cotton-picking cousins from over the hill. If we knew its full history we might not want to frequent the place.

Slave-trade money and freemasonry come to mind, but I think you'll like it.'

'Have you been before?'

'Mmm,' I said. 'Long time ago,' but I didn't enlarge upon my answer. My wife – Vanessa – and I held our wedding reception there. After that we'd come back for a romantic table for two on birthdays and anniversaries. There weren't too many of those. Tonight, hopefully, I was laying a ghost.

Our table was available so we went straight in and sat down. 'This is incredible,' Annabelle said, looking around. Along the edges of the room was a row of desks on high legs, with merchants' names elegantly written on them in gold paint. Blackboards carried the names of breeds of sheep, probably now extinct, with columns for the prices to be written in £.s.d. Portraits of the leading barons in their ceremonial robes, smug bastards to a man, adorned the walls. It wasn't elegant or aesthetically pleasing in any way, but it was authentic and smacked of wealth and all that went with it.

'Would you like the wine list, sir?' a waiter was saying as he proffered a bound volume. He was old enough to have been here when they drowned their sorrows over universal suffrage. Annabelle shook her head when I looked across at her.

'Just fizzy water, please,' I said.

All the other tables were occupied but they were so far apart it didn't matter. We both decided the *halibut dieppoise* with a *salpicon* of prawns and leeks sounded good and settled for that. I was starving so I ordered the carrot and fennel soup and we both asked for pâté.

'How's the soup?' Annabelle asked as I tucked in.

'Delicious, but,' I said.

'But what?'

'But not as good as yours. Same with the bread roll. Have you seen the uplifting slogans carved round the frieze?' I led her eyes upwards. 'The one behind you says: "Blessed are the meek, for they shall inherit the Earth."'

'Good grief, yes,' she replied. 'There doesn't look anything meek about this lot. Yours says: "Out of Prosperity shall come Peace." I suppose I could go along with that.'

'Except when the the prosperity comes from running slaves and peddling opium to the Chinese,' I said.

'It's a fascinating place,' Annabelle observed, glancing around. 'Why haven't you brought me here before?'

'Oh, I just thought I'd keep it up my sleeve,' I told her, laying the spoon across my empty bowl.

'And what else do you have up your sleeve?'

I fiddled with my napkin and focused on the table centrepiece. There was a little silver bowl brimming with primulas, and salt and pepper shakers with a coat of arms on them that featured a sheep hanging by a strap round its middle. I've never understood what that was about.

'Nothing,' I said, softly, looking up into her eyes, bluer than a jay's wing, and reaching a hand towards her. 'There's nothing else, Annabelle. All you see here is all there is.'

Her cheeks flushed. She picked up her fork and pressed the points into the cloth until she realised what she was doing and replaced it. We were too far apart to hold hands so I had to settle for a little smile from her.

An all male party, about eight of them, were at a table in the far corner. We could hear them chattering but they weren't too bad. As the waiter brought the pâté they all burst into raucous laughter.

'I must apologise for the noise, sir,' the waiter said. 'I assure you they are not regular customers.'

'It's not a problem,' I told him.

One of the group was now on his feet, as if to make a speech. A bread roll bounced off his dinner jacket and he sat down again to loud cheers from his cronies.

'It's not how we prefer our guests to behave,' the waiter said, hurrying off.

'Tell me about the restaurants,' I said to Annabelle. 'And this designer you're meeting.'

'I don't know much about it myself,' she replied, leaning forward. 'Xav's meeting me off the train and I expect I'll be whisked away to a meeting, or a working lunch. Working lunches are very popular in this business.'

'I bet they are.'

'Xav sent me some drawings of the interiors of the restaurants, sort of three-dimensional plans, looking inside, if you follow me . . .'

'I think they're called isometric sketches,' I said, although I was guessing.

'Are they? I was wondering if you'd have a look at them with me, when we go home. Will I be able to colour them, to compare how different designs would look?'

'Of course you will,' I replied, smiling. Ever since we met I've broken the rules to involve her in my work. Now she was doing it with me. A roar went up from the rowdies in the corner. I looked across and Annabelle turned in her seat. One of them, jacket off and sleeves rolled up, was pretending to sing, using a Liebfraumilch bottle as a microphone. The others started chanting: 'Sit down you bum, sit down you bum.'

'This used to be a posh place,' I said by way of an apology.

'I think we picked a bad night,' she replied.

The manager, tall and elegant, scuttled out of the kitchen

and headed towards them, a diplomat dashing to quell trouble with the natives. Behind him the chef took up a position in the doorway, meat cleaver in his hand. He looked like a cross between Pavarotti and the King of Tonga. I decided to be on his side.

The manager knew what he was doing. His hands flapped as he spoke, faces nodded at him, smiles broke out and hands were shaken. He went back to his retreat and the chef closed the door.

We ate our pâté and Annabelle told me that the next Luxotel would be on a new complex near West Midlands Airport. Hopefully, she'd be in from the start with the decor of this one. It was nearing completion and decisions needed making in the next few days. I could understand her enthusiasm.

The halibut was superb. I was asking Annabelle if she'd like to change her mind about the wine – a glass of dry white would have gone well with it – when there was another commotion in the corner. They were all on their feet, hooking jackets off the backs of chairs and reaching for wallets.

'Breathe easy,' I said. 'They're leaving.'

'Thank goodness for that.'

They filed towards us, threading between the tables in line astern, bellies thrust forward as they swayed with a curious grace, like sailors on a moving deck, and stifled their belches. They could have been the descendants of the men in the paintings, fat and arrogant but minus the class.

Fifth in the line was Darryl Buxton. He was wearing a cream tuxedo with red cummerbund and dicky bow, and a frilly shirt. Each frill was edged in black, in case you hadn't noticed it. He looked like something from the Great Barrier Reef.

'Well, well, well,' he shouted as he saw me, raising an arm above his head in a parody of a bullfighter, 'look who it fuckin' isn't.'

The man in front turned and grabbed him. 'C'mon, Darryl,' he said.

'That's the bastard who's trying to frame me,' Darryl declared. 'I didn't know cops ate 'ere. I wouldn't have suggested it if I'd known cops ate 'ere.'

The parade had shuffled to a halt at our table. My only thought was with Annabelle. We were in a situation that was not of my making, so how could I extract us with minimum embarrassment and maybe even earn a bit of kudos for myself? Was it to be Gregory Peck in *The Big Country*, or Stallone in . . . whatever? Freud would have loved me.

'Take him away, please,' I said to his companion, my hands spreadeagled on the table so he could see I wasn't going for my gun.

'He's a fuckin' cop,' Darryl told the restaurant.

'C'mon,' his pal said. 'He's not worth it.'

They started to bundle him away and I looked across at Annabelle. Her face was white but she was staring defiantly at him.

'I'll fix him,' I heard Darryl say. 'I'll fuckin' fix you,' he shouted, further away.

The manager was with us, apologising. 'I assure you sir, we won't be accepting a booking from them again, and I'm most sorry for any inconvenience or upset caused to you. Please try to enjoy the rest of your meal. Allow me to bring you a complimentary bottle of wine? Sir? Madam?'

'Who are they?' I asked.

'They said they were estate agents. A company called Homes 4 U, I believe. We took the booking about a week ago. It is the last time they will eat at the Wool Exchange, I promise you. Now, about that wine, sir?'

I shook my head. 'No, we're all right, thanks.' Annabelle had pushed her plate away, cutlery neatly laid on it. I felt the same way.

'I think we'll just have the bill,' I said.

He trowelled the apologies on like marzipan and offered us coffees or liqueurs. I told him that the halibut was excellent but we'd lost our appetites, so he knocked ten pounds off the bill and hoped that we'd eat there again. I promised him we would.

I held the car door open for Annabelle and carefully closed it behind her. I walked round and took my own seat. I pulled my seatbelt on but didn't start the engine.

'That didn't quite work out how I'd planned it,' I said.

'It wasn't your fault, Charles,' she replied, putting her hand on mine.

'I'd wanted tonight to be special.'

'I know.' She smiled, and said: 'Up to then, it had been.'

'Well, at least it wasn't dull,' I chuckled.

'You can certainly say that again. Who was he, that obnoxious man?'

'That was Darryl Buxton, acquitted of rape five times and in the frame for another.'

'*Five* times!'

'That we know of.'

'That's . . . horrible. Be careful, Charles,' she said, 'he looked dangerous.'

'Only with women,' I assured her. 'I can handle the Darryl Buxtons of this world any time at all.' There's no harm in a flash of macho, now and again, as long as you keep it under control.

As we drove out of town I said: 'I think the Wool Exchange must be jinxed for me.'

Annabelle asked me why, and I told her about my wedding reception.

'Oh, Charles, I am sorry.'

'Tell me about yours,' I said.

'My wedding reception?'

'Yes. Where was it?'

'In Kenya.'

'Whereabouts?'

'A little township called Navashonga, in the north.'

'Go on. I like to hear you talk about Kenya.'

We were at the traffic lights. They changed to green and I eased forward, Annabelle's hand on my knee. When I was in top gear again I put mine back on it.

'It was the start of the long wet season,' she began, 'so the acacia trees were in blossom. The church was made of breeze blocks and flattened oil drums, with a piano that had several keys missing. After the service we had a picnic, everybody invited. People came from miles around – half of Africa must have been there – and the Samburu danced for us. It was wonderful.'

I could picture it, through her eyes. She'd shown me her photographs and books and the images were as vivid to me as if I'd been there myself: the flat-topped feverthorn trees, the cattle, swirling dust and pogo-stick dancing of the Samburu, close cousins of the Masai. She was happy when she reminisced, and that usually made me happy, too.

But tonight it was different. Tonight, as I listened to her reminisce, her voice far away, on another continent, with another man, the ache in my stomach felt as if something was trying to suck my entrails from me, and I knew it wasn't the halibut.

'Am I invited in?' I asked as we drew up outside the Old Vicarage.

'Of course, silly. Besides, we're home a little earlier than expected.'

'Mmm, that's true.'

We spread the drawings of the restaurant on the refectory table in her kitchen. The paper wasn't substantial enough for watercolours, so I suggested she purchase coloured pencils from the art shop in town. Using an HB which she found I demonstrated how to do it and watched as she tried herself. Some people have a knack for drawing, some don't, and to them it's like being tone deaf. A foreign language. Annabelle had the ability, but had never practised. It was only colouring squares, so she'd soon get the hang of it. She explained her ideas, for my approval, and I told her about the silver and gold pens you could buy. They'd do for highlighting the borders.

'Do you want me to take you to the station in the morning?' I asked as I finished my mug of decaff and stood up to leave.

'It's kind of you Charles, but I've ordered a taxi. For six thirty, would you believe?'

'You know I'd be happy to take you down there; go with you.'

'No. We want to take a look at a couple of restaurants in the West End and Docklands. See if they inspire us. There's a limit to how many times you can do that in a weekend.'

'So when are you coming home?'

'Monday.'

'You'll put on weight.'

'Probably.'

I put my arms around her for my customary goodnight

kiss. She melted into them but buried her face in my neck.

'You're a very thoughtful person, Charles,' she said as we separated.

I pecked her on the nose. 'Goodnight.'

'Goodnight.'

Halfway out of the door I hesitated. I wanted to tell her not to go to London. Not to go running to this mysterious millionaire with his grandiose schemes whose spell she'd fallen under. 'Annabelle, what would you say if I asked you not to go?'

But I didn't. If I'd asked, and she'd not gone, it would always have been there between us, like an invisible strand of barbed wire with bits of wool dangling where something had blundered into it. I pulled the door shut and strode down her garden path.

I drove straight off, but stopped around the corner at the end of her street. Perhaps I should have said more? Maybe I should go back? But what would I be going back to? Her eyes had been on the edge of tears as we said that last goodnight, and I was scared of the reason. I put the car in gear and drove away, fairly close to them myself.

Darryl Buxton's Mondeo was in his spot outside the Canalside Mews, but there was no light showing in his apartment. I don't know what I'd expected. I sat and watched for fifteen minutes but nobody came, nobody went. 'Go home, Charlie,' I said to myself. 'Go home. You shouldn't be here.' Common sense got the better of me, for once. I went home.

The ansaphone was beeping. A visit from the mailman used to be a delight as you anticipated the message he'd brought, read the envelope and wondered who it was from. Now, envelopes with windows contain bills or computer-generated claptrap that makes your heart bleed for the rain-forest dweller that your personal consignment has rendered homeless. You scan the pile on the doormat and dump the lot in the bin without a second thought.

Not so the ansaphone. It still has the power to raise a minute thrill of expectancy as you press the replay button. Double glazing companies and charities do not leave junk messages on ansaphones. They *know* you're not going to ring them back. And, now of all times, there was the possibility that it was Annabelle . . .

The electronic lady told me that I had one message. There were the usual bleeps and clicks, followed by a brief silence and the noise of a handset being replaced, breaking the connection. 'Your message timed at eleven sixteen p.m.,' the lady told me, which made it about ten minutes ago. I pressed 1471 and she gave me the number for Heckley police station.

'Hello, Arthur, it's Charlie Priest,' I said when they answered. 'You've been after me.'

'Hello, Boss – that's right, a few minutes ago. We've contacted DS Newley and he's taken it, so you can go to bed safe in the knowledge that it's all in good hands.'

'What was it?'

'Girl – well, a young woman – on the Sylvan Fields estate. Badly beaten up. She staggered into a neighbour's and they drove her to the General.'

'Right. I think the young Mr Newley should be able to handle that. Let me know if there are developments.' In other words, if she dies.

'Will do, Boss. And thanks for ringing.'

On the other hand, I was still wearing my shoes and jacket, the car engine was warm, and sleep was about as far away as the cure for snoring. I squealed the tyres as I set off, just to let the neighbours know that the forces of law are vigilant around the clock.

A Heckley panda was parked outside the Accident and Emergency entrance. We always used to call it Casualty. Inside I found a PC I knew and WPC Kent, who I didn't.

'Hello, Graham,' I said. 'What have we got?'

'Hello, Mr Priest. DS Newley's here, you know.'

'Is he? I must be slowing down in my old age. Where is he?'

'Talking to the doctor in IC.'

'What happened?'

'The hospital contacted the station, after she was brought in. They say she's obviously been done over pretty bad. She's called Samantha Teague, from an address on the Sylvan Fields.'

'What happened to the people who brought her in?'

'They've gone home.'

'OK. In that case let's find Nigel.'

I led the way to Intensive Care. It was a journey I knew too well. As we followed the yellow line painted down the length of the corridor floor I turned to WPC Kent and said: 'I'm sorry, I don't know your first name.'

'It's Claire, sir.'

'And you don't mind me calling you Claire?'

'Of course not, sir.'

'Good. Pleased to meet you. I'm Charlie Priest. I object strongly to you calling me sir, unless it's absolutely essential. Graham will tell you all about it.'

Nigel and a ridiculously young doctor were standing outside the doors of IC, deep in conversation. They turned as we approached and Nigel introduced me. 'She's stable,' the doctor said. 'We'll have her in surgery in the morning and she should be able to go straight on to a ward, if we've picked up everything.'

'What are her injuries?' I asked.

'Broken jaw, depressed fracture of the cheek, several broken ribs, concussion, extensive bruising and a few lacerations. I'd say she was given a good thumping round the head and then he put the boot in.'

'Nice man,' I said. 'You mentioned concussion, when can we talk to her?'

'She's drifting in and out of consciousness. You can try having a word, for a minute or two, but she won't be able to speak.'

'Thanks.' I turned to Nigel and suggested that he take Graham to the Sylvan Fields and they interview whoever brought her to the hospital. Maybe they knew her assailant.

Which left me with Claire Kent. I hadn't planned it that way, it was just how things worked out. 'Let's have a word with Samantha, then,' I said to her.

From the contours of the sheet draped over her it was easy to see how thin she was. There was a skeleton under there, and little else. The face was a different story. An oxygen mask covered her nose and mouth, resting uncomfortably on the swelling. One eye was closed-up completely and the other was blackening. Her left cheek was the colour of a dipso's liver and in the midst of the bruising I could see three, then four, small deep lacerations.

'What do you think caused those?' I asked the doctor. Claire leaned over to inspect them.

'I wondered if he was wearing a ring,' he suggested. 'A signet ring or, say, one of those with a sovereign in it.'

'But wouldn't that have made a sharper cut? These are, like, intense bruises, with the skin bursting in the middle.'

'Yes, I see what you mean. Unless he was wearing gloves over the ring.'

'Well done, Doc,' I said. 'I think you're right. We'll have them photographed.'

'There's two more down here,' he said. He slackened off the elastics holding the oxygen mask, saying that her face was still swelling, and pulled it down to reveal her mouth and jaw.

'She had a ring through her lip,' he told us. 'We found it in her mouth, hanging on by a strip of skin. That didn't help.'

'Oh, you poor kid,' I whispered. 'You poor kid.' I straightened up and took in the battered face. Man's inhumanity to Woman in all its glory. Some men have the need to do it, some women endure it for years. This was as bad as it got – the next step was murder.

Her hair was spread out to one side, loose and flowing against the crispness of the linen, and the words of the song flashed through my mind: 'Your head upon the pillow in a fair and a golden storm.' What if it did come from a bottle? Nobody ever said Marilyn Monroe was a natural.

I put my hands on the rail at the bottom of the bed and turned away. The walls were revolving around me.

'Are you all right?' the doctor asked, laying a hand on my arm.

'I know her,' I said. 'I know her.'

'You know her?'

'Yes.'

I sat on the edge of the bed and leaned across her. 'Samantha,' I said, softly. 'Can you hear me?'

The third time I asked she opened her good eye.

'Hello, Samantha,' I said. 'My name's Charlie. I saw

you last week, in your office. Remember?' There was no response.

'I came to see Darryl,' I continued, 'and he sent you out to do some shopping while we talked.' I swear her body tensed at the mention of his name, and I wondered if the instruments wired to her recorded it. Her face was incapable of showing emotion.

'Can you hear me, Samantha?' I asked. 'Blink your eyes if you can hear me.'

She did better than that. She gave a barely perceptible nod of the head.

'She nodded, Mr Priest,' I heard PC Kent say.

'I know,' I replied. 'She's a brave girl. Do you remember me, Samantha?'

Little nod.

'You're in hospital, Samantha. Someone attacked you. But you're safe, now. No one can hurt you here. Do you understand?'

Nod.

'I'm a policeman, Samantha. I want to catch the person who did this to you and put him in jail, where he belongs. Can you hear what I'm saying?'

Nod.

'That's very good. You're doing well. Now listen very carefully to this next bit, Samantha. Was it Darryl who did this to you. Was it your boss, Darryl Buxton?'

Her head jerked sideways, away from me, and she winced with pain.

'Was it Darryl?' I repeated.

No response.

'I think that's enough, Inspector,' the doctor said.

'OK,' I told him, raising a hand to fend him off for a few more seconds. 'Samantha, look at me.' Her head came back round and the good eye pointed in my direction. 'This lady,' I said, reaching out towards PC Kent, 'is called Claire.' She came and stood by me. 'She's going to stay with you, to make sure you are safe. Outside there are ten policemen with guns, just to look after you. That's twice as many as Prince William has. Claire is in charge of them. All you have to do is have a good rest and get better. Understand?'

She nodded.

'Good. There's nothing to be frightened of, now.' I stood up and turned away.

The doctor walked to the door with me and I beckoned for Claire to join us. 'I'll send for the photographer, get those wounds recorded, if that's OK, Doc?'

'Mmm. No problem.'

'Thanks. Claire, have you heard of a dying declaration?'

'Yes sir, Mr Priest. You mean that if she thinks she's about to die she might change her mind about telling us who did this to her?'

'That's right. She works for a man called Darryl Buxton who is a right thug. There's a good chance this is his handiwork. Keep your notebook with you just in case.'

She looked concerned. 'Do you think it might come to that, sir?'

I turned to the doctor, deflecting the question in his direction. 'I'd say she was off the critical list,' he told us, 'but we don't know how bad the internal damage is. She's not out of the woods just yet.'

I was dozing behind my desk, feet on radiator, when Nigel rang. If I'd been at home in bed I wouldn't have slept a wink. It's as if you need some discomfort to divert your attention. It was just before one a.m., Saturday morning.

'We've spoken to the neighbours,' he said.

'Go on.'

'Samantha lives in a council house that she rented with her boyfriend, but he left months ago. The neighbours who brought her in say they heard a noise at their door at about a quarter to eleven and found her slumped on the floor. They don't have a phone so the husband decided to bring her in himself, thought it would be quicker. The neighbours at the other side heard a car door, possibly a bit before that, and the sound of it driving away. Nothing special, possibly a diesel.'

'Or a taxi?'

'Possibly.'

'Great.' I told him who Samantha was, and that I was going to ask uniformed to arrest her boss, Darryl the Rapist.

'On what grounds?' he asked.

'On the grounds that Samantha was scared stiff when I mentioned his name. Whoever worked her over was wearing gloves. If we can find them we have him. See you here about ten, eh?'

'Ten it is, Boss.'

'Get some sleep. Darryl and his solicitor are about to have theirs disturbed.'

It took another hour to organise lifting Darryl and searching his house. I rang a lady magistrate I do regular business with and she agreed to sign a warrant. We despatched a panda to collect it. After that I went home and set my alarm for seven o'clock, five hours away. I slept quite well, but was waiting for the alarm.

I drove straight round to Canalside Mews. Two pandas were parked outside and young Graham opened the door for me.

'Any luck?' I asked.

''Fraid not, Mr Priest. We haven't found any gloves at all. There's three gold rings in the bedroom, and SOCO's taken imprints.'

'Right,' I said.

The flat was a dump. Men who live alone are granted a certain amount of dispensation in the field of housekeeping, but this went beyond that. His white tux and the frilly shirt were thrown on to the settee, next to several days' tabloids. A dirty plate and mug were on the table, and my detective skills told me that his last meal had been sardines. I wandered through the rooms, taking in the squalor and wondering what his classy neighbours would have thought. He hadn't washed up for two days and his bedroom smelled like a horsebox. I opened a window. On a chair was a pile of pages from newspapers. I picked a bundle up and thumbed through them. He'd saved every page-three girl for the last six months.

'Gather round, boys and girls,' I called out.

There were three of them, Graham's partner – Claire – still being at the hospital. When I was a rooky PC on nightshift my partner was David Sparkington. Such is life.

'I appreciate it's Saturday and you should all be home in bed,' I said, 'but are you all right for staying a little longer?'

They nodded.

'Good. I want to widen the enquiry. First of all, though, let's have a think about Darryl's movements.' I told them about Samantha and gave a brief résumé of what we presumed had happened.

'If he was wearing gloves,' I went on, 'It's imperative that we find them. Let's suppose that he did go round to Samantha's and did beat her up. How did he get there?'

'Taxi?' one of them suggested.

'It looks like it. So he does the deed. How does he get back here?'

'Another taxi?'

'How do you get a taxi in Sylvan Fields at eleven o'clock at night?'

'Ring on your mobile. He sounds the mobile type.'

'Very good,' I said. 'He rings for a taxi on his mobile. Meanwhile what does he do? Wait at Samantha's? Or sit under a street lamp?'

'Start walking?'

'What do you think?'

They all agreed that he'd start walking home, looking out for the taxi coming to collect him.

'Right,' I agreed. 'And I reckon he'd walk downhill towards the town centre. And maybe he got rid of the gloves on the way. I'll organise some more help. When it arrives, start looking for the gloves along the route he might have taken. I'll have a word with the taxi firms. Meanwhile, there's something else, but it's off the record.'

I told them about the rape, and asked them to make a note of anything that gave a clue towards his sexual inclinations. It wouldn't be admissible as evidence, but these days nothing is if it incriminates the accused.

Mr Turner didn't look pleased when I passed him in the foyer of the nick, waiting to be taken to his client. Nigel was in the office, brewing up.

'You're early,' I told him.

'Eager,' he replied.

'I think I'll let you talk to Buxton,' I said. 'Keep the enquiries separate. Otherwise they might just assume that I'm pursuing a vendetta against him and not take it seriously.'

'That might not be a bad thing,' Nigel suggested.

'Mmm, perhaps. Thing is, I'm not so sure myself. Samantha was scared when I mentioned his name, but that's hardly evidence. No, you do it.'

We gave Mr Turner twenty minutes with his client before Nigel went down to record an interview. I rang Mr Wood at home to let him know what was happening in his nick and arranged for another crew to assist in the search for the gloves. Then I had a bacon sandwich in the canteen and walked into town to buy another shirt from M and S's Casual but Smart range.

Turner's car had gone when I arrived back, and Nigel was in my office, reading the contents of my in-tray. He slid a report about the effects of police radios on officers' hearing back on to the pile and pushed a cassette across the table.

'According to that you'll be deaf as a post before you're fifty,' I said, nodding towards the report.

'You've seen a ghost behaving shifty?' he replied. For Nigel, it wasn't bad.

'Is this it?' I asked, holding up the tape.

'For what it's worth. He was at the Wool Exchange until about nine, nine fifteen, with a party of managers from Homes R Us . . .'

'Homes 4U,' I interrupted.

'Sorry, Homes 4U. It was their Christmas gathering. Claims he has a foolproof witness.'

'Ta da! Me. Go on.'

'They had a few more bevvies in the pub over the road and dispersed. One of his fellow high-flyers offered him a lift home but he asked to be dropped off at the Sylvan Fields. He walked the last bit, to Samantha's.'

'So he admits being there.'

'Mmm, but he didn't see her. He said the place was in darkness, so he knocked once, he says, very softly, and then he realised it was a bit late and went home.'

'Realised it was a bit late! Him? He won't realise it's a bit late until Old Nick's handing him a shovel and pointing at the pile of coal. How did he get home?'

'Walked towards the town centre and stopped a taxi.'

'That's more-or-less how we'd guessed it. So if we find anyone who saw him near Samantha's he has a ready-made excuse.'

'Quite.'

'What was his manner?'

'Cocky as you can be with a hangover. Turner had to pull him into line once or twice.'

'What about?'

'Oh, he started slagging you off.'

'I bet. Was Turner his usual obstructionist self?'

'He wasn't too bad. I don't think he was pleased about having to come over. How long are you keeping Darryl?'

'Is the custody sergeant grumbling?'

'He's pulling faces.'

'We'll let him stew a bit longer, see if anything turns up. We need to check his story with the bloke who gave him a lift – I'll leave that with you. Thanks for doing it, Nigel, I'll have a listen to the tape later.'

My phone rang while I was finding an envelope for the tape. Nigel answered it. 'Yes, he's here,' he said. 'Good, good. I'll tell him.' He lowered the mouthpiece and said: 'They've found the gloves.'

They were floating among the reeds at the edge of the canal. They'd been thrown off a bridge and landed in the water. I had them rushed straight to City HQ so the SOCOs could examine them, but it looked as if Darryl's luck was still holding.

Nigel went straight home but I stopped for a shoppers' special at the Indian restaurant on the way. As I drove into my street I saw an elderly Austin Montego sitting on a neighbour's drive. It was the best news of the week. Mrs Tait is the lady who normally irons my shirts for me. She'd visited her daughter for the holiday period, and now she was back. I hooked a bundle of coathangers over my fingers and thumbs, stuck the box of Black Magic under an arm and went to say how much we'd all missed her.

It's not normally done, but I'd taken the tape of Nigel's interview of Buxton home with me. His brief, Mr Turner, had a copy, so there was no question of tampering with it. When I came back from Mrs Tait's I slid the cassette into the player, turned the volume up and put the kettle on. I brought my tea and the biscuit box into the front room and thumbed the TV remote control. There were a few seconds' bedlam until I found the right button and wound the TV sound to zero. The choices were: horses running from right to left; a black and white Gregory Peck film; horses running from left to right or various soccer pundits talking about Manchester United's match that kicked off in an hour. I zapped them all to oblivion.

Nigel was saying: 'You were drunk, weren't you?'

'Yeah, I'd 'ad a few,' Darryl admitted.

'So you thought you'd go round to Samantha's for your legover, eh?'

'No, it weren't like that.'

'Were you in a sexual relationship with her?'

'What if I was?'

'So you said goodnight to your cronies and got one of them to drop you off near her house. Did you tell them that you had it laid on? Did you tell them, Darryl, that your secretary was waiting for you to go round and give her a good seeing-to? Is that your style? Is it?'

'No, you've got me wrong.'

'And what happened when you got there?'

'I told you. She wasn't in, or she was in bed. I realised it was late and started walking 'ome.'

'I think she was in, Darryl. I think she said: "You're not coming in here in that state. You're not going out enjoying yourself without me on a Friday night and getting pissed and thinking you can come round here for a bit of the other any time you want." Isn't that more like what happened, Darryl?'

Turner said: 'Sergeant, my client has made it perfectly clear to you that he did not speak to Miss Teague on the night in question.'

'So you lost your rag,' Nigel went on. 'You gave her a good hiding. You don't like it when someone turns you down, do you, Darryl?'

'I really think that's enough,' Turner said. 'My client is perfectly willing to answer questions but I cannot allow you to harangue him in this way.'

I went through into the kitchen and listened to the rest of it while I washed up. The state of Buxton's flat had strengthened my resolve to be tidier.

The SOCO was watching the football match on a little portable when I walked into his office in City HQ. 'Who's winning?' I asked.

'They are, two-nil,' he replied, switching it off. He ambled over to a lab table under the window and retrieved a plastic bag containing a pair of brown leather gloves. Handing them to me, he said: 'Men's, large size, relatively new. Lining worn and leather stretched near base of right index finger, suggesting they have been worn over a large ring. Sadly, they'd been lying in shallow water for several hours and it rained quite heavily through the night. That would be about the equivalent of a colourfast cotton cycle in a washing machine. I've dried them out very carefully and sprayed them with reagent, but there's no trace of blood. We've taken fibre samples from inside, which don't mean anything at the moment, and scrapings from the outside.'

Nigel hadn't asked Buxton about the gloves because he hadn't known about them. If they were his, we needed forensic evidence to link Samantha to them. If he said they weren't his, we'd then need our brainy friends to link him to the gloves.

'And the dinner jacket and shirt?' I asked.

He shook his head. 'Sorry. I'll keep looking, but what marks I've found are probably ketchup and gravy stains.'

'Fair enough,' I said, disappointed. 'Thanks for staying over. Can I take these?' I held up the gloves.

'We've done all we can,' the SOCO replied. 'I'll send the samples to Weatherton for microscopic examination.'

'Right, cheers.' Their electron microscope can see the fluff in a virus's navel, and make individual blood cells look as big as dustbin lids.

As soon as I walked into Heckley nick the duty sergeant collared me. 'Your prisoner's grumbling,' he said, 'and his solicitor gave us hell before he left.'

'Give me ten minutes,' I replied, 'then we'll let him go.'

I ran upstairs and read the reports about the search of his flat. They'd found a few porn magazines but nothing you wouldn't find at most all-male establishments. Tearing out and saving the page three girls was peculiar, and the pair of combat knives told us a lot about the man. Tucked in the back of a drawer they'd found an armband with a swastika on it.

'Gimme the keys,' I said to the custody sergeant when I went back downstairs, 'and lock up your wimminfolk. Let's get him off the premises.'

He was sitting on the bunk with his head in his hands, looking up as I raised the flap in the door.

'God, you look rough,' I told him.

'What do you fuckin' expect?' he snapped back at me.

'Are these your gloves?' I asked when I was inside. I took them from the plastic bag and threw them towards him. He caught one and the other fell to the floor.

'Never seen 'em before,' he said.

'Are you sure?'

'Positive.'

'Try them on for size.'

He opened the neck of the glove he'd caught and started to push his fingers into it.

'Oh no!' he declared, and hurled the glove back at me. 'I'm not trying it on. You're not fuckin' fitting me up like that.'

'Please yourself,' I told him. 'C'mon, you can go.'

We signed him out and returned his property. I didn't offer him a lift home.

There wasn't enough daylight left to do anything in the garden, which was all the excuse I needed. I had a shave and shower and settled in my favourite chair, inevitable mug of tea nearby. It grew dark around me. It's a time I usually enjoy, the gathering gloom emphasising the silence, the shadows, the womb-like comfort.

Trouble was, I had too much on my mind. For a start, I was hungry, but didn't feel like cooking. Then there was Darryl. We'd get him, one day, but how many more people would he hurt before we did? And on Monday it was back to the murder hunt. Somebody was out there who put a gun to the head of a highly respected doctor and blew him to kingdom come. But most of all, more than all these, was my little problem with Annabelle and Zorba the Greek.

The meal at the Wool Exchange had been a disaster. Our relationship was a long catalogue of broken dates, late arrivals and hurried meals. I tried to involve her in the job, but there's a limit to how far you can do that. I could retire in less than two years, but wasn't sure if I could hold on to her that long. I put the light on and found my book of telephone numbers.

Eric Dobson used to be a motorcycle policeman. He retired early and started his own business, Merlin Couriers. I designed his logo and painted his first van. We've kept in touch. I rang the office first but he didn't answer. If he had, I'd probably have hung up. I didn't want a job that would require me at five o'clock on a Saturday afternoon. He was at home.

'Hello, Charlie,' he said. 'Ringing up for a job?'

'Yes,' I told him.

'Seriously?'

'Seriously.'

'Why? What have you done?'

There is a general expectancy among people who know me that one day I'll 'do something'. 'Nothing,' I told him. 'I'm just sick of it. If I leave, what's the chances of finding a simple and undemanding occupation to tide me over?'

'Not with us five minutes and already you're after my job,' he replied in a mock Jewish accent. 'What are you like on a six-fifty Kawasaki?'

'Cold and scared.'

'It'll have to be the Transit then. Is this a firm enquiry or just speculation, Charlie? You haven't been caught with the Chief Constable's wife, have you?'

'Have you seen her? He'd probably recommend me for a QPM. I might set the wheels in motion, see if they can do without me. I don't mind the job, but it's mucking up my personal life, and at my age . . .'

'Tell me about it. We could always fit you in, Charlie. Fact is, if you wanted to invest some money, we could expand a little. What I need is a depot on the outskirts of London. I could treble my business overnight if there was someone down there I could trust. You'd be just the man. How about that, then? Five minutes ago you were staring at unemployment, and now you're a partner in a thriving courier business. Can't be bad.'

'Sounds interesting, Eric. I'll think about it and have a word with pay section on Monday.'

We chatted a while and some of his enthusiasm transferred to me. The weather forecast had said that tomorrow was going to be fine and clear. I found another number and booked myself into a guest house in Keswick for the night. Three hours later I was eating rabbit pie in a Lake District pub, my down jacket over the back of the chair and hiking boots on my feet.

Sunday morning I had the compulsory full English and walked over Helvellyn and Striding Edge. There was a thin covering of snow on the hilltops and the air froze the cilia in your nostrils as you breathed it, feeling like shards of broken glass being stuffed up your nose. I screwed my eyes into pinholes against the glare and absorbed the wonder of it all. There's a well-known conundrum about noise. Does a sound exist if there's nobody to hear it? I feel the same about beauty. Is beauty wasted if you've nobody to share it with? I think it is. I ate my bar of mint cake and strode off downhill.

Weekdays, I do murders. I told Mad Maggie about the weekend's adventures with Darryl and told her to keep an eye on things. If forensic couldn't come up with anything and Samantha didn't make a complaint we'd done all we could. I asked Mr Wood if he could join us and pulled a few chairs around the white board in the main CID office. Sparky re-drew the chart, bigger and with more colours. I was peeved. I'd wanted to do it.

'Right, Dave,' I said as the super joined us. 'You're on your feet so you might as well do the honours.' I rocked my chair back until it was leaning against the top of a radiator. After a few minutes I could feel the heat striking through my shirt.

Sparky ran through our list of suspects, although acquaintances was a more accurate description of them. No one leaped off the board as a fully fledged, twenty-four carat suspect. The doc was a popular character, with lots of friends and colleagues ready to say what a splendid fellow he was. He'd have had no trouble at all getting HP from a double-glazing company. But there is always a dark side to popularity. Success breeds jealousy, and that can fester away inside you like a malignant worm. More so if the person you envy just happens to be screwing someone you love. Reading between the lines, there were plenty of people who might have been glad to see Mr Jordan dead.

Trouble was, they all had cast-iron alibis.

'Maybe it was a contract killing,' Nigel suggested.

'OK. So who might have the necessary connections with the underworld?'

'Perhaps someone came into the clinic for a face-lift. Or someone's wife.'

'And just happened to say they were an assassin?'

'Not like that. They might have got to know them over a period of time. First of all as friends, and then perhaps the conversation worked round to it.'

'It's a possibility,' I admitted.

'I think we're getting a bit fanciful,' Mr Wood said.

'If it was a contract killing,' Sparky began, 'I'd place it back with Ged Skinner and his friends. They've got the contacts.'

'Why would they want him dead?'

'Because he was refusing to play ball.'

'So we're back with drugs?'

'Yes.'

'What about his showbiz friends?' Maggie asked.

'Good point,' I said. 'Is any of them about to play the part of a murderer? It'd be just like one of them to get into the role by indulging in homicide.'

'This isn't being helpful,' Mr Wood protested.

'Sorry,' I replied. 'Truth is, we're floundering.'

'OK,' he said. 'Let's be thoroughly unprofessional. Dave, who's your favourite for the deed?'

Without hesitation Sparky said: 'Him,' stabbing a finger against Ged Skinner's name. 'Or one of his cronies,' he added.

Gilbert nodded. 'I don't think we need to go into motives. Nigel?'

'Dr Barraclough,' he replied, again without hesitation.

'Go on,' Gilbert invited.

'Professional jealousy, plus possible sexual angle, but I don't know what.'

I let my chair drop on to its front legs with a clomp.

Nigel's theory was interesting. There was the added attraction that I hadn't liked Barraclough, but I'd never let a personal opinion affect an investigation. Much.

'And,' Nigel continued, 'there's always the possibility that he's in cahoots with someone else.'

'You mean . . . they're giving each other alibis?' Gilbert suggested.

'Mmm.'

'Don't!' I protested, clamping my hands over my ears. 'Please don't!'

Jeff Caton was with us. He thought Skinner was worth another look at, but was interested in the malpractice suit against the doctor.

'Barraclough's supposed to be finding me details of that,' I said. 'Maggie, when we've finished how about if you go round there and see if he's found the information? You might even learn something about the man himself from his secretary or the other staff.'

'Will do, Boss.'

'Meanwhile, Margaret,' Gilbert said, 'who's your favourite for the killer?'

'Hey, we should be running a book on this,' Sparky said.

Maggie studied the chart. 'I haven't been in from the beginning,' she said, 'but there's an awful lot of grief down there.' She nodded to the box that said 'Abortions, X 10,000'. 'That's where I'd be looking.'

'And you, Charlie?' Gilbert asked.

I folded my arms and shook my head. 'None of them,' I replied. 'None of them.'

In a way, I was right. But then again, in a way, I was wrong.

Chapter Nine

Maggie went off to the White Rose; Sparky and Nigel rang the wife of the registrar, ex-lover of the late doctor, and made an appointment to see her while hubby was at work; and I settled down with the reports. Mr Wood's conclusion, after our meeting, was that we should pursue all the alibis until the Pope himself was a more likely suspect. I decided that some lateral thinking was called for and made another list. Melissa, the mysterious sender of Christmas cards was on it, followed by Mr Farrier, husband of the receptionist at the White Rose. It wouldn't hurt to have a word with George, his chum from college. To prove my impartiality I added Mrs Henderson. Maybe Dr Jordan hadn't chatted her up first, and maybe she thought he should have done. Lastly I wrote 'Malpractice'. That was a gaping hole in our investigation that needed looking into, pronto. I drew a line through 'Mrs Henderson' and a thick box around 'Malpractice'.

The SOCO had made a video of the murder scene. I collected it from the associated property store and watched it in the CID office. It showed general views of the doctor's kitchen, where he'd been found, followed by close-ups of everything in sight. The doc died with his eyes open, a look of terror and surprise carved on his features. The camera zoomed in close and moved slowly over his chin, nose and sightless eyes, like a helicopter tour of Mount Rushmore. His shirt was undone and he was in his stocking feet.

We were taken on a journey across his carpet, the shiny toecaps of the SOCO's shoes bobbing into the bottom of the picture like two bald headed men on a see-saw at the other side of a wall. The camera panned over his kitchen cupboards and along the worktop. In a corner I saw the plastic bin that I'd thought about stealing, between the electric kettle and a box of muesli. The doctor's tie was draped over a chair back, given an extra turn to prevent it sliding to the floor, and his shoes were just inside the door.

The office was quiet. Everyone was out. I switched off the video and reached for the telephone.

'Pay section?' I asked, when someone answered. 'Oh, good. This is DI Priest, at Heckley CID. I was wondering if you could work out for me what terms I could expect if I took early retirement?'

Maggie returned as I was finishing the video and we watched the last few minutes together.

'Learn anything?' she asked as I ejected the cassette and returned it to its envelope.

'Mmm. He knew his killer, as we suspected. The doc's shoes were just inside the door, so when his visitor rang he must have opened the front entrance for him and let him come up to the apartment, not gone to meet him downstairs.'

'Sounds sensible.'

'And he was male.'

'How do you work that out?'

'It's a guess, but the doc's tie was hanging over a chair. If his visitor was female I think he'd have whipped it back on, and his shoes. Did you see Barraclough?'

'Yes. He's a charmer, isn't he?' She opened her notebook and slid it across my desk. 'That's the party who made the complaint – Rodney Allen. His mother, Mrs Joan Allen, was a fit and active sixty-year-old who liked to have a good time. She was booked in to the General for an hysterectomy. The operation was done succesfully, as they say, by Mr Jordan, but the patient died. She had an aortic aneurism later that day, right out of the blue. According to the rules there had to be a post mortem, and this found that her condition could not have been anticipated by the pre-operative investigations. However, her son, Rodney, has learning difficulties. He's forty, by the way. Mrs Allen had been comfortably off and he was left everything, in trust. The trustees, who are a firm of solicitors in Scarborough and a retired GP in Heckley, decided to sue the hospital and Mr Jordan for malpractice and negligence.'

'For a fee, no doubt,' I said.

'No doubt. But the inquest brought in a verdict of natural causes and the case was dropped. I've had a word with the retired GP. He was a friend of the family, before they moved to Scarborough. He says he was opposed to the action but outvoted. Rodney, he told me, was deeply disturbed by the thought of his mother's body being cut open, and dwelt on it for months.'

'And he probably still blames the hospital,' I said. 'We need a word with him, soon as possible. Nigel was checking with the GMC. We'll make sure the official version tallies, then we'd better see what Rodders has to say. Thanks, Maggie, that's a good day's work.'

'There was one other thing,' she began.

I sat back, inviting her to continue.

'I think you have a fan.'

'A fan?'

'Yes,' she said. 'One Cicely Henderson, receptionist at the White Rose. I was supposed to be asking the questions, but she wanted to know all about you. She's an attractive lady.'

'I had noticed,' I admitted, 'but she's not my type. What did you tell her?'

'That you were a very nice man – single – but you had a girlfriend who you were besotted by. Did I do right?'

'As always, Maggie. Did you ask her about her colleague, Mrs Farrier?'

'Yes, we went over it again, but she didn't come up with anything new.'

'Do you think she's jealous of her?'

'Cicely jealous of Mrs Farrier?'

'Mmm.'

'No. She told me that she was off men. She left her husband eight years ago and since then has found all the companionship she needs in her cats. However . . . I think meeting you may have stirred the ashes of some long-forgotten fires.'

'Gosh, how odd,' I said.

'Just what I thought,' she replied, stifling a smile.

I lunched at the cafe in town and went walkabout. There was one avenue that I could follow without too much effort and no charge to the budget. When the squash craze started a few of us from the office tried it, but we had to book a court weeks in advance and quickly lost interest. I found it too claustrophobic. The boom faded and has now settled down to a healthy core of enthusiasts. Heckley Squash Club had financial difficulties, was taken over, converted a couple of courts for other activities and is now doing quite nicely. Several of the woodentops work-out there. I wandered in and asked to see the manager.

I recognised him, when he came, as a footballer with one of the local teams who never quite made the grade. I could sympathise with him. I had trials with Halifax Town and turned out for the second team when I was at art college. We lost, seven-one. I was the goalkeeper. They didn't invite me back.

I introduced myself as a policeman, not a footballer, and asked what had happened to him.

'Knee problems,' he said. 'Cartilage, then ligaments. You name it, my knees have had it. There came a time when enough was enough, but fortunately I was a qualified sports administrator by then. When this job came up I applied for it and stopped kidding myself about soccer.'

We were talking across the front counter. He invited me to take a chair at his side and lifted the flap to let me through. Two young men came and asked for a squash ball.

'Giving up football must have been hard for you,' I said, when they'd gone. Shouts of encouragement came echoing from within the building and the air smelled of sweat and chlorine. That was enough to put me off.

'I had plenty of time to think about it, get used to the idea. Now, I enjoy myself. Life's good. When Bill Shankly said that football was far more important than life and death he was talking out of the back of his head.'

'I've always thought it was a pretty stupid thing to say. I'm investigating the death of Dr Clive Jordan. He was murdered just before Christmas – you probably read about it in the papers.'

'Never read a paper, but I saw it on the telly. He was a member here, you know.'

'Yes,' I said. 'Hence my visit.'

'Obviously,' he replied. 'Sorry about that. What can we tell you?'

'First of all, why did he stop coming? Apparently he was a keen player, then, quite abruptly, he wasn't. Any reason for that?'

He nodded. 'That's easy. Same problems as me – damaged knee ligaments. He knew I'd been through it and we talked a lot. There're two methods of treatment: rest or surgery. I was a professional, my livelihood depended on my legs, so I went for the knife. For an amateur, just playing for amusement and to keep fit, there was only one sensible option. He packed in, thinking that maybe one day time would heal it and he'd be able to play again. Work was taking up a lot of his time, and he was courting a bird off the telly – she's in *Mrs Dale's Diary*, you know – so there was no real choice open to him.'

'Right,' I said. 'That clears up one little mystery. What can you tell me about the man himself. Did he have any particular friends in the club?'

'Not really,' he said, after giving it some thought. He was tall and angular, his shoulders bulging through too much work with the weights. He wore streamlined leggings with a stripe down the side and a Heckley General heart research T-shirt. 'He usually played with a crony from the hospital. Not always the same one, rarely with any of the other members. Squash is a bit like that, if you don't enter the competitions.'

'And he never did?'

'No. His working hours wouldn't let him. He was popular enough, though. He'd have a drink in the bar and chat away to anyone. People liked him. I certainly did. I thought he was a smashing bloke. Have you any ideas who killed him?'

I shook my head and said: 'We are following certain lines of enquiry,' enunciating the words to make it plain that this was a euphemism for not having a clue.

'I'll tell you what the doc was like,' the manager began, a smile of affection on his face as he recalled some anecdote. 'He did enter one competition. We were standing here, me and him, talking about our knees, would you believe, and this girl was pacing up and down, just there,' he pointed into the foyer, 'with her kit on, waiting for her partner to arrive. The doc started to chat to her. At the time there was a mixed doubles competition on, strictly for couples – husbands and wives or boyfriends and girlfriends. It was light-hearted, just to try and get partners interested, make it more a family thing, if you follow me.'

'Sounds an admirable idea,' I said.

'It was, wasn't it? Well, apparently, this girl and her boyfriend were due to play in the first round. The other couple were already on the court, having a knock-up, waiting for them. She was starting to get a bit upset. We were looking at the sheet with the draw on it and the doc noticed that the boyfriend was called . . . would it be Davey? Was the doc's middle name David?'

'Yes, it was,' I told him.

'Right, that was it, Davey. She'd entered them as . . . I can't remember her name. It might have been Sue, or Sandra. Anyway, she'd put them down as Sue . . . Smith, or whatever, and Davey. Just Davey. "I'm called David," the doctor said. "I could pretend to be your boyfriend. Come on, let's give them a game." And they did. And they won. Blow me if they didn't win the next round, too. She was over the moon about it. That's the kind of bloke he was.'

'It sounds Mills & Boon,' I said. 'Did she fall hopelessly in love with him? Did he seduce her?'

'No, I don't think so. They had a laugh about it afterwards and went their separate ways, as far as I know. She was a bit, you know, plain. Not really his type.'

'But was he her type?'

'I suppose so. We all dream, don't we? But she seemed a sensible kid. I think her feet were on the ground.'

'Is she still a member?'

'I'm not sure, and I can't check if I don't remember her name. I don't think she comes any more. I haven't seen her for ages.'

'When did all this happen?' I asked.

'Oh, about two years ago.'

'And when would you say she stopped coming?'

'I couldn't tell you. I don't see some people for months, even though they play every week. It all depends on what time they book the court for.'

'But she could have stopped playing round about the same time as the doctor did?' I suggested.

'Probably,' he replied, nodding. 'About then, at a guess. Do you think that's significant?'

'No,' I admitted.

Three women in leotards and leg warmers walked past us, eyes righting as they said hello to the manager in loud voices. I watched them retreat, several layers of even louder lycra clenched tightly between their buttocks.

'Aerobics,' he explained.

'Are they comfortable?' I asked, wincing.

'They like to look the part.'

'I'm interested in this girl,' I told him, pulling myself back to the job. 'How can we find her name? Will it still be on the computer if her membership has lapsed?' I nodded towards the terminal that sat on the counter.

'Oh, nobody ever comes off the computer,' he replied, 'but we're talking about over two thousand entries.'

'To me, that's nearly as good as a fingerprint. You think she was called Sue or Sandra?'

'Something like that – Sue, Sandra, Sally – but I'm just guessing. I only saw her about three times.'

'Can't we just ask it to find all the females beginning with S?'

'Er, you might be able to, but I can't.'

'Me neither. We must have headed too many footballs.'

'And I'm not even sure about the S. My assistant can do it, when she takes over.' He looked at the clock on the wall behind him. 'She should be here in about an hour.'

'Do you mind if she runs a full membership list off for me?' I asked.

'No problem. I'll give you a ring when it's ready. And I've just remembered who the doc and this girl played in the first round of the mixed doubles. He's one of our stalwarts. I'll ask if he or his wife can remember her name – they probably had a drink together, afterwards.'

'That'd be a big help,' I said.

I did my reports back at the office, and had a discussion with Luke, our civilian computer expert, about rehashing our standard interview documents, targeting them more specifically at this offence. Nigel and Dave came back, looking dejected.

The registrar's wife admitted that she'd had an affair with Dr Jordan, which went back several years. It started as just a fling, she told them, which developed into a habit. Her marriage was sound, but her husband was not very adventurous in bed. It was imperative that he didn't find out.

'As he did know about it,' Sparky said, 'he must have had his reasons for keeping quiet.'

'Perhaps he was waiting his opportunity for revenge,'

Nigel suggested, adding, 'she's a bit older than I expected. I'd have thought the doc could have found someone nearer his own age.'

'Experience, Nigel,' I said. 'There's no substitute.'

'I'll take your word for it.'

'Maybe her husband was having it away with someone, himself,' I suggested, 'and was happy for her to have her little games with the doctor. Grateful, even.'

'That's what I'd wondered,' Sparky claimed. 'Or maybe he just couldn't keep up with her, and was grateful for someone to help him out. It can't be easy, married to someone like that.'

'Cor! I wouldn't mind giving it a try,' Nigel enthused.

'Sounds like penal servitude to me,' I said. 'Look into it. See what the word is among the nursing staff. What about their alibis?'

'Engraved in stone,' Nigel told me. 'We've talked to everybody at the party. They started arriving shortly after seven and stayed until the early hours.'

'So neither of them pulled the trigger.'

'No way.'

I altered the number on the chart next to their names to three – foolproof.

Chief Superintendent Isles sent a message via his secretary apologising for not being able to attend my little presentation that morning and wondering if I could give him a quick run-through of the case so far in his office, first thing tomorrow? I said: 'Yes,' naturally, and before I went home I asked Luke to redraw the charts in a more portable format.

I had an hour's snooze in an easy chair, catching up on the radio news, and dined on chicken tikka makhani. That's choice pieces of chicken breast, marinated in a garam masala, coriander and fenugreek sauce and served with turmeric rice. It only took six minutes in the microwave. I followed it with tinned grapefruit and a pot of Earl Grey.

Sparky had loaned me the video of Oliver Stone's *JFK*. I swivelled the chair round so my feet would reach the settee and settled down, the teapot within easy reach of my right hand. The phone rang in the middle of the newsreel sequence of the assassination, as we saw the fatal shot to Kennedy's head, the secret serviceman diving on to the cavernous trunk of the Cadillac and Mrs Kennedy trying to climb out of the back. History captured on film, as it happened, and telling us less about the President's killers than we know about King Harold's. I found the stop button on the remote control and picked up the phone.

It was Annabelle. 'Hello, Charles, I'm home,' she said.

'You should have told me when you were coming,' I told her, sinking back into my chair. 'I could have met you at the station.'

'I'm sure you have much better things to do. Have you eaten?'

'No, I wouldn't have anything better to do, and yes, I'm afraid I have eaten.'

'Never mind. What did you have?'

'Frozen curry.'

'Sounds delicious,' she laughed.

'It was OK,' I told her. 'I was just settling down to watch a video. Sparky lent me *JFK*. It's about a District Attorney from New Orleans, Jim Garrison, who took out a prosecution against some gangsters over the Kennedy assassination.'

'I've heard of it. It's on my list of "must sees".'

'Do you want me to save it for another time?'

'That would be nice,' she said. 'I was going to invite you round for a meal. We could watch it afterwards.'

'Great. When?'

'Tomorrow?'

'Super. That's something for me to look forward to. How did your trip go?'

'Very well, Charles. I'll tell you all about it when I see you.'

We said our goodbyes and I put the phone down a happier man than when I picked it up. I rewound the tape and tried to pick up the threads of *The Bill*. It wasn't too difficult.

Les Isles nodded approvingly when he saw my fancy computer-generated diagram. 'It's nice to see that my older officers are embracing the new technology,' he said, grinning.

'It was on the flip-chart until late yesterday,' I confessed.

'Don't disillusion me, Charlie. What does it tell us?'

I went through the list of characters, starting with Ged Skinner and making a diversion to tell him about Darryl Buxton and the rape. He listened, nodding and sucking his teeth.

'What's happening with this one?' he asked, tapping Rodney Allen's name with the tip of his pen.

'The malpractice allegation,' I said. 'DS Newley's contacting Scarborough CID this morning. If he's available we'll dash over to interview him.'

'Is that where he lives?'

'Mmm, but he originates from Heckley. Apparently he's a bachelor, not very bright, lived with his mother, hence the grief when she died.'

'It sounds better all the time,' Les declared. Middle-aged

men living with their parents always attract suspicion, even if their only crime is to be unlucky in love.

'It does, doesn't it?' I agreed.

'And then there's this lot.' He pointed to the box marked 'Abortions'. 'God knows what we can do about them. Keep working at all these alibis, Charlie, but cross your fingers that Rodney doesn't have one. It's him, I can feel it in my water.'

We'd all said that about Ged Skinner, but I didn't remind him.

Nigel was in the office, typing a report. I clicked the switch on the kettle and asked him what was happening.

'Waiting for Scarborough to ring me back,' he replied. 'I've faxed the details to them. Sparky and Maggie are paying a return visit to the White Rose Clinic, encouraging the nursing staff to gossip about their medical director.'

'Dr Barraclough,' I sighed, for no reason other than to give a name to the title. In this job, we deal with individuals, not positions.

'What did Mr Isles have to say?' Nigel asked.

'He's happy enough. Thinks it's Rodders what did it. Carry on as we are, no extra staff.'

'Great.'

'It won't be great if we don't arrest someone soon and it goes to review. Then it'll be: "What have you been playing at for all this time?"'

I brewed myself a mug of tea, paused with the teabag dripping off the spoon as I looked for somewhere to put it, said: 'Oh, sod it,' and dropped it in the bin.

Nigel was on the phone when I turned round, looking as if the lottery unclaimed prizes crew had finally tracked him down. 'Scarborough CID,' he hissed at me, briefly covering the mouthpiece as he listened. 'One moment,' he told them. He moved the instrument away from his face and said: 'They sent a DC round and he's now in hospital. Rodders laid about him with what he thinks was a double-barrelled shotgun and he's barricaded himself in. Fancy a trip to Scarborough?'

'You bet!' I told him.

'We're on our way over,' he told them. 'It'll take us about two hours. You'd better give me some directions.'

We needed a breakthrough and this looked like it. You have a murder on your conscience, there's a knock at the door and when you answer it a detective flashes his ID at you and asks your name. You panic. The more I thought about it, the better it looked. I drove while Nigel phoned City HQ to get a message to Mr Isles. No harm in letting him know that his hunch was paying off.

It's a fast road to Scarborough, on a Tuesday in winter. As soon as the days lengthen and the sun comes out for more than an hour it clogs with caravans and a procession of coaches and asthmatic family cars that have seen more polish than petrol. But not today. Driving can be a pleasure on empty roads, even when the temperature is hovering just above zero and sleet is in the air. Going to catch a murderer adds a sense of purpose to the journey.

A Scarborough panda was waiting for us in a layby on the outskirts of town. I pulled in behind him and Nigel dashed out to introduce himself. They led us to a little estate of bungalows, ideal for retired couples, on the north side.

'Brrr! It's freezing,' Nigel had complained as he got back in. His coat was spotted with raindrops.

It was circus time on the estate. The street was cordoned off but everyone was out to watch the excitement, wearing big anoraks and woollen hats against the weather. I expected the ice-cream man to pull round the corner anytime, jingle blaring, desperate for a sale. The wind was coming straight off the North Sea, and tasted of salt. I pulled my down jacket on and we went looking for whoever was in charge.

'DI Charlie Priest, from Heckley,' I told the uniformed inspector, when we found him, 'and this is DS Nigel Newley.' I explained our involvement, and why we wanted to talk to the man barricaded in the house, namely Rodney Allen. He was grateful for the information. Up to then, he'd been struggling to know what it was all about.

'How's the DC who was assaulted?' I asked.

'Not too bad, Charlie,' he replied. 'It's just a scalp wound.'

'But Rodney hit him with a shotgun?'

'That was the first story, but since then the DC has changed his mind. He thinks it might have been a length of pipe, wrapped in a plastic bag.'

'What, to look like a gun?' Nigel asked.

'Possibly. The DC can't be sure, but now he says it didn't feel like a shotgun.'

We all smiled. 'Is he an expert on how it feels to be bashed on the bonce with various tubular devices?' I wondered.

'I think I know what he means, with the emphasis on the *think*, but we can't take chances.'

'Of course not,' I said. 'Have you seen Rodney?'

'Oh, yes, he keeps appearing at the window, brandishing what could be a gun, or a piece of pipe in a bag. There's a phone in there, but he won't answer it.'

'So what's happening?'

'Nothing until we get some reinforcements. I've sent for a negotiator, too. Up to now we've just concentrated on housing him. Soon as I've a few more bodies I want the street clearing and some form of communications setting up. In the light of what you've told us I'd say we need the TFU, as well.'

'What do the neighbours say about him?'

'That he's a bit simple. Lived with his mother until she died, now he's alone. He's a voluntary patient at North Bay House – that's a psychiatric hospital on the edge of town. We've sent someone there to find out if he has a doctor or anyone who can come and talk to him.'

'Do you mind if I ring him?' I asked.

'Be my guest.' He dictated the number and in a few seconds I was listening to the ringing tone, but he didn't answer.

I turned to Nigel. 'Fancy a burger?'

'We passed a place down the road,' he replied.

'Mind if we leave you at it?' I asked the local man. 'You know where we'll be.'

We lingered over the burgers. I rang Annabelle to tell her where I was in case I was delayed, although I was determined not to be, but she wasn't answering, either. We had a couple of hours at the scene of the siege and briefly saw Rodney at a window, brandishing his weapon, whatever it was. A superintendent took charge of proceedings and used a loud-hailer to no avail. I tried on the mobile again, with similar lack of success. Rodney was deaf to our efforts. Unsmiling policemen from the tactical firearms unit, in baseball caps with chequered bands around them, took up positions in gardens and windows. They brandished their Heckler and Koch MP5s as if they were the latest fashion accessories. We had another cuppa at the burger house, which was rapidly becoming the siege canteen, and went for a last look at Rodney's neat little bungalow, with its pocket handkerchief lawn and plastic window boxes.

'Ah, there you are,' the superintendent said, when he saw us. 'This is Dr . . .' he stumbled over a name with too many syllables – it sounded like 'ram in a woolly jumper' to me, '. . . who is Allen's pychiatrist at North Bay House.'

I shook hands with a plump grey-haired lady who wore a fur coat over pantaloons. 'How do you do, Doctor,' I said, wondering if the fur was fake, deciding it wasn't. We sat in her car and I told her what I understood about the post mortem on Rodney's mother, about the malpractice charges and Dr Jordan's subsequent murder.

When I'd finished Nigel asked: 'What exactly are Rodney's problems, Doctor?'

She chose her words carefully. '*Exactly* is not an expression we recognise in psychiatry,' she replied. 'Rodney came to us for the first time after the death of his mother. He had a morbid fascination for her, possibly brought on by dwelling on the details of the post mortem. He suffers from anxiety, panic attacks and depression. There may be incipient schizophrenia. He has not been sectioned and we do not regard him as violent in any way. He comes to us on a voluntary basis, usually as an out-patient, at the recommendation of his GP. Most of the time he gets by in the community, which is as much as we can hope for, these days. We take him in if we can, when things are getting too much, but generally speaking we don't have room for him and he is quite capable of existing by his own resources.'

'Would you say he was capable of shooting the doctor?' I asked. No point in beating about the cabbage patch.

'No more than you or I, Inspector,' she replied, which wasn't very helpful but made a lot of sense.

Nigel said: 'Has he sufficient nous to travel to Heckley by public transport?'

'Oh, yes. He has certain difficulties, what you might call being slow, but can function normally in society. He's sick, not stupid.'

She started her car engine and set the blower on maximum to clear the condensation. The lenses in her spectacles were thick enough to start a forest fire on an overcast day. It was dark outside, and flakes of sleet slid down the windows. A floodlight illuminated the outside of the bungalow.

'When did you last see Rodney?' I asked.

'New Year's Day,' she replied, without hesitation.

'You were open New Year's day?' I queried.

'We're not a corner shop, Inspector,' she admonished. 'We are there for the benefit of our patients. Holiday times can be particularly stressful for them.'

'And the rest of us,' I sighed.

'Actually,' she said, 'we do not have out-patients at holiday times, but sometimes we have vacancies and can take certain vulnerable cases in for a few days. We felt Rodney fell into that category.'

Why did Nigel shuffle uncomfortably in his seat? Why did I suddenly wish I was somewhere else, like having a prostate biopsy?

'He was with you for a few days?' I said.

'Yes. Some of our regulars went home to their families for Christmas, which meant we had some spare beds. There are many temptations and pressures for someone like Rodney at Christmas, so we felt it desirable to keep him with us.'

'Temptations like alcohol?' Nigel wondered.

'Alcohol and loneliness are a potent combination,' she replied.

'So how long was he with you?' I asked.

'Ten days.'

I couldn't do the sums. 'The doctor was killed on the twenty-third,' I told her, 'at eight thirty in the evening. Was Rodney Allen an in-patient at North Bay at that time?'

'He came in during the afternoon of the twenty-second, Inspector,' she replied. 'The following evening – the day before Christmas Eve – we had our party. Rodney earned everybody's displeasure by hogging the karaoke machine. If that is when the doctor was murdered then I can assure you it wasn't Rodney who pulled the trigger. I'm afraid you've had a wasted journey.'

I told the superintendent that Rodney had been given an alibi and thanked him for his cooperation. Before the enormity of my words registered in his brain we were in the car and driving away. As we pulled on to the main road an ARV and a van load of the heavy mob sped in the opposite direction. When they'd vanished from my rear-view mirror I slapped my thigh and declared: 'Well, that's nicely cocked-up their overtime budget!'

Nigel laughed. 'I'm just grateful that you were with me,' he said. 'It goes on your record, not mine.'

'Think positive,' I said. 'It's another suspect we can draw a line through – eliminate from enquiries, as they say. And it's probably the best bit of excitement they've had since the candy floss stall was condemned by the health inspector. We're asking all the right questions – it's just a pity that we're asking them in the wrong order.'

As we headed inland the sleet turned to rain. There was no moon and the night was blacker than the bottom of a gipsy's chip pan. I was surprised how much commuter traffic was heading east, towards the coast, a pre-dinner sherry and the little woman. Nigel fiddled with the radio and found a country music station. A cracked voice was wailing: 'I left you tied to the hitching rail and my best friend rode you awayee . . .'

'Do you think that's meant to be a metaphor?' he asked, pressing the off button.

'What's a metaphor?' I mumbled, squinting against the glare of headlights. I was thinking about Rodney, and North Bay House. Did his trustees pay his bills when he was admitted? It sounded to me as if they had a few vacancies over Christmas, so they rounded up their regular reserves to fill them. I'm paid to have a suspicious mind.

'Why,' I wondered aloud, 'did Mrs Allen have her operation in Heckley when she'd already moved to Scarborough?'

'Waiting lists,' Nigel explained. 'She'd probably been on the General's waiting list for about two years.'

'Of course. Thank you.'

This side of York, heading towards the A1, I swung into a layby and hit the brakes. 'I'd better ring Annabelle, I'm running late,' I explained, reaching into the back for the telephone, in the pocket of my down jacket. I pressed the last number recall button and held the phone to my ear.

'WHAT YOU WANT?' a voice boomed at me. A male voice, close to hysteria. 'Why not you leave me alone?'

I jerked back in my seat and stared at the instrument. 'It's him!' I hissed. 'It's him!' The last number I'd dialled hadn't been Annabelle, it had been Rodney!

Chapter Ten

'Hello,' I ventured. 'Is that Rodney Allen, please?'

'Yes!' he snapped. 'Why you not leave me alone?'

'My name's Charlie,' I told him. 'Do you think we could have a little talk?'

'What about?' he asked, his voice wavering with fear. I could imagine him, quailing in a corner of his little room.

'Oh, this and that, Rodney. Are the policemen still outside your house?'

'Yes, they are. Lots of policemen.'

'Well, I'm not with them, Rodney. I was, about an hour ago, but I'm fifty miles away, now. I've decided to go home for my tea and leave you in peace. Tell me this: do you have a gun?'

'Not a real gun. Don't have a real gun. Real guns dangerous.'

'Very dangerous, Rodney. I'm glad you don't have a real gun. Did you make it yourself?'

'Yes. Rodney made it.'

'What with?'

'Some pipe and a piece of wood.'

'That sounds very clever. All those policemen are fooled by it. Why did you make a gun, Rodney? What did you want it for?'

'To scare lads and lasses.'

'What lads and lasses, Rodney?'

'Lads and lasses that come round and throw stones at windows. Say Rodney's not all there. Bad people.'

'They gave you a bad time.'

'Yes.'

'Did you point your gun at them?'

'Yes. Rodney point gun at them.'

'Did they run away?'

'Yes.'

'And did they stop coming round?'

'Yes, but tell police.'

'I see.' The local youths had given him some hassle, and then we had. My contribution hadn't helped at all. 'Listen, Rodney,' I said. 'Listen very carefully to what I say. Can you hear me?'

'Yes. Rodney hear you.'

'Where are you sitting?'

'On floor, in corner.'

'Right. Are you sitting in the dark, in there?'

'Yes. Not put light on. They shoot me if I put light on.'

'No they won't. Nobody will shoot you unless you start pointing your gun at people. Have you got your gun with you?'

'Yes. Is here.'

'Good. Do you want me to help you get out of this, Rodney? If you do as I tell you the policeman and the lady doctor from North Bay House will look after you. Are you listening?'

'Rodney frightened.'

'I know you are. I'm frightened, too. Will you promise to do exactly as I tell you? Then you'll be OK.'

'Promise to do as you tell me.'

'Good man. I want you to unwrap the gun, Rodney, and throw it to the other side of the room. Have you done that?'

There was a pause, then: 'Done that.'

'OK. Now this is the bit where you have to be brave. I want you to stand up and put the light on. Then I want you to put your hands above your head and walk very slowly to the window and stand there, so they can see you. Do you understand what I'm saying, Rodney?'

'Surrender. You want me surrender.'

'I want you to give yourself up. You've made your point, Rodney, and we don't want anyone else to be hurt, do we?'

'Rodney not want to hurt anyone.'

'Good man. When they come to get you they will shout at you, but they won't hurt you. Some policemen like shouting, but they don't mean it. I promise that. They'll tell you to lie on the floor. Just do as they say, very slowly. Nobody will hurt you. Understand?'

'Rodney know what you mean. See it on telly.'

'OK, Rodney, this is what you do. Stand up. Put the light on. Walk very slowly to the window and stand there with your hands above your head. Understand?'

'I understand.'

'There's a good man, Rodney. Do it. Do it now.'

I heard a rumble and a scrape as he laid the handset on the floor, leaving the line open. I thought I heard the click of the light switch, but it may have been my imagination. A trickle of sweat ran down my spine, zigging and zagging an inch at a time, like the raindrops on the windows.

'Just pray that one of those trigger-happy bastards doesn't open fire,' I whispered, holding the phone at arm's length.

'Keep still!' we heard someone bellow, quite distinctly,

followed by what might have been a Heckler and Koch's rifle stock being slammed into the extended position.

'Put your hands on your head!' They had a very loud voice.

'Now! Slowly. Kneel down.'

'Face down on the floor.'

'Stretch your arms out.'

I counted to ten, to give them time to put the cuffs on, and shouted: 'Hello! Hello! Anyone there?' into the phone.

More rumbles and scrapes, before a voice demanded: 'Who is this?'

'This is DI Priest of Heckley CID,' I told him. 'Who are you, please?'

'Oh, er, Sergeant Todd, sir. Tactical firearms unit.'

'Good evening, Sergeant. Rodney is a friend of mine, so treat him kindly. Remember, he did give himself up. Please tell the superintendent that I'm glad to have been of assistance. Goodnight.' I clicked the phone off and clenched my fists in a gesture of triumph. Nigel was grinning like a fireplace.

'You jammy so-and-so!' he said.

I rang Annabelle, the long way, and told her we were running late but homing in on a fair wind and a wide throttle.

'You sound happy,' she said. 'Have you been drinking?'

'Nothing stronger than tea has passed these lips,' I told her. 'Coming to see you always fills me with the joy of life.'

Nigel tutted and looked away.

Guns have a language all their own. You cock a single-action revolver by pulling the hammer back with your thumb. Pawls mesh into gears and rotate the chamber one sixth of a turn, bringing the next cartridge in line with the barrel. The resulting *c-click* has been used in a thousand westerns to terrorise goody, baddy and audience alike as the gun was pressed against someone's head.

It's different with an automatic. You slide the mechanism back to bring the first cartridge from the clip into the breech, with a *ka-chink* that is as familiar to armchair fans of gangster films as the smell of a smoke-filled speakeasy or the tinkling of a honky-tonk.

A sawn-down repeater shotgun says *chunk-chunk* as the next round is jacked into the chamber, and you know that death or serious bleeding is coming to someone.

But the Heckler and Koch is a disappointment. There's nothing like that with the Heckler. You put the safety to fire and you're away. The gun comes with an extending rifle stock and they usually snap it into position silently, in the privacy of the van, before moving into position. For more intimate situations a few officers have invented a little strategy that's not in the manual. They will have the stock loosely extended but not locked. At the right moment they will bark their instructions at the target and yank the stock home, hard. The resulting *chuck* of catches snapping into place is mundane and meaningless, but in the psychology of brinkmanship it strikes terror in the already sweaty palms of the hearer.

Annabelle had cooked one of my favourites – trout and almonds – for me, followed by home-made cheesecake. We'd called at the Granada services on the M62 and I'd bought a bunch of carnations, to put me in the good books, and the *JFK* video, to save time collecting Sparky's copy from home. Only trouble was, I was wearing the clothes I'd been sitting and standing about in all day and was unshaven. I apologised for my appearance and told her about Rodney, which was a mistake. All her sympathy immediately transferred to him.

'So,' I said, after I'd topped up her glass with the last of the Spanish red we both like, 'how did the trip go?'

'Very well,' she replied. 'I'll show you my ideas.' She stood up and left the room. We'd eaten off the large refectory table in her kitchen. I cleared our crockery away and when she returned we spread the drawings out.

'Unfortunately the fabrics have already been ordered,' she said, 'so we have to work around them. Actually, it makes it easier, I suppose.'

They were architects' impressions of the interiors, and Annabelle had coloured them in. Her schemes looked good, although her skills with the pencils required polishing. 'Use the edge, like this,' I said, and coloured a wall on a spare drawing. 'And make the end of the wall that is nearer to you a little bolder. If you're doing it quickly, for an immediate impression, use big zig-zags, full of confidence. Don't be faint-hearted. Like this.'

I handed her the pencil and made her show me. We were talking about drawing, which I know about, and avoiding discussing her trip to London, which I didn't. She was grateful for the diversion, I accepted it.

'These are very good,' I told her, pointing, meaning it. 'You have brilliant colour sense, and you're prepared to be adventurous. Zorba should be delighted.'

'He's called Xavier,' she reminded me.

'Sorry. So when is your next expenses-paid jaunt?'

'I have to go to the new site, near West Midlands Airport, to meet the architects, sometime on Thursday.'

'Will you stay down there?'

'I think so. It's called market research. If it's a morning meeting it might be easier for me to go down tomorrow night. I'll stay at the Post Chase – our big rivals – to see what I can learn, and consider ways of improving upon same.'

'It sounds fun,' I admitted.

'Mmm, it is. I'm enjoying myself.'

'Will you drive down?'

'Yes, I'll have to. I can manage the West Midlands.'

'You know you've only to say the word and I'd gladly take you.'

When she smiles at me like she did I know there is nothing I wouldn't do for her. I almost wished some great catastrophe would overtake us, some suffering we could rise above that would hold us together for ever. But all I had was a lopsided grin and a few stumbling phrases.

'I know you would, Charles,' she said. 'You're very kind to me. Shall we take our tea in the other room and watch the video?'

I was a child of the Kennedy era. We believed we were poised on the brink of a new age, when war would be waged against poverty and ignorance, and not against our fellow men. 'Let us begin,' he told us. Those shots at Dallas didn't just kill a president, they blew out the dreams of a generation. I'd never known that a prosecution had been brought against factions of the mafia and their Cuban connections. New Orleans District Attorney Jim Garrison pursued his case until it almost destroyed his family, but in the end he lost the trial and saved his marriage. I'd call that success.

Annabelle's head was on my shoulder as we watched it, my arm around her. I had cramp for the last hour, but bore it stoically. 'Do you think we'll ever know the truth?' she asked, as we washed the supper dishes.

'Not really,' I replied. 'Where does this go?'

'In there, please.'

'We'll know it, but not recognise it. It's there, somewhere, along with all the other stuff.'

'Do you believe there was a conspiracy?'

'Yes,' I replied. 'I'm a pathological believer in conspiracies.'

I stayed the night. We went to bed and made love, because that's what grown-ups do when they go to bed together. Afterwards, I lay awake for hours, wondering what might have been. I think Annabelle did, too. She was snuffling in her dreams when I sneaked away at about six thirty, my car engine rattling like a clarion call in the stillness of the vicarage close.

I was close-shaved and clean-shirted when I took the morning meeting. The petty criminals of Heckley hadn't taken a day off while I went to the seaside, so there was plenty to talk about. After that the first team met in my office for an update on the doc's murder. I let Nigel tell Sparky and Maggie all about the Siege of Scarborough.

'And the psychiatrist is calling in the local nick this morning to make a statement,' he finished with. Sparky put a number three in the appropriate box on his chart and looked glum.

Nigel had a report to write and the computer to update. Sparky and Maggie were investigating ways of breaking the confidentiality rules around the abortions at the clinic. Barraclough was the obvious approach, or perhaps their counsellor might be helpful. He'd told us that all the potential mothers were given counselling. We didn't want copies of all the records – a nudge towards someone they'd had concerns about would do nicely.

I rang Les Isles with the bad news and spent the rest

of the morning on paperwork. Les said not to worry, it had been worth a try, which was seven orders of support away from what he'd claimed yesterday. In the afternoon I went to the regional inspectors' meeting. We're supposed to talk about trends, developments and tactics. As usual we discussed pay, tenure of office and the precarious nature of the chief inspector rank. I didn't hear a word of it. My mind was elsewhere. Before I left Annabelle's, earlier that morning, I'd written her a letter and left it propped against the electric kettle. Now she knew exactly how I felt, and what my plans were.

I called in the office on my way home, in case there was anything brewing that I needed to know about. It could all wait. I had the place to myself, so I rang the force medical officer. He's an old pal of mine. We wished each other a happy New Year and had a long chat. He complained that he and his wife hadn't seen me for a long time and, pleasantries over, confirmed what he'd told me a few years earlier about the state of my health. I promised to go for Sunday lunch in the near future and dialled my next number.

Our divisional chief inspector (personnel) was still at his desk. 'No,' he said, as soon as he recognised my voice.

'You don't know the question,' I argued.

'The answer's still no.'

'So, if my question was . . . oh . . . "Are there any disadvantages if I retire at the weekend?" the answer is still no?'

'Bugger!' he exclaimed. 'It's no wonder you've got to where you are. Happy New Year, Charlie. What can I do for you?'

'Happy New Year, Bob. I've just rung Doc Evans and he's confirmed that I can still go on ill health, if I so desire. I've had a word with pay section and they're calculating my terms. All I want now is the go-ahead from you.'

'You're wanting out?'

'I think so.'

'I don't blame you, Charlie. I've had enough, myself. It's a different game from when we joined. You haven't been sick, have you?'

'No, it's the old war wound. There's still a couple of shotgun pellets floating around inside me that could cause trouble anytime. The doc tried to persuade me to go when it happened, but I didn't want to leave, then. Now I want to sort out my private life, so it might be better to jump, before I'm kicked out.'

'Are you still with the tall lady? Annabelle, was it?'

'Yeah. Maybe if I put as much effort into this relationship as I've put into the job we might make something of it.'

'There's a lot of sense in that. You've over twenty-six and a half in, haven't you?'

'By a couple of years,' I replied.

'OK, so you'll go on the full two-thirds, and your pension will start right away. How much leave have you left?'

'All of it.'

'And your white card?'

That's our record of days owed for unpaid overtime and holidays worked, except that inspectors do not recognise overtime. 'I've stopped filling it in,' I replied.

'OK. So just send me your minute sheet, saying: "I hereby inform you that I wish to retire on such a date . . ." Give us a month, as required. Meanwhile, try to negotiate yourself some of the leave that's owed you. With two weeks leave you could be gone in a fortnight.'

'As simple as that?'

'As simple as that.'

'It's a bit frightening, all of a sudden.'

'I know, but it'll overtake you, one day soon, if you don't take the plunge, Charlie.'

'I'll think about it. Thanks, Bob. Keep your eye on the post.'

'Invite me to the bash. See you.'

A fortnight! I could be gone in a fortnight! On full terms! I had to tell someone. I rang Annabelle, but there was no answer. I stood up, walked round the office, sat down again. Gilbert wasn't in, either. I thought about treating myself to a meal at the Bamboo Curtain, but I wasn't hungry. I strolled round the main office, reading the papers on the desks, the notices on the walls. Jeff Caton's sweater was still over his chair back. One of the others had a framed picture of his motorbike on his desk. Two cartoons torn from newspapers, brown with age, were pinned on the board, both featuring someone called Charlie. What was it Herbert Mathews said? 'Once you leave, you're history.' It'd be a wrench, but I could do it.

It was drizzling outside, but it felt right. I unlocked the car and started the engine. Ideally, I'd have liked to have walked home, feeling the rain on my face. I'd have plenty of time for walking, unless I took the offer of a partnership from Eric Dobson. There were decisions to be made, discussions to be held, and fast. Two more weeks! I put the car in gear and eased out of the station yard. There was a strange feeling in my stomach, churning at my innards. I think it was fear.

I called in M and S for a few ready meals and some fruit. There'd be more time for shopping. The girl at the till gave me an extra special smile, as if she shared my secret. I called in the travel agent's again for some more brochures to go with the ones I still hadn't shown Annabelle. California, this time, and the Seychelles.

The ansaphone was beeping. I put the stuff in the freezer, hung up my jacket and changed my shoes. Annabelle didn't answer when I pressed her button, so I listened to the tape. It was her, message timed at 10.12 a.m.

'Oh, er, hello, Charles,' she said, rather hesitantly. 'It's Annabelle. I, er, I found your note, after you left. I don't know what to say. I'm driving down to the West Midlands Airport this afternoon. There's a meeting with the architect tomorrow, at the Post Chase. I'll be staying there overnight and will probably come home after the meeting. I'll talk to you then. 'Bye.'

So now she knew. We'd been cruising along quite nicely for all this time, in an eternal courtship. It's usually regarded as the happiest time of your life – it was mine – so why spoil it? But the human condition is not to be content with what we have. We need to consolidate, to constantly renew, to mark our territory, build a nest. Maybe Xav had done me a favour, galvanised me out of my state of happy lethargy. Perhaps that's what Annabelle had in mind all along? I smiled at her unexpected guile. 'I bet he's a four-foot Saddam Hussein with bad breath,' I said to my reflection in the bathroom mirror.

I could make the West Midlands Airport in an hour and a half. That would make it about eight o'clock. I asked directory enquiries for the number of the Post Chase and dialled it.

'I believe you have a Mrs Wilberforce staying with you,' I said. 'She checked in sometime today.'

'Mrs Wilberforce? Yes, that's right.'

I asked to be put through to her room, but she didn't answer the phone. Probably using the pool, I thought, wishing I were already there, with her.

'Would you like me to page her, sir?' the desk clerk asked.

'No, but I'd be grateful if you could take a message for her, leave it under her door, or whatever. Could you tell her that Mr Priest is coming down, and will be there about eight o'clock?'

I dressed nonchalantly smart, with a tie from the flamboyant end of my range, and hit the streets. The M1 was busy, as usual, but there were no hold-ups. I stuffed Dylan's *Before the Flood* live concert tape into the cassette and sang the words of every song, tapping time on the steering wheel with my fingers. We were just starting the opening number, *Most Likely You Go Your Way and I'll Go Mine*, for the second time as I tried to decipher the jumble of signs on the approach to the airport, peering between the sweeps of the windscreen wipers. A Mercedes glided across my bows and turned in the direction I needed. Nice car, I thought, pressing the eject control and swinging after it.

It had all changed since my last visit, when I picked up Sparky and family after a fortnight at one of the Costas. Somebody was investing a lot of money around here. I eased over the speed bumps, past the raised barrier, into the Post Chase car park. The Merc stopped under the canopy at the entrance; I kept going, round to where the hoi polloi left their motors. It was nearly full. These places cater for businessmen on expenses. They are chock-a-block through the week and empty at weekends. Annabelle had been lucky to get a room.

I found a space and dashed towards the entrance, slowing to a walk as I reached the shelter of the canopy. The passenger from the Merc was having a last word with his chauffeur, probably telling him to beeswax his polo pony or rake the gravel in the wine cellar, as a flunky hovered nearby with a huge umbrella, shivering patiently in his bum-freezer jacket. I strolled to the desk and waited for some service.

An attractive girl in a burgundy cap smiled at me and asked if she could help.

'You have a Mrs Wilberforce staying here,' I said. 'Could you please ring her room and tell her that Mr Priest is at the desk?'

She consulted her VDU screen and dialled a number. I turned to scrutinise the place. Market research, Annabelle had called it. They hadn't skimped on the size – it was immense. Three piece suites were dotted about like atolls in the Pacific, with copses of shrubs, real or otherwise, contributing to the feeling of space. First impressions were good, and most visitors wouldn't have a chance to form any others. I nodded approvingly. It was an ideal place for pursuing two of my passions: sipping tea from a china service and people-watching.

'Mrs Wilberforce doesn't appear to be in her room sir. Would you like me to page her?'

A silver-haired man in a silver suit came through the revolving door, adjusting his cuffs and taking a cursory glance around the foyer. Judging by the lack of raindrops on his jacket he was from the Mercedes. He was about sixty and obviously knew where he was going, in more ways than one. He struck off across the hinterland of the foyer and I noticed a discreet sign pointing towards the restaurant.

'Shall I page her for you, sir?' the girl was repeating.

'Pardon,' I replied.

A woman stood up. They faced each other for a moment, his arms held open. She moved into their embrace and he kissed her on both cheeks. She returned the kiss, but on his lips. They exchanged a word or two and he gestured towards the restaurant. The last I saw of them they were walking towards it, his hand on the small of her back, she turning to speak to him, animated and lively.

'Sir?'

'Er, sorry?'

'Shall I page Mrs Wilberforce for you?'

'No,' I said. 'It doesn't matter. Thank you.'

I sat in the car for a long time. I don't remember how I got there, but I could feel the wetness striking through my clothes. Feel it as an observation, oblivious of the discomfort.

'It's Charlie,' I said, when the duty sergeant answered the phone, when I felt coherent enough to speak. 'Could you do me a PNC check, please?' I gave him the number.

'Are you all right, Boss?' he replied. 'You don't sound your usual chirpy self.'

'Tired, Arthur, just tired.'

'Don't go away.'

He was back on the line in a minute or so. 'You don't mess about with nonentities, do you, Chas?' he said. 'It's come back as a smoke silver Mercedes 420, keeper details: Audish Trading, at a London address. Do you need chassis and engine numbers?'

'No, that's fine thanks.'

'Anything else?'

'No. I'll try not to bother you again. Goodnight.'

'No bother. G'night, Boss.'

So that was Xavier Audish. I didn't need telling who the woman was. We were old friends, or I thought we were.

Apart from the Gary Glitter CD, on which they had deliberately left the price tag showing that Woolworth's had sold it at a loss, Sophie and Daniel, Sparky's kids, had also given me Nigel Kennedy's *Four Seasons*. It was totally inappropriate, so I put it on. I'd arrived home safely, after cruising up the motorway in the slow lane and having a long stop for supper at the Woodall services. I sat in front of the fire, my coat and shoes still on, nodding my head in time to the music and occasionally conducting with a raised finger. Love him or hate him, he plays like an angel. Each time it ended I pressed the replay button and heard it again, until the heat from the fire was burning my legs and stinging my eyes.

I crawled into bed with Vivaldi's frantic rhythms pulsating through my head, leaving no room for other thoughts. At two o'clock a cat started yowling in next door's garden; at three I heard a train pulling a heavy load up the gradient towards Manchester – the wind must have been from the West; and at four thirty my central heating switched itself on with a *clunk* that reverberated through the house. I had a shower and found some clean clothes.

Unpredictability is a quality I've tried to cultivate over the years. If I realise I've fallen into a habit, I change my behaviour. It wasn't habit that took me to work that morning, it was a determination not to do what anybody might have expected of me. I could have driven to Cape Wrath and studied the sequence of the waves. I could have put my boots on and hiked over Black Hill and Bleaklow until hunger drove me off the tops. More sensibly, I thought about ringing Sparky's wife and offering to take Sophie and Daniel off her hands for the day. Two films at the multi-screen, followed by a beefburger and chips, with all the fixings, would have been a handy diversion. But I went to work.

I cruised through the morning briefings, deployed the

troops, feigned interest when answering the phone. I read reports and information sheets, made notes and generally created an impression of busy-ness. At ten to twelve I received a message from Scarborough saying that Rodney Allen had been granted bail on condition that he stayed at North Bay House. He was off my list of suspects. He couldn't possibly have shot Dr Jordan. It was just the excuse I needed to dash over there to see him.

The home wasn't in the same league as the White Rose Clinic. It dated from early in the century and every attempt at modernisation had gone to the lowest tender. The walls were dirty above the easy reach of an underpaid cleaner and ribbons of electric cables for phones, power and monitoring were stapled on top of oak panelling that would have had the green lobby crying into their tofu. I saw Rodney but hardly spoke to him. He didn't remember our phonecall, the siege or hitting a policeman. There are stories about Yorkshiremen knowing when to be slow, but his condition had been encouraged by the application of certain class B substances. They'd doped him to make him docile. The doctor hadn't found time to make a statement, so I persuaded her to write me a brief assurance that Rodney had been at the home on the night of the crime, and I left. I had fish and chips in Scarborough and sat in the car for nearly an hour listening to the news and watching waves crash over the Marine Drive. A scientist in California was claiming to have identified a gene for homosexuality and an MP had been found dead in his Westminster flat with a plastic bag over his head and his trousers around his knees. Foul play was not suspected. As my mother used to say, there's always someone worse off than yourself.

Sometimes, before an interview, I run through all the likely answers. I choose my questions carefully and consider as many responses as I'm capable of imagining. More often, these days, I just make it up as I go along. I ask a few sighting questions, to test the range and the direction of the wind, then let go with the big guns. This time I didn't know what to do, because I knew the outcome was already settled.

Annabelle's little car was on her drive as I reversed in behind it. I'd been home and shaved. I was going to change my clothes but decided not to. What you see is what you get. I switched off the engine, pulled the brake on and left the gear in neutral. It was ready for a smooth, unhurried getaway.

I pushed the doorbell, but didn't go in.

'Hello, Charles,' she said, softly, when she saw me standing there. 'I thought I heard a car. I wasn't expecting you.'

'I won't keep you long,' I said, following her in. She sat at one end of the settee, but I stayed on my feet. 'About the note I left,' I said.

She was wearing grey trousers in a silky material, with an emerald green blouse outside them. Her face looked pale against the bright green. 'I . . . I was going to ring you,' she began. 'I don't know what to say . . .'

'I'll make it easy for you,' I told her. 'The note is withdrawn. I rang your hotel last night and left a message. Did you receive it?'

'A message? No. I received no message. What did you say?'

'I said I was coming down to the Post Chase, to take you to dinner.' She swallowed and looked shaken. 'I was asking for you at the desk when Audish walked in. I saw you with him, Annabelle. I saw you kiss each other. I saw the way you tilted your head as you spoke to him, and watched the swing of your skirt as you walked away from me.'

Her eyes were filling with tears. 'I've got to say this,' I went on, 'although I know the answer. We could start again. We had something special, Annabelle. You don't throw that away lightly. I don't know anything about Audish, except one thing: he's not for you.' I left it at that. Slagging him off would be counter productive. 'Come with me,' I begged. 'Now.'

Tears were running down her cheeks. She sniffed and wiped them away with her fingertips. 'I didn't want to hurt you, Charles,' she sobbed. 'You've been so good to me. I didn't know what to do.'

'I thought you loved me.'

'I did love you. I still do.'

'So come with me.'

She shook her head.

'You love Audish more?'

'Yes,' she sobbed.

'Right,' I said. 'Right. You can keep my things. Take them to the Oxfam shop, if you still remember where it is.' At the door I turned back to her. 'I always knew I'd lose you, Annabelle,' I told her. 'Deep down, I knew that one day you'd hurt me, that I could never hold on to you. But I thought it would be the kind of hurt I'd cherish for the rest of my life. I thought you'd be in Africa or India or somewhere, maybe married again, but we'd always be friends. I'd get a card from you, at Christmas; that sort of thing. I knew you'd hurt me; I never dreamed you'd . . . you'd . . . do this to me.' I never dreamed you'd disappoint me. That's what I nearly said.

I opened the door. 'You know where to find me,' I told her. 'But I won't be waiting.'

* * *

I'd run out of things to do, places to go, dogs to kick. You can only drive up on to the tops so many times to watch the lights in the valley until they blur together in a yellow swamp. I was a big boy, now. I tuned-in to the country music station, because I can't stand country-fucking-music, and drove home.

The postman had been. Lying on my doormat was an envelope with a window, postmark and style of typing that told me exactly from where it came. It was the same as the ones my monthly salary statements come in, except the next one wasn't due for another three weeks. That was quick, I thought. Pay section had been on the ball, for once. Maybe they wanted rid of me. I put the envelope on the telephone table, unopened. If I didn't open it I could always swear I hadn't received it.

I love my shower. When I'm lost for something to do, or have twenty minutes to spare, or people in the office start giving me sideways glances and moving away, I have a shower. I do some of my best thinking with the hot jets impinging on my back and soap running into my eyes. Annabelle had given me some smelly stuff for my birthday. I finished it off with a lavish portion that had the plug hole struggling to cope with the foam. Tonight I'd smell nice, for nobody in particular, and one reminder of her would be consigned to the bin.

I pushed my thought processes in other directions. Rodney would be in a drugged sleep. Maybe he was the lucky one. I turned the temperature control up a few degrees and rinsed my hair. It was now too hot, but I left it at that. Tomorrow we'd have to start looking at the abortions, all five thousand of them. Most of the shampoo suds had gone. I slicked my hair back with my hands and turned my face into the hot jets. If there really was a gene for homosexuality, like the scientist in California was claiming – the so-called gay gene – surely they would all have died out by now, wouldn't they? I opened my mouth and let it fill with water, struggling to inhale through the storm. Autoerotic asphyxiation, that's what the MP died of, with his head in the plastic bag. They say it increases the intensity of the orgasm. I tipped my head forward so the water ran from my mouth, grabbed a breath and looked back into the spray. I reached up and swung the shower head to one side, keeping my face directly under it, and leaned back against the tiled wall.

And I made a discovery.

Chapter Eleven

They were gathered around Sparky like the apostles around Jesus, expressions of beatitude on their upturned faces. I'd been up to see Mr Wood to tell him what he didn't want to know – that we were roughly in the same place in our enquiry as we were when Dr Jordan's body was found. I didn't mention the rape and he didn't ask, and I certainly didn't tell him about my revelation in the shower. He wasn't ready for that, yet.

Sparky was in full flow: '. . . and the French television reporter looked at them and said: "Wait a minute, wait a minute . . ."'

'*Un moment! Un moment!*' Jeff Caton interrupted, one hand raised with the fingertips together, as if plucking a grape.

'I'm translating for Nigel's benefit,' Sparky told him.

'Oh, sorry.'

'That's all right. So this Frog reporter says: "Wait a minute. You don't like our wine. You don't like our food. You don't like our ladies. So just why do you keep coming back to France all these times?" And the Siamese twin on the left says: "It's the only chance I get to drive."'

They drifted away, morale boosted, back to the tedium of reports and observations and the frustrations of court. Nigel and Sparky stayed behind.

'Where's Maggie?' I asked.

'She went straight to the clinic,' Nigel said. 'Wanted to collar Barraclough before the daily grind of executive meetings started. I've told her I'll join her, soon as I can, if you don't need me.'

'Fair enough.'

'There's a package on your desk,' Sparky informed me. 'Special delivery from Wetherton. A hell's angel from traffic brought it a few minutes ago.'

'That was quick,' I said. 'I only rang them at half past seven.'

'You could tell he was happy at his work,' Sparky declared.

'Who?'

'The biker.'

'How?'

'He had dead flies on his teeth. What's in it?'

'In January? It's just a little something I wanted to borrow,' I replied. 'I'll tell you all about it when I've had a think. Meanwhile . . . I'm going to set you some homework.'

'This sounds omnibus, Nigel,' Sparky complained.

'It does, doesn't it?' he replied.

'Nigel, are you still going out with that red-headed WPC from City?' I asked. He opened his mouth to speak but I cut him short. 'On second thoughts,' I said, 'are you going out with anyone?'

'Er, sort of,' he answered.

'Right,' I said, turning to Sparky. 'And you're still in a blissful relationship, I presume?'

'Ye-es,' he replied, cagily.

'OK, here's what I want. Tonight you will both make love to your respective partners in the shower, and be prepared to discuss same tomorrow. Understood?'

'Is that all?' Sparky said. 'I was expecting something exciting.'

'Forget the "respective partners" bit, if it helps,' I suggested.

'Will, er, you be joining in this research?' Nigel wondered.

'No,' I told him. 'I did the initial fieldwork; your job is to confirm my findings.' I didn't mention that I was alone at the time.

When they'd gone I pulled the piece of equipment I'd borrowed from Wetherton lab from the package and found the instructions. It sounded simple. I tested it against the palm of my hand and discovered that I was fit enough to survive the day. In that case, I'd carry on. On the way out I stopped at the front desk to see if there was a female officer available to accompany me, but I was out of luck. Ah well, never mind.

Janet Saunders was in when I knocked because I could hear Radio 2 filtering quietly through the door. I knocked again and the volume lowered. There were footsteps inside and a key turned in the lock. The door opened a fraction and she peered out at me, a chain bridging the gap.

'Yes?' she asked, timidly.

I held my ID in front of her face. 'DI Charlie Priest,' I said. 'I met you when you came to Heckley Police Station. I wonder if I could have a word with you?'

'Who is it, Mummy?' a tiny voice asked, and I looked down to see a little face framed with platinum blonde hair gazing up at me.

'I didn't recognise you,' Janet said, steering her daughter to one side so she could close the door to unfasten the chain.

She led me through into the living room and invited me to sit down, 'If you can find an empty seat.' There was a scattering of toys and clothes, but the place was clean and fairly tidy.

'You must be Dilly,' I said to the angel face that came to stand alongside me. She nodded.

'And how old are you?'

Dilly looked up at her mother for a prompt.

'Tell the gentleman how old you are,' she said.

'I'm five.'

'Five! You're a big girl for five. I thought you were at least six.' Sparky would have been proud of me. 'And how long have you been five?' I asked.

She thought about it, swinging her body from side to side. 'Um, since my birthday,' she calculated.

I decided I was out of my depth and looked across to Janet for rescue. She suggested that Dilly go up to her room and put some different clothes on, suitable for a trip to the shopping mall.

'She's back with you,' I said, when we were alone.

'Yes,' Janet replied, walking over to a portable radio and switching off Terry Wogan or one of his clones. 'Her father is working away – Edinburgh – so I've got to have her, all this week.'

'You appear to have a civilised relationship with him.'

'Yes, we try to have.'

'It must be difficult, arranging your lives around Dilly.'

'It is, but we manage.'

'She's a lovely little girl,' I said, smiling. 'It's easy to see who she takes after.'

It was a stupid thing to say. Janet coloured slightly and asked: 'What did you come for?'

Shelter from the storm? 'I'm sorry,' I told her. 'I

shouldn't have said that. Maggie is busy, otherwise I wouldn't have come alone. Maybe I should have waited.'

We sat in silence for a few seconds. 'Maggie has told you all about Buxton?' I said.

She nodded.

'He's done it before,' I continued. 'More than once.'

'I know. Maggie told me.'

'Right. I need to break his story, Janet. He says that on that night – Christmas Eve – you did it the first time in the shower.'

She gave a sigh that came from right down in her cheap trainers. 'No. I'd just come out of the shower. He dragged me into the bedroom and . . . and . . . and did it to me on the bed.'

'He says you consented.'

'He's a liar.'

'He says you were a willing participant.'

'He had a knife at my throat.'

'But you didn't have sex in the shower?'

'No! For what it's worth, I've never had sex in a shower, either here or anywhere else.'

'OK. I needed to know. I'd like you to make a statement to that effect in the next few days. Maggie can take it, if that's all right.'

She nodded. Her hands were in her lap, engaged in a subconscious wrestling match, and her feet were shuffling about as if the floor was too hot to bear.

There was an uneven clomping on the stairs as Dilly came down, leading with the same foot on every step. She dashed to her mother and posed for inspection and approval. She was wearing fluorescent tights and a blue dress.

'Have you got them on the right way round?' Mummy asked.

Dilly nodded.

'Good girl.'

'She's, er, colourful,' I observed.

'You're a little rainbow, aren't you?' her mother said, swinging her up into a cuddle. Dilly giggled.

'Is it all right if I have a look in your bathroom?' I asked.

'Yes, of course it is. It's at the top of the stairs, facing you.'

The staircarpet was threadbare. The welfare state considers rent and food bills when calculating its allowances, but carpets and repairs to washing machines and a host of other expenses are considered non-essential. I closed the bathroom door behind me and slid the bolt across.

There was no radiator in there, just an electric heater high on the wall. The element was covered with dust, showing that it hadn't been used all winter. Those things eat electricity. I took my jacket off and hung it behind the door, next to a white towelling dressing gown and a tiny pair of pink pyjies with yellow teddy bears on them.

The shower worked straight off the taps, which isn't the best way to do it, and fingers of mildew were eating their way along the grouting between the tiles. I pulled the curtain out of the bath and turned the shower on for a few seconds. It didn't take me long to decide that Buxton and Janet almost certainly had not had sex in there. Problem was, could we convey that certainty to a jury? I had a pee. Down the side of the toilet was a plastic seat, designed to reduce the size to that of a child's bottom. I smiled, acknowledging that although I would have liked kids, having none has plenty of compensations. I was flushing the toilet when I noticed something on the windowsill that caused a jolt of recognition.

It was a miniature swing bin, just like the one that Dr Jordan kept his teabags in. I picked it up and flipped the lid open. It was half filled with remnants of soap tablets; that final flake that breaks in half and tells you that trying to use it any longer is not worth the effort. Janet saved them for recycling. Thrifty girl. I washed my hands and went back downstairs, taking it with me.

Dilly had gone outside, and Janet had her coat on.

'I, er, saw this,' I said, waving the bin at her. 'I've been looking for one, all over.'

'That,' she said with a shrug. 'It's called a mini-bin. I just keep bits of soap in it. You can have it, if you want.'

'No, I wouldn't dream of taking it. I'd like to know where you got it, though.'

'It came from Magic Plastic.'

'Magic Plastic? Never heard of them. Where are they?'

'They don't have a shop. Well, they might, somewhere, but a man comes round. He leaves a catalogue and comes back a week later to collect it and take your order, if you want anything.'

'I see. And how often does he come round?'

'I'm not sure. Once a month, I imagine, but most of them don't last that long. I ordered something because I felt sorry for him, but the next time I didn't buy anything – it's all a bit expensive – and he didn't come any more. An empty coffee jar would have been just as effective.'

'I don't suppose you still have the catalogue?'

'No, sorry. I left it hanging on the door handle – that's what you do – and it vanished. I suppose he collected it.'

'Right, thanks,' I said, placing the mini-bin on the table. Gilbert would have to wait for his used-teabag receptacle. 'Thanks for your help, Janet,' I said. 'It's been most useful. If you're going into town I can give you a lift.'

'No thanks,' she replied. 'The bus stop's just outside.'

'But I'm going that way.'

'It's all right, thanks.'

Have it your way, lady, I thought. I was driving past the mall while they were probably still waiting for a bus. They're not exactly as numerous as the daisies in the fields in that neighbourhood. Recently they've gone back to two-man crews – driver and shotgun.

On an impulse I hung a right at the traffic lights, completely wrong-footing a woman pushing a pram across the road, and parked outside Heckley Squash Club. I made a mental note to paint a little silhouette of a baby carriage on my door, next to the hedgehogs, cats and traffic wardens.

A young woman with that healthy outdoor look you used to see on Syrup of Figs posters was standing behind the desk, drinking an isotonic concoction from the neck of the bottle. Orange juice with a pinch of salt is just as good and a fraction of the price, but it doesn't have that certain cachet. Magic Johnson drinks the real stuff, whoever he is. She was wearing green jogging bottoms and a polo shirt with a kangaroo embroidered on the left pocket and sweat spots in delightful places. I averted my gaze.

'Hello,' I began.

'Hi,' she replied.

'Your manager,' I went on, 'tells me that as well as being highly proficient with bat, ball and dumbells, you are also a whizzkid on this.' I tapped the top of the computer VDU.

'Yer what?' she demanded.

I flashed her my ID and crossed her off my list of possibilities. 'Charlie Priest, Heckley CID,' I said. 'He promised me a printout of all your members' names; said he'd ask you to run it off for me.'

'Aw, gee, the printout!' she exclaimed. 'Completely slipped my mind.'

'I'd be very grateful for it.'

'OK, but it'll take ages. Tell yer what, are you at the police station here in town?'

'Uh uh.'

'Right.' She delved under the counter and came up with a large manilla envelope that had been used. 'Why don't you just cross out our address and write your own there, and I'll set this thing going right now and drop it in on my way home. How does that sound?'

'Very cooperative. Thanks a lot.' I reinstated her as a contender.

'Did yer want them in alphabetical order?'

'Yes please, if possible.'

'No problem. Nice meeting you, Inspector.'

'And you.'

The office was empty. I ate the prawn sandwich I'd bought on the way back and shut myself away. A plan of action was required. I wrote my reports to clear my mind and made notes on a sheet of A4. First thing we needed was a suitable venue. I put my coat back on and drove to City HQ.

Superintendent Isles wasn't in, which suited me fine.

'Are the old Bridewell cells still in use?' I asked the desk sergeant. City HQ is attached to the town hall, and parts of it date back to Victorian times. The old cells, known universally as the Bridewell, were down in the basement. He seconded a young PC to help me and we went exploring.

The one we chose was used to store sports equipment. We manhandled a wobbly ping-pong table into the cell next door, along with assorted cricket pads and a one-armed bandit. The PC, called Martin, tried the fruit machine and wondered if the social club would let him have it.

There was a bit of dust around, but not enough to make the place uninhabitable. We'd ask the cleaning ladies to give it a quick once-over. There was a power point and the fluorescent light on the high ceiling worked. The walls were covered from top to bottom in white tiles, broken only by a thin blue line running round the room at waist height. I ran a hand over them, wondering how many frustrated prisoners had found their glazed surface unyielding to scratch or skull. You couldn't buy tiles like these any more. They had curved edges and special corner pieces, and were as hard and unforgiving as tungsten carbide. Just what I wanted.

I took Martin upstairs and introduced him to the technical support wizards. They found one of the portable tape recorders we used before the new interview suites had them built in, and showed him how to drive it. I dithered over a video camera, then decided to go for it. They gave Martin a crash course on that, too. We carried the lot down to the Bridewell and I left him practising. I told him to make sure the batteries were charged, the tapes were blank and the lights worked. If all went well, I'd buy him a fruit machine. He nodded enthusiastically and went to fetch a table and some chairs.

Maggie was in when I arrived back at Heckley. 'How did it go?' I asked.

'Like drawing teeth,' she sighed. 'Slow and painful. Patient confidentiality, all that crap. I don't know who they think they are.'

'Did you tell them that our investigation overrides any duties of confidentiality they may have towards their patients?'

'Till I was blue in the face.'

'So how have you left it?'

'I had a long discussion with the counsellor who talks to all the young women who go in for abortions. She said most of them know exactly why they are there and are not interested in counselling. A few sad ones seize the opportunity but usually decide to go ahead. Not many back out. She said that she has had one or two disturbing cases, possibly unbalanced, and nothing they did would surprise her. One involved an irate boyfriend. Trouble is, she wouldn't name names. I had a word with Barraclough and suggested that if she told him they might then be able to come to some arrangement where he could pass the information on to us, whereby she wouldn't have contravened the etiquette of her profession.'

'Mmm, maybe. I'd rather you leaned on them. Tell them that we are not interested in their consciences or the sexual transgressions of their clientele. We're trying to catch a killer. Make that a serial killer. Say we have reason to believe that one of them is next on his list. That should focus their attention.'

'Ha!' she laughed. 'Some serial killer. He's only done one, so far.'

'That's the best time to catch them, Maggie. That's the best time to catch them.' I decided to change the subject. 'Have you,' I asked, 'ever heard of a company called Magic Plastic?'

'Magic Plastic?'

'Mmm.'

'No. What have they done?'

'They haven't done anything. I want to know where they are. They produce a catalogue of a hundred and one things for the home that you never thought you needed, and employ door-to-door salesmen. I'd appreciate it if you could track them down and tell them to send me a catalogue, soon as possible.'

'Right, no problem. Is this police work?'

'Maggie!' I exclaimed. 'Of course it's police work. When did I ever do anything else?'

If you sit still too long in this job everybody learns that you are at your desk and rings you. By five o'clock my right ear was numb and my brain was reeling, so I trudged upstairs for a decent cup of tea with Gilbert. The atmosphere is always more relaxing in his office. I refused to answer questions about crime but told him that I was on the verge of solving the great teabag disposal problem. He wasn't impressed.

We were on the way out, walking past the front desk, when a voice shouted: 'Mr Priest!' I turned to see the desk sergeant coming out of the office. 'Packet for you,' he said, reaching under the counter. He handed me the self-addressed envelope I'd left at the squash club.

'Thanks,' I said, taking it from him.

'A big green Sheila brought it in,' he told me. 'Said it was special delivery, for you and you alone. Wish you'd tell me how you do it.'

'That's the problem with Australian women,' I replied, winking at him. 'They keep coming back.'

I drove out of town on the old Oldfield road, quiet now, since the coming of the motorway. There is a transport cafe, famous for its wholesome meals and warm atmosphere, where all the truckers stopped on their journey over the Pennines. It has had to contract, grass over the lorry park, and change the menu, but it has, thankfully, survived. Nowadays they make a decent living from a handful of drivers who remember where they are and hordes of senior citizens who know where to find a tasty bargain. And now me. One time, I was a regular at all the cheap eateries. I'd have to start finding my way around them again. No more sneaking away at lunchtime for trout in almonds at Annabelle's. I'd miss that. I ordered lasagne, with salad, and sat facing the telly, to give me something mindless to think about.

A man in a jacket the colour of a ruptured gall bladder was reading from a sheet of paper. 'For five points, Dorothy,' he whispered intimately, as if asking for her dying testament, 'can you tell me the name of . . . the first man to run the mile in four minutes?'

'Roger Bannister!' she screeched, as the camera panned to an open-mouthed matron clutching her hands to her head. The whole world was ganging up on me. I moved to the chair at the opposite side of the table, my back to the telly.

The lasagne was not bad, for lasagne. I followed it with rhubarb crumble and a refill of tea. Today, I'd eaten well. Annabelle would be proud of me. No, she wouldn't. There I go again, I thought.

When I reached home I took the envelope in with me. A list of a couple of thousand names and addresses is my idea of bedtime reading. The mailman had left an avalanche of correspondence spilling halfway along my hall. I gathered them up and took them into the kitchen to look at while the kettle boiled. One from the bank was put to one side for future reference and I binned missives from the AA, Damart and Reader's Digest. A note from my window cleaner said I was three payments behind. I put fifteen quid in an envelope and took it round to my neighbour's. The final piece of mail was from the Playhouse, containing two tickets for *Romeo and Juliet*. It was hard to believe, but Annabelle had never seen a stage performance of it. The repertory theatre in equatorial Africa prefers Shakespeare's more violent offerings. They were for Monday evening, and I'd wanted it to be a surprise. I placed them back in their envelope and stood it behind the clock.

There was a programme about the mating habits of termites on Channel 4, so I watched that until I remembered the list from the squash club. She'd used half a roll of Sellotape on the envelope, but I eventually made it to the contents.

I have a lot of sympathy with the Chinese. I usually read the front page of a newspaper first, then the back page, then work through it from back to front, like they are supposed to do. I'm sure it's more natural. I'm equally convinced that we drive on the wrong side of the road in Britain, and the Continentals and most of the rest of the world have it right, but I rarely put that one into practice. The list was on the type of computer paper with sprocket holes down the edges, in a continuous concertina of folded pages, about a hundred, although I didn't count them. I started at the last name – Younghusband, William Defoe, 'Carrickfergus', Cotswold Manor Garth, Heckley – and slowly started to work my way upwards on the long journey towards Abbott, John, 143 Sheepscab Street.

I studied them methodically, unhurried. I'd read each name and dredge my memory for a spark of recognition. One or two sounded familiar, but the addresses were wrong. A couple were policemen I knew. Then I'd read the address and try to visualise where the member lived. I studied them all, but I was mainly interested in the women. If I didn't find anything we'd have to put them in the computer and let that search through them.

Two hours later my eyes were burning. I'd be reading names, flicking through them, and realise that nothing was registering. I'd go back a few places and try again. I thought of playing some music, but when I glanced through my collection I found nothing that wouldn't have been a distraction. Just reading the labels reminded me of Annabelle. After a great deal of dithering I marked the place I'd reached in the list and rang her number. The ansaphone came on. I put the receiver down, had a think about it and dialled again.

'It's me,' I said. 'Hello. Last night . . . I may have said things that I didn't mean . . . I'm not sure if I said them or just thought them . . . anyway, I take them back. I was upset. The last five years have been the happiest of my life, and I'm grateful to you for that. You're a big girl, and you must do what is best for yourself.' I wanted to say a lot more, but ansaphone tapes are not very long. I finished with: 'I hope it works out for you. Don't write or anything . . . It's not necessary . . . But you know where I am, if you need me. Oh, and I meant what I said in the note. Every word. Goodbye, love.'

I'd made another mug of tea and was arranging the sheets on my lap to recommence the search when the doorbell rang. I looked at the clock – it said just after ten. I refolded the pages with my pen marking the appropriate place, about halfway through, and went to answer it.

Maggie was standing there, pale and grim, her coat buttoned up around her throat. 'I'd like a word, Boss,' she said.

'Come in,' I invited, holding the door wide.

She walked through into the lounge and sat down, leaning over to see what the printout was about.

'Heckley Squash Club,' I told her. 'Membership list. Dr Jordan was friendly with a girl there, called Sue or Sheila or something. I was looking through them for inspiration. So, what's happened? Is something wrong?'

'I'm . . . not sure,' she replied.

'Are you taking your coat off?'

She shook her head.

'Cup of tea? The kettle's just boiled.'

'No. I don't want a tea.'

'Right. In that case, you'd better tell me why you're here. Sadly, I'll assume it's not a social visit.'

The fingers of her right hand screwed up the belt of her coat and smoothed it out again. I've known Maggie a long time. We have a good working relationship but there's something above that between us. She's listened to my problems and chided or encouraged me, as required. I've leaned on her. They say that there's no such thing as a platonic friendship between a man and a woman, but I'm not sure I agree.

'No,' she said. 'It's not a social visit.'

'So what sort of a visit is it?'

'What you just said, a moment ago . . .'

'What?'

'You said: "Sadly I'll assume it's not a social visit."'

I shrugged. 'So?'

'It's flirting. You do it all the time, Charlie. I don't think you know you're doing it.'

I was puzzled. 'I'm not flirting with you, Maggie,' I told her. 'I'm being pleasant, or at least I thought I was. If I've got it wrong . . . if you have a problem with it, I'll change. I'll be an arrogant bastard like most of the others. Is that what you'd prefer?'

'No.'

'Well I'm not in the mood for a lecture on political correctness, Maggie, from you or anyone else. I treat everybody the same, and you know it. I respect our differences, and work round them, but as long as we're all pulling together I don't give a toss about them.'

She unbuckled her belt and unfastened the top buttons of her coat. 'I know,' she sighed. 'It's just that . . .'

'Just that what?'

'This morning. You went to see Janet Saunders.'

So that was it. 'Oh,' I said.

'She rang me. You scared her, Charlie. Have you any idea what she went through?'

'I like to think I have.'

'No, you haven't. I thought she was pulling round, learning to trust us, but now . . .'

'Maggie,' I said. 'It was ten o'clock in the morning. You weren't available. No one else was. I played it by the book, and for God's sake, her daughter was there.'

'You commented on her looks.'

'Yes,' I admitted. 'And I meant it. It was an observation, not a come-on. The last time I went to the cinema I made a similar remark about John Travolta's smile, but I've no desire to hop into bed with him. It was a crass thing to say, under the circumstances. I realised that, as soon as the words came out, and I apologised.'

'She said you went up into the bathroom and tried the shower, where Buxton says it happened.'

My elbows were on the chair arms, my fingertips pressed against their opposites in front of my face. I drummed them together in a rhythm that Dave Brubeck never mastered. 'What are you trying to say, Maggie?' I whispered. 'What are you implying?'

'I don't know, Charlie.'

'If you're suggesting that I went round there in the hope of having sex with Mrs Saunders, I want you to leave, now. Make a formal complaint, if you want, but leave.'

'I tried to tell her that you'd have a good reason for what you did, Charlie. I said you were a person who cared, like nobody else I know, but you frightened her. I told her that if she wanted to make a complaint about you, that I couldn't handle it. There was a procedure . . . It'd have to be someone higher up the ladder. But I assured her she was wrong, she'd misunderstood. I offered to have a quiet word with you, and she agreed.'

'So that's what this is: a quiet word?'

'It looks as if I've made a balls of it.'

I shook my head. 'No, you haven't. I'm grateful for you coming, and I'm sorry if I upset Mrs Saunders – that was the last thing I wanted. But I've a job to do. If she's like this after I visit her, how will she be on the stand, with Buxton's brief implying that she's every kind of slag under the sun?'

'Do you think it will come to that? Go to court?'

I looked across at her. 'Trust me, Maggie,' I said. 'Trust me.'

'OK,' she replied. 'That's good enough for me.'

I walked her to her car. Her husband, Tony, was sitting in the driver's seat. She'd brought backup. 'Hello, Tone,' I said.

'Hi, Charlie. All sorted out?'

'I think so.'

I waved them away and slinked back inside, shivering with cold. I closed the door and leaned against it. Not you, Maggie, I thought. Don't you desert me, too.

Chapter Twelve

I told Nigel to have the first team assembled in my office for when I returned from seeing Mr Wood. I declined a coffee with the super on the grounds that I was busy and might have something for him later, and as soon as he was updated on the Heckley crime wave – actually, it's more of a strong tide – I dashed back downstairs.

Sparky was extolling the merits of his Ford Escort to Nigel, who's been dreaming about something sleek and sporty for as long as I've known him. Maggie was sitting apart from them, sipping coffee and looking at a back number of the *Police Review*.

'It's an old man's car,' I declared, taking my jacket off and hanging it behind the door.

'Just what I said,' Nigel agreed.

'Some old men are very discriminating,' Sparky argued.

'Never mind that,' I said. 'Pin back your ears and listen. This morning I propose to arrest Darryl Buxton and interview him on tape and video. I think we can break his story about having it away in the shower.'

'Yes!' Maggie exclaimed, thumping the magazine on the table and knocking over her polystyrene coffee cup. A river of khaki liquid shot across my desk and vanished under a pile of papers.

We all jumped up and started pulling tissues and hankies

from the recesses of our clothing. Nigel dashed out and came back with a roll of paper towelling. No damage was done and when everything was dry we resumed our seats.

'Sorry, Boss,' Maggie said. 'Put it down to excitement.'

'I suppose it's better than drinking the stuff,' I replied. 'Now listen. This is what's happening. Dave and myself will arrest Buxton and take him to City HQ. We will interview him there.'

Maggie opened her mouth to object, her eyes wide with disappointment, or indignation. I turned to her. 'It's not how you think,' I told her. 'I know you've been in on this case from the beginning, and that you were present at the initial interview, but I believe it will be more productive if Dave and myself conduct this one.' She didn't look convinced. 'Darryl Buxton is a misogynist,' I explained. 'He hates women because, deep down, he's scared of them. When it's one-to-one, and he's had a few drinks, it all comes to the surface and he can bully them, but in other circumstances he's lost. You would intimidate him, Maggie, in a situation where he couldn't fight back, so I'd prefer it to be an all-male affair.'

Sparky turned to her. 'You are a very intimidating lady, Maggie,' he confirmed. 'I've often remarked on how intimidating you are. Isn't that so, Nigel?'

'Often, David,' Nigel agreed, adding: 'Nice intimidating, though.'

'That's enough,' I told them. 'I want to play it all-the-lads-together, Maggie. Get him talking, trying to impress us. Appeal to his machismo. Dave and me are the best two to pull it off.'

She gave me a nod of understanding and I left it at that.

'So what's changed?' Nigel asked. 'What do we know today that we didn't know last week?'

I drummed my fingers on the desk. 'Don't ask,' I said. 'If it works, Dave will tell you all about what a superb piece of detective work it was. If it doesn't, it will be consigned to the U-bend of CID history, and Buggerlugs here will be sworn to silence under threat of me telling you all about the time he went to interview a window dresser who turned out to be . . .'

'All right! All right!' Dave interrupted. 'I get the message.'

'In that case,' I said, 'let's go. If you need us, we'll be at City HQ.' I pulled the package from Wetherton lab out of my bottom drawer and unhooked my jacket.

As we drove into Heckley High Street Sparky said: 'You'd better tell me all about it.'

'Right,' I replied, wondering how to begin. We were in my car. I filtered into the righthand lane at the traffic lights and said: 'Did you do the homework I set, last night?'

'No,' he answered. 'The wife said: "Tell that pervert Priest to get his vicarious kicks through someone else," or something like that.'

'Oh. You weren't supposed to tell her it was my idea.'

'Sorry. You didn't make that clear.'

'So now I'm in your Shirley's bad books?'

'No, not any more.'

'How's that?'

'Well, thinking about it must have put her in the mood. This morning she said: "Tell Charlie thanks."'

'Great. Anytime.'

'So what's it all about?'

I stopped at a pelican crossing as an elderly couple hobbled across, the odds against them dying that day reduced to single figures until they were safely on the pavement at the other side. I moved off again and began to tell him about my own adventures in the shower.

We were parked in the back street behind Homes 4U by the time I finished my story. Buxton's Mondeo was in its usual spot. Sparky grinned and nodded his approval. 'Sounds good to me,' he confirmed.

'In that case,' I said, 'let's get on with it.'

We walked through the alley into the front street and entered the shop. A girl of about sixteen was behind the counter, reading something on her lap and chewing gum at the same time. One of the brighter ones. She looked up at us and smiled without interrupting the chewing motion. Her hair was straight and black, reaching down to her shoulders; her lipstick was white and her eyelashes wouldn't have looked out of place on a pole, poking from a chimney. I'd seen her before – she did *Puff the Magic Dragon* at the Isle of Wight.

We both showed her our IDs. 'We're police, love,' I said, quietly. 'Is Mr Buxton upstairs?'

'Er, D-Darryl?' she stuttered. 'Y-yes, he's in. Sh-shall I ring him, tell him you're here?'

I put my hand over the phone. 'No, not yet. How long have you worked here?'

'J-just since Wednesday. Three days.'

'How long have you known Darryl?'

'The same. W-we were in a pub, me and some mates. He started chatting to us, and said he was looking for a secretary. I was unemployed . . .' She shrugged her shoulders to finish off the story.

No previous experience required, I thought. Sparky raised the flap in the counter and walked through. He lifted a PVC coat from a hook on the wall and held it open for her. She glanced from me to him and back to me, like a rabbit choosing between a ferret and the shotguns. 'Go home, love,' I told her. 'There is no job.'

She put her arms into the sleeves and Sparky hitched the coat over her shoulders, pulling the top together across her throat like a concerned parent might. She was about the same age as Sophie, his daughter. As she came to my side of the counter I saw that the coat matched her miniskirt and knee boots. I held the door open and gave her a weak smile as she passed through. She didn't return it. I closed the door, dropped the latch, slid the top and bottom bolts across and turned the sign to closed.

Upstairs, we found Darryl in his executive chair, smoking a cigar and reading *What Car?*

'Hello, Darryl,' I said, walking into his office. 'Just pricing up a Ferrari Testosterone, eh?'

'What the fuck do you want?' he blustered, pushing the magazine into his drawer in a gesture straight from his childhood. Guilt and disapproval were still dogging him.

'We want you, down at City HQ, for a taped interview.'

'I can't leave the shop, just like that. How did you get up here? Where's Jemima?'

'We sent her home,' Sparky told him.

'Sent her home? You've no right to . . .'

'Darryl Buxton,' I began, 'I am arresting you for the rape of Janet Saunders you do not have to say anything however it may harm your defence if you do not mention when questioned something which you later rely on in court anything you do say may be given in evidence get your coat.'

I glanced across at Sparky for approval.

'Word perfect,' he confirmed, producing a pair of handcuffs.

'Oh, I don't think they're necessary,' I said. 'Darryl usually cooperates with us. No need to be so heavy, is there, Darryl?'

'I want to ring my brief,' he said.

'Good idea. Might save a few minutes. Tell him that this time you'll be at City HQ. He'll know where it is.'

We locked the back door of Homes 4U's Heckley branch and in less than twenty minutes we were showing Buxton into my makeshift interview room. Martin, the young PC, came and sat with him while we went to the canteen and waited for Mr Turner to come from Manchester. This time he drove straight over.

'First of all,' I began, when we were all assembled, 'I'd like to apologise for the surroundings.' I waved a hand at the walls and the high ceiling, my words ricocheting like bullets off the tiles. 'We came here because the interview rooms at Heckley are being decorated, but unfortunately there's been a burst and the rooms upstairs are out of use. Would you believe, all the pipes are lead? You'd think in a police station, of all places, the pipes would be made of copper, wouldn't you?'

Nobody agreed. Nobody laughed.

'So,' I continued, 'I'll ask Martin here to start the tapes rolling and we'll begin.' Martin switched on the big Grundig twin-cassette recorder that sat on the desk and adjusted the video camera on its tripod. 'Martin is our chief grip, today,' I explained.

'Best boy,' Sparky suggested.

Martin smiled and nodded to me.

'Right, let's go,' I said. I read out the time and date and asked everybody to introduce themselves. 'We are here,' I continued, the formalities over, 'to record a substantive interview with Darryl Buxton, formerly known as Burton, concerning the alleged sexual assault on Mrs Janet Saunders on Christmas Eve last . . .'

'An allegation that will be vigorously denied,' Mr Turner interjected.

'Quite,' I said. 'We are in a situation where allegations have been made and denied. One way or another I would like us to lay this one to rest; this morning, if possible. It is not fair to either party for it to drag on. In the absence of independent witnesses we have to study the evidence, which so far consists of statements by the two adversaries, and decide whether it is worthwhile making a submission to the CPS. I would therefore like to clarify Mr Buxton's statement made on January 2nd and give him the opportunity to add to it or explain in any other way the events of that night. Does this make sense?'

Turner and Buxton nodded.

'Gentlemen!' I chided, raising my hands. 'For the tape, please.'

'Yes, Inspector,' Turner agreed, drowning Buxton's mumbled assent.

'In that case, Darryl, would you tell us again what happened that night, starting in the Tap and Spile, just before it closed at midnight.'

'I've told you once,' he complained.

'I know,' I replied, with forced patience. 'But this time it's for real. You've had time to go over what happened, to perhaps remember things which had slipped your memory before. You were in an unpleasant situation, under stress, accused of rape. Maybe you weren't thinking too clearly. Let's hear it again, eh? For a start, how well did you know Mrs Saunders?'

'Janet? You mean Janet?'

'That's right. How well did you know her?'

His hair looked newly cropped and his face was fat and puffy, with glowing cheeks. A face like a slapped arse, to use Sparky's expression. 'Depends what you mean,' he replied.

'Had you ever been out with her before?'

'No.'

'But you'd spoken to her?'

'Yeah, course I 'ad.'

'You were on nodding acquaintance?'

'A bit more than that.'

'You knew her name?'

'Just her first one.'

'Did she know yours?'

'Yeah, I fink so. Yeah, she did. I remember her calling me Darryl.'

'Did you buy her a drink on Christmas Eve?'

'Yeah, a couple, free, maybe.'

'So you were standing at the bar, talking to her when she had the opportunity, and you bought her two or three drinks.'

'That's right.'

'Wasn't it a bit too crowded to have a conversation?'

'Yeah. We didn't do much talking, if you know what I mean.'

'These drinks you bought her. What were they?'

'I don't know.'

'You don't know?'

'No.'

'I'd have thought a man of the world like you would have remembered what she drank.'

'Well you're wrong. I'd say: "Have one yourself," and she'd give me my change and say: "Fanks, Darryl,"

I don't know what she had. Maybe she just kept the money.' He'd scored a point, and swelled in his chair, his arrogance slowly returning, inflating him like a hot air ballon.

'So what happened next?'

'They closed at midnight. Janet didn't 'elp much with the clearing up and left nearly straight away. I said I'd walk her 'ome, but she said that people would talk. She asked me to give her five minutes and follow her.'

'Were you surprised?'

'Yeah, I was, a bit.'

'Did she give you her address?'

'Yeah.'

'What is it?'

'What's what?'

'Her address.'

'Oh, no, she just described it. The first 'ouse on Marsden Road, wiv the street light outside.'

'And you followed her?'

'Yeah, just like she said to.'

'Go on,' I invited.

'Well, I got there and we messed about a bit and . . .'

'Not so fast,' I interrupted. 'How did you get in?'

'She left the door open for me.'

'OK. Go on.'

'Like I said, we messed about a bit and she said she needed a shower. I asked her if she'd like her back scrubbing and she said . . . something like . . . "You scrub my back and I'll scrub yours."' He grinned with satisfaction. He'd used an epigram, so it must be true, as any politician will confirm.

'And then?' I prompted.

He didn't need much. No doubt he'd realised that all

this would go on his court documents – his depositions – and if he did find himself in jail on remand they'd be useful currency with his cellmates.

'We went upstairs and she turned the shower on. I took all my clothes off, and then I 'elped her take all hers off. We got in the shower . . .'

'Was it warm enough?' Sparky asked.

'No,' Buxton remembered, after some thought. 'It took a bit to warm up. I was behind her, holding her, like, while we waited. She was getting really turned on.'

'Like the shower,' I said.

'Yeah,' he grinned.

'Sorry. Go on.'

'We got in and snogged a bit. I had to slow her down. She wanted it, there and then, no messing. I soaped her, all over, then got her to do it to me.'

'And then?'

'And then we did it. She wouldn't wait any longer. She was desperate for it, I'm not kidding.'

'Standing up in the shower?'

'Yeah.'

'Isn't that dangerous? I'd have thought you'd fall over.'

'Nah, course not. You lean on the wall, don't you.'

'What, both of you?'

'Christ, 'aven't you ever 'ad it against a wall? She leans on the wall wiv 'er legs open and you do it to her; it's no different.'

'A good old knee trembler!' I declared.

'Yeah, a knee trembler. In the shower. You got it.'

I pursed my lips and thought about things. After a moment I said: 'Let's get this clear. I've led a sheltered life and it's all new to me. You're standing in the shower, both of you, covered in soap. You take her by the shoulders and gently lean her on the wall and . . . hey presto, you're away. Is that it?'

'Yeah, more or less.'

'Didn't she protest?'

'Protest!' he echoed. 'What about? She was begging for it. I leaned her on the wall and she couldn't wait for it inside her. She didn't do no protesting.'

I worried about the double negative, but decided his meaning was clear. 'None at all?' I asked.

'None,' he assured us, adding, 'She was desperate for it.'

'Did it take long?' I wondered.

'No,' he admitted, grinning modestly. 'We was boaf a bit too eager.'

'So was she disappointed?'

'Nah, not a bit. But I like to give satisfaction, if you know what I mean. Well, we all do, don't we? We got dried and I took her in the bedroom and we did it again, on the bed. This time I waited for her. She lapped it up, I'm telling you.'

'Sounds fun,' I said, nodding appreciatively. I turned to Sparky, who'd pushed his chair back from the table. 'What do you think?'

He leaned forward. 'A fair f- f- f-, a fair, er, very fair, I'd say,' he replied.

I allowed myself a little laugh. 'Have you ever had it in the shower?' I asked him.

'No,' he replied. 'I'm strictly under the blankets, with the lights off.'

'Do you talk to your wife while you're doing it?'

'It'd be difficult. We have separate bedrooms.'

This time Darryl joined in with my laugh, and even Mr Turner allowed himself a little smile.

'Well,' I said, 'I reckon that just about concludes it. We'll let you have a copy of the tape and video, Mr Turner, and a transcript. Can you think of anything else, Dave?'

'The tattoo,' he replied. 'Don't forget the tattoo.'

'God, the tattoo!' I exclaimed, bashing a palm against my head. 'It'd completely slipped my mind.' I opened my notebook and thumbed the pages, first in one direction, then the other. 'Here we are,' I said, flattening the pages. 'Do you, Darryl, have a large tattoo on your back?'

Turner looked at him and raised a hand before Darryl could answer. 'I think I'd like to consult my client in private,' he said.

I nodded my approval, 'No problem,' and slid my chair back.

'I ain't got no fuckin' tattoo,' Darryl blurted out. 'Tattoos is for fuckin' weirdos.'

'Maybe we should have a talk,' Turner said.

'It's OK, Mr Turner,' Darryl assured him. 'I ain't got no tattoos.'

I turned to Turner. 'Nasty case,' I said, grimacing. 'Another rape. We have to ask, I'm sure you understand. The chap who did it – the woman said he had this big tattoo on his back. Apparently she had mirrors on her ceiling, and he didn't realise.' I consulted my notebook. 'According to her, it was a mural of someone called . . . Bart Simpson, riding a Harley Davidson motorbike. Does that mean anything to you, Darryl?'

'Bart fuckin' Simpson,' he scoffed. 'Get real.'

'Should I know who he is?'

'He's a cartoon character, Boss,' Sparky informed us.

'Right. And you don't have a likeness of him reproduced anywhere on your torso, Darryl?'

'No.'

'Fair enough, but to eliminate you from enquiries I have to confirm it. Unfortunately your word is not enough. With Mr Turner's approval, would you be good enough to remove your shirt?'

Turner shrugged, Darryl stood up and slipped his jacket off. He unfastened his tie and started unbuttoning his shirt, determined to prove his innocence of this one. His stumpy fingers had problems with his cuffs, but in a few moments the shirt was draped over the back of his chair. He turned round and flexed his muscles.

'Let's have you on film,' I said, looking at Martin. Darryl held the pose as Martin checked the viewfinder. He nodded at me and I said: 'That's fine, thank you.'

Darryl relaxed and turned back to us, rotating his shoulders as he reached for his shirt, obviously pleased with his performance. He was well built, but turning to fat. His shoulders were overdeveloped and the muscles on his neck could have buttressed a small cathedral. His shape reminded me of one or two Olympic athletes who fell foul of the drug testing procedures.

'Just a moment, please,' I said as he lifted his shirt from the chair. He paused as I got to my feet and let the shirt fall from his fingers. I approached him, flapping my hands like a novice curate addressing his flock.

'This . . . sex in the shower thing,' I said. 'I'm still a bit baffled as to how you did it.' I stepped past him and gestured to the wall of the cell we were using. 'Just . . . stand here a moment, please, if you don't mind.' He moved to where I'd indicated, looking uneasy. Turner's chair scraped on the floor but he made no objection.

I moved forward until I was standing almost toe-to-toe with Buxton. 'Let's just say,' I suggested, 'that you are her and I'm you.' He looked wary, his cockiness rapidly evaporating, but didn't protest. I raised my hands and held them palms towards him, but not quite touching. Touching is deemed an assault. 'Now . . . you said . . . that you leaned her back against the wall . . .' I shuffled forward until I could smell last night's beer on his breath and see the wrinkles of skin through the stubble on top of his head. I inched my palms towards him and he leaned backwards against the ancient glazed tiles of the Bridewell.

'Whaa!' he exclaimed, jerking upright.

'What's the matter?'

'It's fucking freezing!'

'Just lean back again,' I insisted.

He tried again, flinched and stepped forward.

'OK,' I told him. 'That'll be enough. It looks as if I'll never know how to do it against a wall.' I passed him his shirt and sat down. We watched him refasten the buttons and stuff the flaps into his trousers. When he was back in his seat I said: 'You're a big lad. You obviously work out.'

'Yeah,' he agreed. 'Now and again.'

'At a gym?'

'Yeah.'

'Which one?'

'It's in Manchester.'

'I see. We had a gym in Heckley, once. A good one. Unfortunately the proprietor killed someone.' I paused, studying his face, then added: 'I put him away for life.'

Turner shuffled and said: 'Is any of this relevant, Inspector? I've other places to be and I'd be grateful if we could bring this interview to a conclusion. My client has fully and satisfactorily replied to your questions and I suggest that there is therefore no case to answer to.'

'He was on steroids,' I continued. 'He killed two people in a fit of 'roid rage. Are you taking steroids, Darryl?'

His mouth was set in an expression of hate, his head lowered, eyes fixed on mine. 'No,' he said.

'Not ever? You've never been offered any at the gym?'

'No.'

'You've never done any . . . *stacking*, I believe it's called?'

'I don't know what you're talking about.'

'Pity,' I told him. 'Nowadays it can be used in mitigation. I don't know if it makes any difference, but it gives the defence something to pontificate about. We're not letting you go, Darryl. I want you charged with the rape of Janet Saunders and in front of a magistrate tomorrow morning. We'll be opposing bail.'

'This is proposterous,' Mr Turner protested. 'On what grounds can you do this? My client has made it clear what happened. At the previous interview he told you that Mrs Saunders became hostile when he tried to leave and demanded money. She has a reputation in her locality for being a woman of some sexual experience.'

'*Some sexual experience!*' I gasped. 'And what about *his* reputation?'

'If my client has any sort of reputation it is inadmissible as evidence.'

'But hers isn't?'

'No.'

'Does that strike you as fair?'

'It's the law. Fairness doesn't enter into it.'

'Mrs Saunders says Buxton raped her, at knifepoint.'

'And he says she consented. I suggest you release my client and pass the file to the CPS for their consideration. I can safely say that they will not entertain it. The words "wasting time" might appear somewhere on their response.'

I was in my shirt sleeves, my jacket draped over the back of the chair. I half turned and retrieved the Wetherton package from a pocket. 'This,' I said, unwrapping the contents and holding it towards Buxton, 'is a digital thermometer. You switch it on . . . here, and press this end against whatever it is you want to know the temperature of, like this.' I held the probe end against the palm of my hand and offered the instrument so his solicitor could read the liquid crystal display. 'Could you please tell us what that says, Mr Turner?' I asked.

'No,' he said. 'I don't wish to take part in this charade.'

'Read that, DC Sparkington,' I said.

'Thirty-six point . . . something,' he replied.

'That's degrees centigrade,' I told them, 'which is blood heat, near enough. That's how you check the thermometer. I am now going to take a reading from the wall where Darryl leaned a few minutes ago. Would all those present like to come and check this?'

Sparky stood and moved round the table but Turner and Buxton remained glued to their seats. I nodded to Martin to join us. I pressed the probe against the tiles and waited for the numbers to settle.

'What does it say?' I asked.

'Twenty-one degrees,' Martin informed us.

'Yep, twenty-one,' Sparky confirmed.

We resumed our places. 'You used to be a bailiff, a repo man, I believe,' I said to Darryl. He didn't answer.

'You have to be able to handle yourself in a job like that,' I continued. 'Fancy yourself as a tough guy, do you?'

He glowered at me, his top lip distorted and his forehead shiny with sweat, but stayed silent.

'Perhaps you just don't like the cold,' I suggested.

'You're a hothouse plant. I'm not. There's nothing I like better than to be out on the moors on a frosty morning with the wind whistling round my ears and the air like champagne.' I did an exaggerated breathe-in and exhaled with a sigh. 'Yesterday morning . . . I visited Mrs Saunders' home. I went upstairs to the bathroom, where you claim intercourse took place. I removed my shirt and stood in the bath, right where you say you did. I leaned back against the wall. Your actual words, a few seconds ago, were: "It's fucking freezing." You were dead right. Her bathroom wall was fucking freezing. It was cold enough to freeze the balls off a . . . pawnbroker's sign. I couldn't lean on it for two seconds. So, I took out my faithful friend here.' I tapped the thermometer. 'And measured the temperature. It was eighteen degrees, a full three degrees centigrade lower than the wall in this room. Your story is a pack of lies, Buxton. Sex in the shower is one of your pathetic fantasies. In the North of England, in winter, in an unheated bathroom, it's strictly for masochists.'

'Inspector,' his brief, Turner, began, raising a conciliatory hand. 'All this is rather far-fetched. What happens in the clinical conditions of this interview room cannot be compared with the high passions that were running that night. The cocktail of lust and alcohol that both parties were under the influence of would surely overcome any chilliness of the tiles in her bathroom, don't you agree?'

'Mrs Saunders doesn't drink,' I said. 'But your client was no doubt under the influence of alcohol, and probably anabolic steroids, too. A simple drugs test will show that. Meanwhile, we'll let a jury decide about the anaesthetising effects of "high passion", as you called it. I want him in court, and when he is, we'll play it clever, like you usually do. For a start, there'll be women on the jury. We'll make sure that there's an overnight adjournment between them hearing our evidence and retiring. And do you know what they'll do, every one of them, when they are at home or in the hotel? They'll all stand in their showers, stark naked, and lean on the wall. Just like you will, tonight, Mr Turner. And that's when they'll make their decisions.' I leaned back, flicking my notebook closed.

Sparky said: 'And then there's all the other women you've attacked. We'll call them, just for indcntification purposes, of course. "Is this the man you knew as Darryl Burton?" "And when did you last see him?" That sort of thing.'

'You can't do that!' Turner protested. 'It's inadmissible.'

'We'll get round it,' I told him. 'When they learn that your client is probably going away for a long time one or two might be willing for CPS to re-start their cases. Young Samantha Teague might press charges. The phrase I'm wanting to hear from the judge's lips is the one about being put away until no longer a danger to women.' I turned to Sparky. 'How old do you reckon that is, Dave? About seventy?'

'God, older than that, I hope,' he replied. 'Charlie Chaplin put their Oona in the family way when he was about ninety.'

'A long time, anyway.'

'You can say that again.'

'Anything else?' I asked.

Sparky shook his head.

'Mr Turner?'

'Not at the moment, except to confirm that we will be strenuously denying these charges and protesting about the way the evidence of this morning was obtained.'

'Buxton?'

He glared at me, one corner of his mouth pulling in uncontrolled twitches towards his ear. 'I'll get you, you bastard!' he hissed. Turner slapped a hand on his arm to silence him.

'We'll take that as a negative,' I said. 'Interview terminated at . . . twelve forty-seven p.m.'

Chapter Thirteen

We took him to the charge office, read him his rights under PACE and showed him the menu. Our natty paper suits do not come in a full range of sizes, and the one that fitted his shoulders was rather long for him. The crutch was level with his knees and the legs were concertinaed around his ankles. All part of the dehumanising process, of course, but sometimes it doesn't bother me a bit. As soon as he was settled in we left.

As we walked out of the headquarters Sparky thumped me on the upper arm and said: 'Well done, Squire! Bloody brilliant.'

I rubbed my arm. 'You don't know your own strength,' I complained. As we'd missed the Saturday morning remand court we'd have to keep Buxton until he could appear before a magistrate on Monday, and not 'tomorrow', as I'd told him during the interview. It would give him another twenty-four hours to reflect on his misspent youth. I drove us both back to Heckley nick.

'I'll sort out the remand file in the morning, if you don't mind,' Sparky said as he unbuckled his seat belt. 'I promised to take Daniel to the match, if we got done early enough.'

'I've nothing on,' I told him. 'I'll pop upstairs and do it myself. It won't take long.'

'Come on, then. We'll both do it.'

'What about the match?'

'We've plenty of time. Why don't you come with us? I could ring Shirley, arrange for an extra place for dinner.'

I considered his offer for two milliseconds, nodded and said: 'Mmm, thanks, that'll be nice. Let's go upstairs and sign Mr Buxton's card for him, then.'

There was a big white envelope on my desk, where I couldn't miss it. Inside I found a re-sealable plastic bag containing a catalogue for Magic Plastics – 'filled with all those essential things you've been waiting for someone to invent.' I put it where I wouldn't forget it and turned my mind back to Darryl Buxton.

You can work fast when the office is empty and free from distractions. Dave typed and I dictated. The Crown Prosecution Service are interested in two main areas: evidence and public interest. The former didn't look too convincing in print, so we laid it on thick about the risk to the female population.

'That should do it,' Sparky said, tapping in the final full stop. Now it was up to the CPS prosecutor.

I asked him to ring Maggie before we left, so she could inform Mrs Saunders of the latest developments, and then we drove in convoy to Dave's house.

As we arrived, I was surprised to see young Sophie with a team scarf around her neck. She'd changed her mind and decided to come along at the very last moment. Thanks, Sophie, I thought.

We won, four-nil, and celebrated with pints of shandy in the pub outside the ground. Dinner had been postponed until after the match, and Shirley had put in an extra Yorkshire pudding for me. Whisper it softly, but her puddings are better than my mum's were.

Dave washed, I dried and Shirley put them away. 'Are you taking Annabelle anywhere tonight?' Shirley asked.

'Er, no,' I replied, passing a dish back to Dave with a terse, 'rejected.'

He examined it and gave it another scrub. 'Tell you what,' he said, 'why don't we all go to the Eagle tomorrow, for lunch? We'll get in if I give them a ring.'

'That's a good idea,' Shirley agreed. 'Will you and Annabelle be able to make it?'

'No,' I mumbled. 'We've, er, something on.'

'Oh, what a pity,' she said. 'Are you going anywhere special?'

'Yes.'

There was an uncomfortable silence. I started on the cutlery as Sparky emptied the bowl and reached for the first pan.

'The kids ought to be doing this,' Shirley said.

'We're too soft with them,' Sparky concurred.

'Leave them alone,' I protested. As their uncle-by-proxy, it's my role to defend them.

'Now I know why Dave's hands are always so soft,' I told her.

'No, his head's just as soft,' she responded. 'Annabelle loaned Sophie some books,' she went on. 'I'll find them, so you can return them, otherwise they'll be forgotten.'

'It doesn't matter,' I replied.

'Oops, how did that escape,' Sparky said, finding a plate in the bottom of the bowl and passing it to me.

'Of course it matters,' Shirley continued. 'They look expensive. And tell Annabelle: "Thank you," when you see her. As well as having a crush on you, I think poor Sophie has one on Annabelle, too. I'm not sure which I disapprove of more.'

One fib you can get away with. Any more and you start to build a house of cards. That's how we catch crooks.

'I won't be seeing her,' I replied. Before they could comment I went on: 'Truth is, Annabelle and I have finished. We're not together any more.' I carefully dried the Denby plate I was holding and offered it to Shirley. She didn't attempt to take it.

Dave's hands stopped swishing about in the sink. 'Sorry, Chas,' he mumbled. 'I didn't know.'

'Finished?' Shirley repeated, eyes wide. 'Finished? You and Annabelle?'

'Yep,' I managed to say, biting my lip.

'Oh, Charlie,' Shirley began. 'I'm so sorry. I thought . . . I thought you and Annabelle were . . . I don't know, you just seemed so right together. You must be devastated.'

'I'll get over it,' I said, gently placing the plate on the work surface before I dropped it. More lies.

Shirley put her hand on my arm. 'I'm sorry, love,' she said. 'I . . . I'm sorry. Are you sure it's, you know, final?'

'Yep,' I said.

'Oh, I am sorry. Well, you know where to come if you want to talk about it.'

Sunday I dedicated to housework. My parents had lived in this house, but I'd be in big trouble if they could see it now. Decorating it myself was out of the question. I'd ask around, see if I could find anyone who did a good job, cheap. I vandalised all the cobwebs, consigned various books and ornaments to a box destined for Help the Aged and gave the place a thorough hoovering. It was a big improvement. I found several items that belonged to Annabelle: a bottle of Mitsouko; her hiking socks; toothbrush; that sort of thing. I dropped them in a carrier bag and went out to the dustbin, then changed my mind and stuffed it to the back of a cupboard.

Later, I showered and had a can of lager. The Magic Plastic catalogue was on the coffee table, with the squash club membership list, alongside my favourite chair. I made a mug of tea, found my place near the middle of the list, and resumed plodding through the names.

My finger was on Davis, James Ashley, when I realised that my brain hadn't registered a thing for God knows how long. I folded the pages, put them to one side and went to bed. I never looked at the Magic Plastic catalogue.

I'd run out of shirts again. Ever since Mrs Tait returned from her daughter's I'd been struggling to re-establish my routine for taking them round to her for ironing. I found the denim Wrangler with the mother-of-pearl studs and pulled that on. No doubt Mr Wood would make his usual comment about me looking like Jesse James, so I wriggled into the tightest pair of jeans I could find, just to irk him. I can be a real mean hombre, at times. One day, I promised myself, I'd buy a pair of snakeskin boots with high heels and silver buckles. As I was leaving home I saw the theatre tickets behind the clock and put them in my inside pocket. Nigel might have a use for them.

The good news that Monday morning was that Darryl Buxton appeared before a stipendiary magistrate, charged with rape. It's an indictable offence, which means it has to be dealt with by the crown court – the appearance in front of the mags is just to set the wheels in motion. Mr Turner asked for bail but wasted his time. Darryl was remanded in custody and the trial bounced straight to the higher court. Round one to us.

Maggie followed me into my office and told me that she'd seen Mrs Saunders over the weekend and put her straight.

'Fair enough,' I said. 'And now you can tell her that Buxton is in custody and start preparing her to give evidence. It'll be a worrying few months for her. Do you think she's up to it?'

'Would it matter much if she cracked up on the stand?' Maggie asked, by way of an answer.

'No, I don't suppose it would. But I don't send my witnesses out with the intention that they'll go to pieces. I'm quite content for them to answer questions in a controlled manner.'

Maggie looked contrite. 'Sorry, Boss,' she replied. 'I think maybe I'm cracking up myself, lately.'

'It's overwork, Maggie,' I said, adding: 'That catalogue came from Magic Plastic, by the way. Thanks for that.'

'Oh, good. What do you want it for?'

I pulled a face and sighed. 'I don't know,' I admitted. 'Something's gnawing away inside my head, but I can't put my finger on it.'

'The good old intuition.'

'I don't believe in intuition.'

'You say you don't.'

'Maybe. After you've seen Mrs Saunders I'd like you to go through the list of Darryl's other victims. Interview them all, see who might take the stand.'

'Great,' she replied.

'I want you to mother this one, Maggie,' I continued. 'Fax the other divisions; ask them about unsolved rapes and murders, particularly indoor ones and any that have produced DNA samples. Tell them we have a possible candidate. If he's as much as wagged his willy in Stanley Park I want him for it.'

'Super,' she replied, beaming.

'And tomorrow,' I told her, with my wickedest smile, 'you can come back on the doctor's case.'

Nigel was jumping round the office like a squirrel in a wheel. One second he was on the computer, then the phone, and next he'd be maniacally thumbing through the telephone directory.

'Not yet,' he hissed at me, covering the mouthpiece, when I asked him what he was on with.

At half past five, just as I was planning to leave, he burst into my office with a 'Ta Da!' and a two-fisted salute. 'Barraclough!' he announced. 'I've got him!'

I placed the cap on my pen, closed the pad I was using, pushed it away and leaned back against the wall. 'What's he done?' I asked.

'I'll tell you what he hasn't done,' Nigel declared. 'He hasn't passed any medical exams. He's a fraud.'

'Really!' I exclaimed, dropping my chair on to all four legs. 'You mean . . . he's posing as a doctor?'

'Well, not quite. I've just been talking to – wait for it – the San Bernadino Faculty of Transcendental Philosophy and Tantric Learning, in California.'

'It had to be,' I interjected.

'Right. And that's where his doctorate is from. I've run up a heck of a phone bill, by the way.'

'Don't worry, we'll deduct it from your salary. Maybe that's what he does at the clinic, this transcendental stuff. He doesn't practise medicine, does he?'

'He's called the medical director. He flunked his first year medical exams at Leeds University and dropped out. It'd be interesting to know what he put on his CV and application form, don't you think? Maybe Dr Jordan rumbled him.'

'And was killed for his trouble? It's worth knowing Nigel, well done, but I'm not sure if it's a good enough motive. And don't forget he has a cast-iron alibi. Let him know you know, and use it to prise information about the abortions out of him. That's our best avenue, I think.'

'I'm sure you're right, but I can't wait to see his face.'

None of the pubs do meals so early in the evening, so I went to the cafe over the road and had tomato soup, gammon and pineapple, blackberry crumble with custard and a pot of tea. I took my time over it, preferring watching real people go about their mundane activities to watching second-rate television at home. I was about to ask for a refill when the old gimmer at the next table lit his pipe, so I decided to leave. As I reached inside my jacket for my wallet I found the tickets for *Romeo and Juliet*.

I walked back into the station yard, where my car was, and stood there, indecisive, wondering what to do. I'd already been accused once of approaching a witness with a view to obtaining sexual favours; would I be tempting fate?

The performance started in fifty minutes. Sod 'em all, I thought, and marched back into the nick.

Her number was in my book and she answered her phone almost straight away. 'Is that Mrs Henderson?' I asked.

'Yes, it is. Who's speaking?'

'Hello, Cicely. It's Detective Inspector Charlie Priest, from Heckley CID. Do you remember me? I met you at the clinic.'

'Hello, Inspector,' she replied, warmly. 'Of course I remember you. How can I help?'

'It's Charlie,' I told her. 'Please, call me Charlie. Actually, it's not business, it's a personal call . . .'

I told her that I'd been left with these tickets for Romeo and Juliet and forgotten all about them until just now and I was still in my working clothes because I hadn't had time to go home and change and hoped she wouldn't get the wrong impression but I'd intended giving her a ring when this whole thing was over and I realised it was very short notice and if she'd prefer to go with a friend she could have the tickets but it was a shame to waste them because it was a good production and . . .

She said she'd love to accompany me, and could be ready in twenty minutes.

I found the emergency razor and toothbrush in my bottom drawer and made a hasty toilet in the office loos. Somebody had been there before me and left a bottle of aftershave, so I used it liberally, including large dollops in my shoes, like Jon Voight in *Midnight Cowboy*. I tipped myself a wink in the mirror and left.

Cicely looked good. Fantastic, in fact. Not my type, with her heavy make-up, tight-back hair and impossible heels, but I'd have looked twice. Any man would. I imagined her doing the flamenco by the light of a campfire, stomping her sturdy legs, arms aloft, as she danced passionate tales of old Iberia.

It was drizzling, so I dropped her off at the Playhouse entrance and went to park the car. I dashed into the foyer as they gave the two-minute warning and brushed my wet hair out of my eyes. 'You look stunning,' I told her. She'd taken her coat off and was wearing a blue suit, with a black polo-necked blouse and black tights. Her hair wasn't black all the way to the roots, but nature sometimes needs a little help.

'You don't look bad yourself,' she replied, with a smile that I took to have a trace of disapproval in it. I imagined she liked her men in suits.

'Yeah, well,' I mumbled, 'I normally do make a bit of an effort . . .'

'You look fine,' she said, 'and I wasn't looking forward to another night in with the cats. I'm glad you rang.'

'How many cats do you have?' I asked.

'Just two. Sasha and Mustapha.'

'They sound Persian.'

'That's right.'

Ah well, at least they weren't Omar and Khayyam.

It was a good production. It must have been on that year's national curriculum, for several school parties were present. The kids were more familiar with the story and led the laughter at the bawdy bits, which created a happy atmosphere. Cicely had a gin and tonic – I made it a large one – during the interval, and asked me how the enquiry was progressing.

'Not very well,' I admitted. 'We're nearly at a standstill with it. In fact, we're wondering if it might have been a case of mistaken identity.'

'You mean, they murdered the wrong man?'

'It's possible. How do you like working at the clinic?' I was supposed to be asking the questions.

'Oh, it's all right,' she replied.

'Only all right?'

'It's fine. Conditions are good, pay is reasonable and they treat us well.'

'Cheap cosmetic surgery, if and when the time arises?'

'Ha! They're not that generous.'

'What about Dr Barraclough,' I asked. 'How do you get on with him?'

'I hope you didn't bring me out just to grill me about the clinic, Charlie,' she admonished.

'Sorry,' I said. 'Force of habit. No more shop talk. What do you think of the play?'

'He's not a real doctor, you know?'

'Isn't he? Which one's the doctor?'

'I mean Barraclough,' she giggled.

'Oh, that doctor. What is he, then?'

'He thinks nobody knows, but we all do. He's a doctor of divinity, or something, from one of those American universities that sells qualifications. He's never passed any exams.'

Nigel was going to love this. 'Well, well,' I said. 'It looks as if we'd better have another word with Dr B.'

It went downhill in the second half. The kids grew restless and I couldn't understand why the friar and the nurse were taking such apalling risks just to get two spoilt brats into bed with each other. I nodded off a couple of times, towards the end.

'It was a bit like *West Side Story*,' Cicely observed as we filed towards the exit.

'Yes, it was,' I agreed, 'but without the tunes,' and the woman in front turned to give me the look she usually reserves for when she's cleaning up dog sick.

I offered to fetch the car but Cicely said she'd be OK. The rain had slowed to a drizzle and after years of practice she'd mastered the technique of trotting in five-inch stilettos.

'Brrr!' I said, spinning the engine and pushing the heater controls to maximum.

She fastened her seat belt and looked across at me. 'Thank you for a lovely evening,' she said. 'I've enjoyed it.'

'Shakespeare's not to everybody's taste,' I replied. 'Personally, I prefer Ayckbourn.' I smiled at her and she smiled back. There and then, in that light, she looked stunning. In the next fifteen minutes I had to decide if I wanted to see her again. I wasn't sure.

I didn't stop the engine outside her house. It seemed presumptuous to do so. She opened her door and stretched one leg out on to the pavement.

'Thanks again, Charlie,' she said. 'It's been lovely.'

'My pleasure,' I replied, the decision made.

'If . . .' she began.

'Mmm?'

'If I invite you in for a coffee . . . you won't get the wrong idea, will you?'

'You mean . . .' I hesitated. 'You mean . . . you're not really inviting me in for a coffee?'

'No!' she protested, laughing. 'I mean I am inviting you in for a coffee. And that's all. Nothing else.'

'Thank you,' I said. 'I'd love a coffee.'

She hung her coat on a stand in the hallway and led me into her kitchen. It wasn't quite as de luxe as I'd expected, but not bad. Somehow, I'd gained the impression that she was well off, probably because I associated her with the no-expenses-spared surroundings of the clinic. Two bowls of cat food stood on a plastic mat on the floor, but the moggies were absent.

'Can I leave you in charge?' she asked, retrieving milk, sugar, mugs and and all the other stuff required for the seemingly simple task of making two cups of coffee.

'No problem,' I replied.

'Look, Charlie,' she said. 'I want to get out of these clothes and into something more comfortable. You won't get the wrong message, will you? I dress smartly all day and like to be more relaxed when I come home.'

'I know the feeling,' I replied, holding my arms wide

and looking down at my own clothes. 'I promise to behave myself and not get any ideas.'

'Good. And that's the kettle,' were her last words, as she tapped it before disappearing upstairs.

It was one of those kettles that lifts off its base, so you're not dragging the flex across to the sink. I filled it right to the max mark and pushed the button.

I put the mugs on saucers and placed them on opposite sides of the table, with a vase of narcissi that I found on the windowsill as a centrepiece. Cicely had produced a box of biscuits, so I arranged a selection on a plate in a geometric pattern. Might as well demonstrate that I was reasonably civilised. The kettle wasn't making any noises. Cicely returned just as I realised what the problem was.

'Switched off at the plug,' I explained. 'Coffee will be delayed by a few minutes.'

She was wearing a silk kimono, high at the neck, in an ivory colour and heavily emboidered. I was about to pay her a compliment, then decided not to. It might be misconstrued.

'Do you like Lionel Ritchie?' she asked, walking into the adjoining room, where her music lived.

'Some,' I answered, untruthfully, watching her go. She was still wearing her tights, which had seams up the back. I hadn't noticed that before, and her stilettos looked even higher than I remembered them.

A rich voice flooded the room, singing a song I didn't know. Cicely walked back in and put her arms around my neck.

'Let's dance,' she said, 'while the kettle boils.'

We danced, round in circles, in the middle of her kitchen, her face resting on my chest, my fingers caressing her neck.

The song ended. Cicely took my hand and led me into the other room. The gas fire was hissing and the wall lights were low. As we kissed, her hands fumbled between us, undoing the belt of the kimono. She wriggled it off her shoulders and it fell to the ground. It looked as if we were taking a raincheck on the coffee. I held her at arm's length and deliberated on what I saw, taking my time, savouring the experience. She was wearing the kind of underwear you see in the adverts near the back of the tabloids, catalogue sent under plain cover. Her bra was more uplifting than Elgar's 'Nimrod', and if her briefs had been cut any higher she'd have been able to put her arms out through the leg holes.

'Do you like me?' she whispered, suddenly vulnerable.

I didn't answer with words. Words can express everything, which makes them meaningless. This wasn't what I wanted, but going now would hurt her more than if I stayed. Sometimes, I'm just a victim of circumstances. Our tongues tangled as my hands traced the silhouette of her body, following the valleys and making forays into the mountains and forests. She unpopped the top stud of my shirt. Then the next and the next: pop, pop, pop. There's no fumbling with a Wrangler.

Button.

Zip.

She looked down, then up into my face, eyes wide with approval, and, I like to think, just a hint of apprehension.

My hands came to rest on her hips and I gently pressed downwards. We sank to the floor, our legs folding and buckling beneath us, like two disused power station chimneys, after they fire the dynamite.

In the kitchen, the kettle came to the boil and switched itself off.

* * *

It had gone. It wasn't on the side of the sink, where I'd left it, or in the bin for the paper towels. Damn! A toilet flushed and young Caton emerged from a cubicle.

'Lost something, Boss?' he asked, turning a tap on and squirting monkey spunk on to his hands from the dispenser.

'Aftershave,' I replied. 'It was here last night.'

'Can't say I've noticed any. What brand was it?'

'That's what I need to know.'

'Why? Are you thinking of buying some?'

'No. I want shares in the company.'

Mr Wood was at one of his meetings, giving funny handshakes to people he didn't like while standing on one leg saying that yes, it was cold, but it would get colder before it got warmer. In other words, I was in charge. In other words, I had to stay in the office, if possible.

He started sending me to the meetings, but I misread the signals and then invented a few of my own. I think someone must have had a word with him, because he stopped sending me, which is what I'd intended all along. When all the troops were deployed I trudged up to his office to see what the postman had brought him.

I dealt with all of it except a request for a donation to the Chief Constable's retirement present. I decided he might like to handle that one personally. When I'd finished I pushed his chair back, put my feet on the desk and pondered on what might have been.

I'd fucked it up, from beginning to end, home and away, no doubt about it. The job wasn't the same. A few of us, old-timers, stuck together, bonded by ancient loyalties, but nobody would help you out of a jam any more. They couldn't – one step out of line and you were down the road. My offer of retirement was still open, but what would

I do, at home all day, on my own? That was the crunch. On my own.

I'd taken the membership list and the Magic Plastic catalogue up with me, hoping that I'd have a chance to look at them. I reached for the catalogue and flicked through it, wondering where I'd find the mini-bin.

And that made me think about Janet Saunders. What would I do, I wondered, if Mrs Henderson walked into the front office and said that I'd raped her? We'd been to the theatre, as arranged; she'd invited me in for a coffee, all good and proper; and I'd turned nasty and raped her at knifepoint. How could I defend myself against the allegation?

I couldn't. But she wouldn't, would she? Truth was, I hadn't really wanted a date with her. I wasn't complaining, far from it, but Cicely and what she had to offer wasn't what I was looking for. The implication from that, of course, was that I was looking for something.

She'd be at work. I pulled the phone towards me and dialled the number for the White Rose Clinic. Magic Plastic, I noticed, did a device for catching spiders in the bath. Just what I've always wanted.

'Good morning, White Rose Clinic,' a precise voice said in my ear.

'Good morning,' I repeated, holding the phone with a hunched shoulder as I turned the page. 'My name is Detective Inspector Charlie Priest, of Heckley CID. I believe you have a Mrs Cicely Henderson at the clinic.'

There was a pause, before she said: 'This is Mrs Henderson speaking. How can I help you, Inspector.' I could feel the smile in her voice.

'Hello, Cicely,' I said. 'How are you?'

'I'm fine. And you?'

'Excellent. It's amazing what a good night's sleep can do. I just thought I'd thank you for coming to the theatre with me. It was a very enjoyable evening.'

'Yes, I thought so, too. Thank you for the invitation. Shakespeare has taken on a whole new meaning for me.'

'He's full of surprises, isn't he? I was thinking that maybe we could go out for a meal, say, Thursday or Friday. What kind of food do you like?'

'I thought you were busy.'

'I can get away, if I know in advance.'

'I'd rather not, if you don't mind, Charlie.'

'Oh. Some other time, then? Or just out for a drink, over the weekend?'

'Er, no, but thanks all the same.'

'You mean . . . you'd rather not see me again? Is that what you're saying?' I catch on fast, these days.

'No. It was very pleasant, Charlie, and I enjoyed myself, but I'd rather leave it at that, if you don't mind. I don't want any involvement.'

'Fair enough,' I said, 'but I might see you if I have to call in the clinic, sometime.'

'That's all right. We can still be friends. It's not you, Charlie, it's me. You were . . . well, you were . . . magnificent, believe me. I don't want you to think otherwise. It's just that . . . I'd wondered what I'd been missing, all these years. I decided that it was very nice, but not worth all the complications. Does that make sense?'

Bloody good sense, I told her; and damned sporting of her, too. We said polite goodbyes and rang off. Perfect, I thought, replacing the handset. I couldn't have managed it better if I'd written the script. No tears, no regrets, no recriminations, no guilty consciences.

Except. Except . . . It would have been nice to have had a say in it.

The mini-bin was on page twenty-two and cost £6.99. Janet Saunders was right: you could buy a jar of coffee for that and use the jar. There was a nearly empty one on the table where Gilbert makes his brews. I jumped up and tipped the dregs into his new jar, which I had to open, and dropped the pile of drying teabags into the now-empty jar. I stuck a label on it reading: 'used teabags'. There's a penny on the community charge for me to make decisions like that.

I sat down again and resumed my perusing. The only thing they didn't make was a device for recycling useless devices, but it was only a matter of time. I turned the final page and read the ordering instructions on the back. I felt uneasy. There was a space for the agent to place his – or her – name and address. Mine had come straight from head office, so it was blank. I tossed it on to Gilbert's shiny desk top, drummed my fingers several times, and reached for the squash club membership list.

I'd started at the end and worked forward, but couldn't remember where I'd reached. The best thing, I decided, was to start again, at the beginning this time, and stop when I knew I'd gone far enough. Abbott, John, I read. Never heard of him. Next . . .

Five minutes later Gilbert's chair was neatly in place with my feet under the desk and firmly on the floor as I thumped numbers into the phone.

'Heckley Squash Club,' said a male voice.

'It's DI Charlie Priest,' I told him. 'I got the membership list. Thank you. This girl that the doctor played the mixed doubles with – I don't suppose you've remembered her name?'

'Oh, hello, Mr Priest. No, sorry. I've tried to remember, but my mind's a blank.'

'Never mind. You also told me that they played the first round of the mixed doubles competition with one of your regular members and his wife. Have you asked them if they can remember her name?'

'No, sorry,' he replied. 'Paul and Tricia, we're talking about. They go away for Christmas, every year. Have a place in Spain. I'd forgotten. They're back now, I'm told, so I'll ask Paul when I see him. He'll be in tomorrow, probably.'

'Don't bother. Just tell me his second name and I'll ring him.'

'It's Duffy. Paul Duffy.'

I found him on the list and rang his number. I was rewarded with a long buzzing noise – his phone had been cut off. I rang the control room on the internal and asked them to do a person check on Paul Duffy. He was on our files, with a conviction for receiving, dated 1987, and was currently banned from driving for being OPL. Tricia Duffy had been cautioned for perjury, again in 1987. The loving wife sticking up for her bent hubby. I decided that the personal approach was called for.

'You're in charge,' I told the sergeant at the front desk. 'Give me a ring if you need me.'

'Where are you going?'

'Door to door.'

'It's hissing down outside,' he replied.

'Oh. Can I borrow a coat, then?'

He found a waterproof jacket for me and handed it across the counter. I ran to the car with it over my head.

It was a smart house, built from local stone on a hillside. The drive was steep and the gates were closed, so I had to park on the road. I pulled the coat on and slogged up the drive, feet squelching. Mrs Duffy answered the door.

She was average height and comfortably plump. She wore a lilac jogging suit adorned with sequins, and several gold chains, worn on top to remind her of what she'd achieved every time she looked in a mirror. Nouveau riche or market trader; I wasn't sure which. She had the best tan I'd seen in ages. I showed her my ID and she tilted her head back as she inspected it, looking through the bottoms of her spectacles, where the tint was lighter. It said Police on the breast of the waterproof I was wearing, just to confirm my origins.

'Is Mr Duffy in?' I asked, after introducing myself.

The man himself appeared almost immediately, as if he'd been waiting. Maybe they saw me approach.

'I'm Duffy,' he said. 'How can I help you?' He was big and bronzed, with a huge gut and a respectable handlebar moustache.

'I'd like to ask you a few questions,' I replied, 'about Heckley Squash Club. Do you think I could come in?'

'Of course. Come in, Inspector,' he gushed. And why not? He'd nothing to worry about. He'd been out of the country for a month, hadn't he? 'Let's have you out of this stinking weather. Bloody rotten climate. Take your coat off.'

'Your phone doesn't work,' I explained as Tricia Duffy took the dripping coat from me. A large bag of Ping golf clubs stood in the hallway.

'Bloody thing's cut off!' he exclaimed. 'I don't know what this country's coming to. We've been to our place in Portugal for a month and that's what you find when you come home. Going to the dogs, we are. Saturday – at the airport – every face you saw was one of our Commonwealth cousins. Why do we let them in, eh? Bloody taking over, that's what they're doing. I'm telling you, Inspector, as soon as I sort out a few things I'm moving over there, for good. You can keep this place. Have a seat.'

And then you'll be an immigrant, too, just like them, I thought.

They hadn't heard about the doctor's murder, and were suitably saddened. 'How well did you know him?' I asked.

Duffy shrugged. 'Reasonably well, I'd say, but just to have a drink and a laugh, in the bar. He was a good sort. Everybody liked him.' He considered this last remark, then added: 'Well, somebody didn't.'

'Any thoughts who?'

'No. No idea.' He pondered for a few seconds. 'I know it's the done thing to say kind words about somebody after they've died,' he continued, 'but I'm not bullshitting when I say that the doc was one of the nicest people I've ever met. Not that I knew him all that well, of course, but I always thought of him as a gentleman. A good old old-fashioned gentleman.'

'You're not the first to tell us that. If you don't mind me saying,' I went on, 'you look rather, er, large for a squash player.'

He laughed and patted his belly. 'They can't get round me. But you're right. I only do it for some exercise. Golf's my game.'

'And you, Mrs Duffy?'

He answered for her. 'Golf's her game, too. Isn't it, darling? She's the ladies' captain next year.'

'Really. Well done. And how did you find the doctor, Mrs Duffy?'

She smiled at the memory of him. 'He was dishy,' she said. 'I only met him twice, but he could have taken my pulse, anytime.'

'I'll tell you what he was like,' Duffy informed us, emphasising his point with a raised hand. 'This was bloody typical of the man. When we played him and that girl. You remember, don't you, Trish?'

'I'll say. I completely went to pieces.'

'This girl,' Duffy explained. 'Her partner didn't show up. She was upset. The doc started chatting to her, ended up partnering her, against us. He'd no need to do that, had he? Bloody beat us, too.'

'That's what I've come to ask you about,' I admitted. 'The manager told me about it. I don't suppose you remember the girl's name, do you?'

They both looked blank. She shook her head. He said: 'No. Sorry. Ought to do, but it won't come.'

'It was . . . just . . . an ordinary name,' she said.

'Did you have a drink with them in the bar, afterwards?'

'Yes, we did.'

'And how did he and the girl get on?'

'Very chatty,' Mrs Duffy replied. 'Very chatty. But when I was alone with her – we went to the ladies' – I said: "You've done all right there," and she said he wasn't her type. I expected her to be over the moon, I would have been, but her feet were well and truly on the ground.'

'Would you have said that she was his type?'

'No, not at all. She was a plain Jane, and he was going out with her off the telly. Do you know about her?'

'Yes, I've talked to her.' I suppressed the smile that the memory generated. 'I assume the doc and the girl would have to meet again to play in the next round?' I said.

'That's right,' Mr Duffy confirmed. 'They swapped phone numbers, and he told her what times he was most likely to be available. It was awkward for him, being a doctor and on call.'

'I know the feeling,' I said.

'We went to watch them,' he went on. 'Bugger me if they didn't win again. Got knocked out in the semi-final, though. She was thrilled to bits, I remember. Got a little trophy. I think that meant more to her than going out with the doctor would have done.' He turned to his wife. 'You missed that, didn't you, darling?'

'Yes,' she confirmed. 'I had one of my heads.'

I nodded sympathetically. It must be terrible to have heads. 'But you still can't remember the girl's name?'

They couldn't.

'OK,' I said, 'in that case, we'll have a little identity parade.' They looked worried. I'd taken the membership list with me. I unfolded it on the arm of the easy chair and pulled my notebook from my inside pocket. 'I'm going to write four names down,' I explained, 'from the list of members. If you recognise her name amongst them, I want you to point to it. Understand?'

I found three women's names and added them to the one I was interested in. 'Just point, if you think you see her name,' I told Duffy.

'That's her,' he said, without hesitation, placing a fingertip on the second name down. 'At least, it was something like that.'

'Thanks. Now you, Mrs Duffy.'

I moved across to her and a wave of perfume hit the back of my throat like a karate chop. I swallowed and blinked away the tears.

'That's her,' she said, touching the page with the tip of

a nail extension that gave me a pain in my teeth. Writing on blackboards would have been hell for her.

'Are you sure?' I asked. She'd picked the same name as her spouse.

'Yes, definitely. That's her. Susan Crabtree.'

Chapter Fourteen

The door closed behind me and I could almost hear the collective sigh they emitted on the other side of it. No doubt they'd celebrate my leaving with a little snifter or two. I pulled the coat together across my throat and walked down the drive towards the car. The rain was falling straight out of the sky, too morose to slant either one way or the other.

I could have strode away from it. I could have written that letter of resignation, saying I wanted out, and that would have been that. In two weeks, I'd be a civilian. But I didn't. I had a job to do. I didn't make the rules – that's what we pay politicians for. I just applied them.

And every guard in every concentration camp used exactly the same excuse.

I drove to the Canalside Mews, home of the late doctor and also of Darryl Buxton. Eight flats, two definitely empty, a weekday. I'd be lucky to find anyone in.

I got an answer first try. 'My name's Detective Inspector Priest,' I shouted into the hole in the wall. 'I'm making enquiries about the late doctor who lived upstairs. Do you mind if I come in?'

'I'll open the door for you,' the woman replied, as the catch buzzed.

I pushed it open and walked across the lobby to flat

number two. My luck held. Two others were in and answered my questions, not that I had many. 'We're investigating various callers or salesmen who've been seen in the area,' I told them all. 'Have you ever had anyone leave a catalogue for a company called Magic Plastic?'

Heads were shaken. Noses were looked down. Magic Plastic salesmen didn't call at prestigious developments such as Canalside Mews. Perhaps, I thought, they knew that the residents weren't as generous with their money or as sympathetic as the likes of Janet Saunders. The young man in number five wearing a cookery apron offered me a coffee and the lady in number seven showed me her husband's tropical fish.

'Your sergeant was ever so interested in them,' she said.

'I know. He told me all about them.'

I saw a lot of gold velvet and tassels and G-Plan furniture and was definitely unimpressed. I was left with the big question: if the Magic Plastic salesman had never called at Canalside Mews, where did the doctor obtain the mini-bin I'd seen in his apartment? I climbed into the car and wiped the rain off my neck. I couldn't put it off any longer. I started the engine and drove across town to where Susan Crabtree's parents lived.

It was a street of post-war semis with bay windows, similar to the one I lived in. The type of house that middle-class people aspired to, in those far-off days before inflation set the market alight and home-owning became a hedge against it and not a millstone around the pay packet. These had become seedy a few years ago, then regained respectability as the double-glazing salesmen moved in to give the place a face-lift. Now the cycle was being repeated with patio doors and conservatories. As I cruised slowly past their house I saw a woman at an upstairs window, polishing the glass like she'd done every day since her daughter hurled herself off a graceless concrete car park, two Christmases ago. She wore a yellow smock that made her the brightest thing in the street. I parked about six doors away and turned up my collar.

I knocked at the door of the house I'd parked outside and a dog started barking. A woman told it to be quiet and somewhere inside another door slammed, muffling the dog's yelps. A bolt slid back, the latch clicked, and the door swung open.

She was about eighty years old and four foot eleven high. 'Yes,' she demanded.

'Police,' I said, offering my ID. 'I'm DI Priest. Could I have a word, please?'

'Come in,' she ordered.

We stood in the kitchen. 'First of all,' I told her, 'I want to give you a ticking off.'

'A ticking off?' she echoed. 'I'm too old to take a ticking off from you, young man, police or no.'

'You should be more careful who you let in. Don't you have a spy hole, or a chain on the door?'

'I'm eighty-three years old next birthday,' she responded. 'If anything was going to happen to me it would have happened by now, don't you think?'

At what age do you start adding one on instead of taking a few off? How do you argue with someone who believes the Earth is flat? You don't.

'I'm enquiring about people – salesmen – who come round knocking at doors,' I told her. 'Have you ever had anyone call from a firm called Magic Plastic?'

'Magic Plastic? Yes, of course I have. He calls regularly.

Never buy anything, though. Far too dear. He's a nice man, always polite. What's he done?'

'Nothing. Do you know his name?'

'Why do you want to know his name if he hasn't done anything?'

'Because he might have seen something. We don't only talk to criminals, you know. We talk to witnesses, too.' I could give it as good as she could.

'What sort of something?'

'That's what we want to ask. Do you know him?'

'No.'

'Do you still have a catalogue?'

'No, he collected it.'

'When?'

'Weeks ago. Months, in fact.'

I thanked her for her trouble and told her to keep the door chain on, but she wasn't listening.

The next two houses were unoccupied. A middle-aged woman with a headscarf over her rollers saw me knocking and told me that her neighbours had gone to Tenerife for a fortnight. Who'd have a job in crime prevention? Yes, the Magic Plastic man did call, although he hadn't been for a few weeks. No, she never bought anything off him, and no, she didn't have a catalogue.

The woman with the two toddlers who lived directly opposite the Crabtrees bought some stuff for cleaning moss off her patio when he first called, but it didn't work and she hadn't bought anything since. Her labrador insisted on jumping up at me, leaving big muddy paw-prints on the East Pennine Police waterproof. 'He's just being friendly,' she assured me.

And that was that. I'd arrived. It couldn't be postponed a moment longer. I crossed the road, looking up at Mrs

Crabtree, her chamois leather moving round in circles, slowly progressing across the pane of glass like a glider in a crosswind. She paused as my hand fell on their gate and we stared at each other for a moment. I lifted the catch, she reached into a corner for an invisible speck of dirt.

William, her husband, answered the door. As I waited I noticed that the drain next to the bay window was covered with a plastic lid, to prevent the ingress of leaves. A snip at £8.99 from Magic Plastic. 'Hello, Mr Crabtree,' I said. 'I'm Inspector Priest, from Heckley CID. Do you remember me?'

He looked confused and mumbled something.

'I'd like a word with you both,' I told him, stepping forward. 'Do you mind if I come in?'

He moved to one side to allow me past, and when he'd reclosed the door we went into their front room. I took the heavy coat off and suggested he call Mrs Crabtree. He shouted up the stairs to her, saying they had a visitor. He called her Mother. I placed the coat in the angle between a sideboard and the wall, half on the floor, half leaning against the wall.

William hadn't changed much, but his wife had. She'd taken the house coat off and had lost at least a couple of stones since I'd last seen her. Her face was lined and her hair unkempt. We all sat down.

'How are you both?' I began.

They shrugged, mumbling meaningless answers to a meaningless question.

'I was the officer in charge,' I told them, 'when Susan died. I came to see you, but you've probably forgotten me. Christmas brought it all back, and I was wondering how you were.'

'So-so,' he replied, quietly.

'For you,' I went on, 'I don't suppose it ever went away, did it?'

They shook their heads. 'No.'

'And I don't suppose it ever will. In a sense, you probably don't really want it to go away. She was your daughter, your only child, and you loved her. She'll always be a part of you.'

Mrs Crabtree said: 'The Lord moves in mysterious ways.'

'That he does,' I agreed.

She turned to her husband. 'Would you like to make some tea, Treasure?' she suggested.

'I'll put the kettle on,' he replied, stooping forward before making a big effort to rise from his low chair.

'No!' I insisted, raising a hand. 'Not for me, thanks all the same.' William settled back.

I straightened the antimacassar on the arm of my chair. 'I have no children,' I stated. 'But it's hard, even for me, to imagine anything as devastating as losing a child. Except, of course, you lost a grandchild, too. That must be unbearable.'

'Some fell on stony ground,' she said. 'And even as we sow, so shall we reap.'

'Quite,' I replied. 'The Bible must be a great comfort to you, Mrs Crabtree.'

He said: 'Yes, it's been a great comfort to you, hasn't it, Mother?'

She reached out and took his hand. 'We came through it together, didn't we, Treasure? We helped each other and trusted in the Lord.'

In the far corner of the room was a big Mitsubishi television. Stuck on the side of it was a holder for the channel changer. 'Only £2.99 and you'll never again have to search for that elusive remote control.' 'Hey! That's a good idea,' I said, glad to change the subject. I strolled across the room and lifted the controller from its holster. It occurred to me that I could just as easily have turned the telly on while I was there. 'I could do with one of these,' I declared. 'Where did you find it?'

'Oh, we bought it,' he replied.

'From a shop?'

'No. It's someone who comes round.'

'You mean, like the Magic Plastic man?'

'Yes. Them.'

'Magic Plastic?'

'Yes.'

'Right. I'll have to look out for him. I'm told they do some useful stuff.'

'Yes, they do.'

I glanced around the room. It was still filled with all the clutter I'd seen before: commemorative plates, porcelain shepherdesses, cut glass vases. Everything pristine, standing on crocheted doilies to protect the polished surfaces of the furniture. No photographs.

'You don't seem to have a photograph of Susan,' I said.

They glanced at each other. 'No,' he replied, awkwardly. 'We, er, have different ideas about that. I try to forget, most of the time, put her out of my mind. It's my way of coping. Mother's just the opposite. She likes to remember Susan as much as possible, don't you, Mother? We have photographs. They're upstairs. I go in every night, before I go to bed, for a few minutes, but Mother spends most of her time up there.' He was close to tears.

'Would you like to see Susan's room, Inspector?' Mrs Crabtree asked, leaning forward.

'Yes,' I replied. 'I'd like that very much.'

I followed her upstairs, to a room at the back of the house with a crucifix on the door. She pushed the door open and ushered me in.

The hairs on my neck were bristling as if I'd moved into a powerful magnetic field. The only illumination came from electric candles on the walls and at either side of what I can only call a shrine. It had probably been a Welsh dresser, but now it was a repository for religious artifacts and memorabilia of their daughter. There was a big picture of her as the focal point, underneath one representing Jesus Christ as a Scandinavian pop star rather than a Middle Eastern artisan. Susan looked intelligent but you'd never call her pretty. Her hair was hacked and she wore what I believe is called a twin set. Maybe I'd have liked her values. Rosary beads hung across a small photograph of the Pope.

'Are you a Catholic?' I asked, lamely.

'No,' she replied. 'There is but one God, and He is Jesus Christ, our Lord.'

There was an easy chair positioned in front of the shrine. 'Is this where you come, Mrs Crabtree?' I asked. 'Is this where you find your comfort?'

'Yes,' she whispered. 'I spend many hours here. William doesn't seem to understand.'

'I'm sure he does,' I told her. I walked to the door and turned the dimmer switch, brightening the room, and took in the scene. There was a square of clear plastic around the light switch, to prevent a stray fingertip soiling the wallpaper. 'What was the baby called?' I asked.

'Davey,' she replied, so quietly I hardly heard. Davey, of course. I'd almost forgotten.

'Davey. Was that the father's name?'

'No.'

'Do you know the father's name?'

'No.'

'You never met him?'

'No.'

There was no photograph of the baby, and I wondered why.

'There doesn't seem to be a picture of Davey, Mrs Crabtree?' I commented.

She moved towards the shrine. 'Just a small one,' she said, and unhooked a gold locket that was hanging by its chain alongside the picture of Susan. Inside was a little round photo of a baby's face, looking like every other bonny baby I'd seen. 'He was a handsome fellow,' I said.

'Yes, he was beautiful. He weighed seven pounds five ounces, in spite of being five weeks premature.'

'I didn't know that,' I told her. The PM hadn't said anything about him being premature.

'These,' she said, opening the other side of the locket with a fingernail, 'are his hair and his toe-nail clippings. Would you believe, his nails needed cutting when he was born?'

I looked at the wisp of hair and the tiny slivers of protein that were all that remained of little Davey. 'Don't lose them,' I whispered.

Mrs Crabtree clicked the locket shut and replaced it next to Susan. There were other photographs of her, tracing the development of popular photography as well as the girl and young woman depicted in them. Fading black and whites of a little girl in National Health spectacles that she hated, right up to full colour seven-by-fives of her with friends, somewhere at the seaside. She changed over the years, blossomed even, but the glasses singled her out, every time. I saw a little bronze trophy, with crossed squash rackets on it, and my stomach bubbled like a sulphur pool. I picked it up. 'Mixed doubles,' it said, 'Losing semi-finalist.'

'Mrs Crabtree,' I began. 'Did you ever . . .' I replaced the trophy, looked at it and adjusted its position. 'Did you, or Susan . . . ever consider an abortion?'

'No!' she declared, defiantly. 'Never. Life is not ours to take away. By the fruits of your sins shall you be judged.'

'Did Susan think about having one?'

'No.'

'Did she investigate the possibility? Maybe take advice, or counselling?'

'He wanted her to,' she said. 'But he would, wouldn't he? He didn't want the responsibilities of a child.'

'What did he say?'

'He took her somewhere. When she came back she was confused. They poisoned her brain with the devil's works. She soon changed her mind when she was back with her family. The word of the Lord prevailed, but the price of salvation is eternal vigilance.'

I only know one quotation from the Bible. I learned it from my dad. When I was little and he was a struggling PC he drove a motorbike and sidecar. It was his pride and joy. He took great delight in telling people that Moses rode a motorbike. It said so in the Bible. It said: 'And the sound of his Triumph was heard throughout the land.' He'd have loved talking to Mrs Crabtree.

'This boyfriend,' I said. 'He took her somewhere, for advice about an abortion?'

'Yes, but she was too strong for him, for she was filled with the Holy Spirit.'

'But he knew all about abortions?'

'Yes. He was a disciple of Satan. He did the devil's work, here on Earth. The devil finds work for idle hands.'

'What was he called?'

'I don't know.'

'I think you do.'

'I don't know.'

I dimmed the lights and held the door open for her. Outside, after I'd pulled the door closed, I put my hands on her shoulders and looked into her eyes. I could feel her bones, and her face was criss-crossed with fine lines.

'Thank you for showing me Susan's room,' I said.

Downstairs, William was standing close up to the gas fire, warming his legs, even though it must have been eighty in there. He turned as we entered and sat down again.

I made a production of looking at my watch. 'Is that the time?' I said. 'I'd better make a phone call, if you'll excuse me.' I went to the front door and lifted the latch so I didn't lock myself out. I stood on the front step and spoke to the desk sergeant, telling him where I was and asking for a panda to come and stand by.

'It's still raining,' I told them as I took my seat again. They didn't comment. 'Mrs Crabtree was telling me that Susan's boyfriend wanted her to have an abortion,' I said.

William shuffled and looked uncomfortable.

'Do you approve of abortions, Mr Crabtree?' I asked, watching him as I waited for an answer.

'I . . . don't know,' he replied, eventually.

'Do you know the boyfriend's name?'

He shook his head.

'I think you do.'

'No.'

'You were a soldier, I believe.'

He looked at me, startled by the change of tactic. 'I was a conscript,' he replied. 'Called up. We all were.'

'How old were you?'

'Eighteen.'

'Did you sign on?'

'Only for three years.'

'When was that?'

'1950.'

'And did you go abroad?'

'Germany.'

'That would have been quite an experience for a young man.'

'Yes, it was.'

'You'd see all the devastation.'

'Yes.'

'Did you carry a gun?'

He shrugged his shoulders.

'Did you carry a gun, Mr Crabtree?'

'There were guns about. Sometimes we carried one. It was dangerous. We never knew what they were thinking.'

'An Enfield thirty-eight?'

'Possibly. I don't remember. It was a long time ago.'

'It was a long time ago,' Mrs Crabtree repeated.

'Yes, it was,' I agreed. They were sitting with their backs to the window, which meant that their faces were in shadow but I could see out into the street beyond them.

'Losing a child,' I began, 'like you did. And a grandchild. It's the saddest thing imaginable. You must have been about forty when Susan was born. You'd probably already accepted that you'd never be parents. Resigned yourselves to it. And then she came along – everything you'd always wanted. And, all those years later, little Davey, too – the grandchild you never expected to have. If someone took them away from you, caused their deaths, you'd want to kill that person, don't you think?'

He crossed his feet and dug his fingers into the chair arm. She sniffed and pressed her interlocked hands into her lap. Neither spoke.

'You knew all about the doctor she met at the squash club, didn't you?' I continued. 'She'd come home, thrilled to pieces, and tell you all about him. When she fell pregnant you knew he must be the father. He took her to the clinic and she told you that she was thinking of having an abortion. Is that what happened?'

'He was the devil's disciple,' Mrs Crabtree told us. 'He tempted her with the forbidden fruit, then wanted her to resort to murder to avoid the wages of sin. He filled her head with ideas, but with the help of her loved ones the will of God prevailed.'

'And when Susan died, you blamed him.'

'Our Lord is a jealous Lord. "Vengeance is mine," He said.'

She was ga-ga. Stark, staring ga-ga. Outside, a car horn *peep-peeped* and I saw a panda's blue lights slide past above the privet hedge. I turned to William. Maybe he was capable of rational thought.

'You wanted him dead, didn't you?' I said.

He shrugged and stared at the carpet.

'And one day, you remembered the gun. Where was it? Hidden up in the loft, or somewhere, wrapped in grease-proof paper? Whenever we have a guns amnesty it's amazing how many old soldiers bring in weapons that they forgot to hand back when they were demobbed. Do you know what I think, William?' I didn't wait for an answer. 'I think you found the doctor's name and address in Susan's diary, when you went through her things. And then the hatred for him began to fester in your minds. Both of you. The strange thing is, I think it's perfectly understandable. In your shoes, I'd have wanted the same thing. What did you do? Go round, with the gun? But he lived in a block of flats and you didn't know how to get in, did you? So you left a Magic Plastic catalogue in his mailbox, with a note saying that you'd call back. Couldn't you do it, that first time? And what did you think when he ordered a mini-bin from you? Is this about how it happened, Mr Crabtree?'

He nodded, slowly and deliberately, without taking his eyes from the carpet.

'But then Christmas came, with all its images of children, and the feelings became unbearable. Christmas Eve was the first anniversary of Susan's and Davey's deaths. You went back again, didn't you? You said you were the man from Magic Plastic, and he let you in. This time you made him lie on the carpet and you shot him through the head. Am I right – is that how you did it?'

His wife reached across and took his hand. 'Suffer the little children to come unto me,' she said, 'for theirs is the Kingdom of God.'

He looked up at me and nodded. 'Yes,' he whispered.

'What did you do with the gun, William?' I demanded.

He opened his mouth to speak, but she beat him to it. 'He threw it in the canal.'

'Did you?'

'Yes, I threw it in the canal.'

'Whereabouts?'

'Off the bottom bridge.'

That shouldn't be too difficult to find, I thought. I turned to her. 'Could you get your coats and shoes, Mrs Crabtree,' I said. 'I think you'd both better come down to the station.' She struggled to her feet and went to fetch them.

We stood in the hallway and I held her coat while she helped him with his. She fussed around him, checking his buttons and fastening his belt. He thrust his hands deep into the pockets as she placed hers on his cheeks and kissed him.

'Don't worry, Treasure,' she whispered to him. 'Be brave. Mother's coming with you.'

As soon as she was inside her own coat I asked where the key was. She retrieved it from a hook beside the door and handed it to me.

'Right, let's go,' I said. I locked the door behind us and took William by the arm, guiding him up the garden path, Mrs Crabtree leading the way. The panda was parked near my car. When the driver saw us emerge he drove slowly towards the Crabtrees' gate.

Mr Crabtree wrenched his arm from mine as the car stopped. I turned as the gun fired and saw the side of his head blossom like a chrysanthemum and felt the warm wetness of him on my face. He was falling through a scarlet mist. I threw my arms around him but I was off-balance and he dragged me down to the ground. Mine was the embrace that held him in his death throes, but he was already beyond comforting.

The two PCs came running, but there was nothing anyone could do. I took the waterproof coat off and spread it over William's body, the army-issue Enfield revolver still grasped in his hand as his blood spread out across the wet concrete. Mrs Crabtree stood there, rain pouring down her face, spouting her mantras, until she was led away.

'It's come,' Sparky informed me as I returned from the

morning meeting, a week and a half after we'd brought Mrs Crabtree in. He followed me into my office and retrieved a brown Home Office envelope from my in-tray.

'Right,' I said, hanging my jacket on its hook. 'Better ask Nigel and Maggie to join us.'

Sparky poked his head out of the door and shouted: 'You and you. Boss says to get your arses in here, toot sweet.'

Maggie arrived first. 'Nigel's on the phone,' she told us.

'It looks like the results of the DNA tests have arrived from Wetherton,' I explained, showing her the envelope.

'What do they say?'

'I haven't looked yet. Sit down.'

'Let me get this straight,' she said, pulling a chair from under my table and turning it round. 'I wasn't in from the beginning. The Crabtrees were under the impression that Dr Jordan was the father of the baby?'

'Yes.'

'And Jordan wanted Susan to have an abortion?'

'Not quite. According to the counsellor at the clinic he just took her along to explain the options. She listened to them and at first she appeared quite keen to have a termination, but then changed her mind. The counsellor detected that she was under a great deal of pressure from her parents to let the pregnancy take its course.' I sliced the envelope open with the glass dagger I use as a paper knife. It was a present from the team after an earlier murder enquiry.

'And after it was born the depression set in.'

'It looks like it. She blamed them, they blamed the doctor. Sometimes, it helps if we can put the responsibility on someone else instead of accepting it ourselves.'

'And the Magic Plastic Killer was created.'

'Yep.'

Nigel came in. 'Sorry about that,' he said.

'Did she put the gun in her husband's coat pocket?' Maggie asked.

'It looks like it. She said something about coming with him, but I don't know what she meant.'

'Will she stand trial?'

'Mrs Crabtree? I doubt it. She's been sectioned under the Mental Health Act. She'll spend the rest of her days preaching to her fellow inmates. No doubt they'll hang on to her every word.' I thought about it for a second, then continued: 'It's funny, isn't it? If there is a God speaking to her, putting the words into her mouth, you'd think he'd give her the right quotations, wouldn't you?'

Sparky said: 'You know what they say: When we talk to God it's called praying. When he talks to us, it's called schizophrenia.'

'I'll say Amen to that.' I unfolded the letter from Wetherton. 'Let's see what we have here.' There was a silence as I scanned it. 'Tests were conducted . . .' I read out, 'at the request of handsome but self-effacing DI Priest of . . .'

'Get on with it!' Sparky urged.

'Right. Blah blah blah. Here we are – "Conclusions. Examination of the band patterns shows that there is no obvious kinship between the two samples. In answer to the specific question posed, we can categorically state that the donor of sample CP1 is not the child of the donor of sample CP2." That's it. The doctor wasn't little Davey's dad.' Nigel extended his hand and I gave him the letter.

'So who was?' Maggie asked.

'Big Davey? Whoever he is.'

'Are we going to find him?'

'To tell him his ex-girlfriend and their baby are dead? What's the point?'

Sparky said: 'So the doc was just being kind to her.'

'It looks like it,' I replied.

'Every way we've turned, every avenue we've followed, he's come up smelling of roses. He was a decent bloke, all along.'

'You're right. He was a bit of a lad, but why not? Everybody who knew him liked him. He had plenty of friends. Some of them just happened to be a bit dodgy.'

'Who needs enemies?'

Nigel placed the letter on my desk. 'So it was all a waste of time,' he stated.

''Fraid so.'

'All that . . . all that grief was for nothing.'

'Yep,' I agreed. 'All for nothing.' And I've still got the scars to prove it.

I never wrote that letter to personnel saying that I wanted out, and the one from pay section is still unopened. Darryl Buxton appeared before a crown court judge last month and pleaded guilty to a charge of rape. He'll be sentenced in a few weeks. The daffodils outside the court looked magnificent.

When we tried to tell Herbert Mathews the good news we discovered that he'd been admitted to a hospice, and he died shortly afterwards. Maggie and I went to the funeral. His old station was represented by a young WPC who'd never met him. They sent a wreath, everybody else made a donation to Cancer Research. On the way Maggie told me that Janet Saunders had applied for a job as a school dinner lady, which would give her a good chance of regaining custody of little Dilly. She'd decided that life was still worth living, and was putting it back together.

I opened the letter that Annabelle sent me, even though I'd asked her not to write. She said she had to. There was no address, it just said London in the top right-hand corner. I was glad she hadn't put an address. It was the best testimonial I've ever received; when I'd finished it I couldn't understand why she'd ever left me. I slowly tore it into a hundred and twenty-eight pieces, and immediately wished I hadn't.

Her house is empty, with a For Sale sign standing in the garden. I think about her, now and again. Wonder where she is, what she's doing, if she's happy. I hope she is. I don't dwell in the past, but sometimes a memory of her takes me by surprise. All sorts of things can trigger it off, but music is the worst. Some of my CDs I doubt if I'll ever play again, but it can be anything: Barber's *Adagio for Strings*; the *Archers*' signature tune; when it rains; when it doesn't.

Since the Doctor Jordan case I've let Nigel run the show. He'll be promoted to inspector soon, which will mean a return to uniform. Meanwhile, I let him play at detectives. I go walking, most weekends, either in the Dales or driving up to the Lakes on a Friday or Saturday evening. The couple who run the B and B I use have become friends, and he suggested I do some back-packing on the Continent. I wondered about the Blue Ridge Mountains, in the USA.

There's a good library in Heckley. One lunchtime, fired with enthusiasm, I went along to see what I could find in their Travel section and discovered that my membership had lapsed. That's a bit like saying that Maggie Thatcher wasn't a chemist any more.

'Could you fill this in please?' the woman behind the

counter asked, 'and we'll put you on the computer. We have computers now, you know.'

'Whatever next?' I replied, taking the white card from her. She was wearing wire-framed spectacles and her hair was tied severely back. She believed in conforming to type, but couldn't disguise the fact that she was attractive. I was reminded of one of those Barbra Streisand films where the make-up people have drawn on all the skills of their craft in an attempt to make her look dowdy, fooling nobody except the hapless hero.

'Will that do?' I said, handing the form back to her, holding on to it a fraction of a second longer than necessary.

She studied it and looked at me, her cheeks tinged with colour. 'Hello, Charlie,' she said. 'I thought it was you.'

I imagined her in the last reel, where he removes her spectacles and she lets her hair tumble free, revealing the enchantress we knew was there all the time. 'Jackie?' I said, disbelieving my eyes. 'Is it Jacqueline? Well, er, fancy meeting you here.'

Author's Note

This story and all the characters in it are fictional. However, some real names of people and places have been used for dramatic effect. Any implied criticism of the citizens or police forces of the towns mentioned is again for dramatic effect and is not based on experience or reputation.

Huddersfield's Derek Ibbotson set a new world one-mile record in 1957 with a time of 3 minutes 57.2 seconds. The following year, at the White City, London, he became the first person to be timed at exactly four minutes for the distance.

The East Lancashire Regiment was stationed at Fecamp, Normandy, home of the Benedictine distillery, during both the First and Second World Wars. To this day the biggest single market for the liqueur is in the pubs and clubs around Burnley and Accrington.

David Rose, in his excellent book *In The Name Of The Law*, tells of an – alleged – serial date-rapist who has been acquitted seven times. May there be a Charlie Priest waiting for him, soon.

S. Pawson

The Mushroom Man

Stuart Pawson

There's nothing Detective Inspector Charlie Priest hates more than a case involving children. When Georgina, the eight-year-old daughter of local businessman Miles Dewhurst, goes missing, Charlie and his colleagues soon start to fear the worst. And Charlie's suspicions are focused on Dewhurst – is his performance as desolate parent a little too pat?

Meanwhile, these are dangerous times for clergymen. Three have died suddenly, and a picture of a Destroying Angel mushroom has been left beside the body of the most recent victim. It seems that something more than coincidence links the deaths – but why would a serial killer focus on men of the cloth?

As he races against time to find Georgina, and happens upon the first real clue in the hunt for the Mushroom Man, Charlie Priest has another preoccupation – his tentative pursuit of bishop's widow Annabelle. And Charlie's courtship is about to take a dramatic turn – for he is more deeply embroiled in one of the cases than he realises . . .

0 7472 4897 4

HEADLINE